THE LEGACY SERIES

The Mexican Messiah: A Novella & Stories
Jay Kauffmann

Close to a Flame
Colleen Alles

American Animism
Jamey Gallagher

Keeping What's Best Left Kept Secret
David Ricchiute

Soaked
Toby LeBlanc

The Path of Totality
Marie Zhuikov

Shocker in Gloomtown
Dan Libman

The Continental Divide
Bob Johnson

The Three Devils and Other Stories
William Luvaas

The Correct Response
Manfred Gabriel

Welcome Back to the World: A Novella & Stories
Rob Davidson

Greyhound Cowboy and Other Stories
Ken Post

Close Call
Kim Suhr

The Waterman
Gary Schanbacher

Signs of the Imminent Apocalypse and Other Stories
Heidi Bell

What We Might Become
Sara Reish Desmond

The Silver State Stories
Michael Darcher

An Instinct for Movement
Michael Mattes

The Machine We Trust
Tim Conrad

Gridlock
Brett Biebel

Salt Folk
Ryan Habermeyer

The Commission of Inquiry
Patrick Nevins

Maximum Speed
Kevin Clouther

Reach Her in This Light
Jane Curtis

The Spirit in My Shoes
John Michael Cummings

The Effects of Urban Renewal on Mid-Century America and Other Crime Stories
Jeff Esterholm

What Makes You Think You're Supposed to Feel Better
Jody Hobbs Hesler

Fugitive Daydreams
Leah McCormack

Hoist House: A Novella & Stories
Jenny Robertson

Finding the Bones: Stories & A Novella
Nikki Kallio

In this trenchant debut story collection from ghostwriter Pearce, Chicagoans pluck at the fraying bonds of their relationships. . . . Pearce's prose exudes a solid sense of place, but the author's real power lies in his ability to trace the emotional toll of his characters' seemingly small but consequential decisions. It's an accomplished and assured first outing.

—*PUBLISHERS WEEKLY*

Wonderful . . . a love letter to a recognizable Chicago, full of snowbound dibs and Irish bars, hidden storefronts and class conflicts across neighborhoods. Don't sleep on this one.

—*CHICAGO TRIBUNE*

The Plan of Chicago has an unusual structure—nine linked stories set in nine Chicago neighborhoods—and unusual range. The characters —half men, half women—include immigrants from Poland, Mexico, Ireland, and Somalia. . . . Through these varied characters—Black and White, straight and gay, wealthy and working-class—Pearce captures the breadth and depth of the city that sits dead center in America and perhaps better than any other, can reveal its promise and flaws.

—*IRISH AMERICAN NEWS*

This is a terrific collection. I savored it, one story at a time, the way I do the masters of the genre—Trevor or Munro or Gallant. Like them, Pearce creates in each short story a novel's worth of rich characterization with deft artistic compression; and like the masters of geographically linked collections— Joyce, Anderson—Pearce renders contemporary Chicago in loving and brutal complexity from a myriad of vivid voices. And in his own stylish manner, Pearce pulls off, again and again, dazzling plotlines that deeply satisfy. I loved reading this book.

—ANTONYA NELSON
author of *Bound* and *Funny Once*
winner of the Rea Award for the Short Story

The form of Barry Pearce's compelling linked collection of stories, *The Plan of Chicago*, mirrors the city. Each story is allied with a Chicago neighborhood. "Chez Whatever," his haunting Nelson Algren Prize winning story, is connected to South Shore, and there are stories paired with Rogers Park, Humboldt Park, Uptown, and others. The pairing is not merely a clever scaffolding device. The power of Pearce's book rises from the foundational sense of Chicago as city of neighborhoods. *Neighborhood* is the level where the great urban themes—race, ethnicity, minority culture, assimilation, inequality, democracy, the American Dream—that elevate the work of writers like Algren, Brooks, Bellow, Terkel, Cisneros, and Kotlowitz have been expressed, a lineage to which this book belongs.

—STUART DYBEK
author of *The Coast of Chicago*
and *Paper Lantern: Love Stories*

Like James Joyce's *Dubliners*, this collection of stories accumulates a strange cohesive power, and the city itself becomes a character— an arbiter, a friend, an inspiration, a tough customer. The stories are beautifully crafted and carefully written, and while the book is utterly unsentimental, a deep love of place bleeds through the prose. In a culture increasingly bent on the infantilization of its citizens, it's rare to find a book that's genuinely written for grown-ups—a dark, honest probing of what it means to be human and to live, right at this moment, in Chicago. Barry Pearce is a shrewd, fearless writer, and *The Plan of Chicago* is the best book I've read in a long time.

—ROBERT BOSWELL
author of *Tumbledown* and *Mystery Ride*

If only the people of a city could know how necessary they are for each other, they could heal each other and be healed in turn. Will the richly realized characters herein grasp this salvation? Either way, through Barry Pearce's art, we may. Resonant, empathetic, and continually surprising, *The Plan of Chicago* is a glorious, living map by a master storyteller.

—ALEX SHAKAR
author of *Luminarium*

Barry Pearce's Chicago tales cut across the certainties of seasonal change and static divisions in search of connection upon a sprawling flatland. His city dwellers do find light along the way—achingly, bracingly, sometimes incidentally. Yet it is in the insistence of their paths that Pearce captures their resolute spirits while summoning the soul of their city.

—BAYO OJIKUTU
author of *47th Street Black* and *Free Burning*

The Plan of Chicago is a tapestry of interconnected stories exploring the intricate intersections of love, identity, and the desperate gambles we take to survive and belong. Set in 21st-century post-industrial Chicago, where lives teeter between chaos and connection, these narratives delve into the complexities of human vulnerability—how past choices and present fears shape us, how love both binds and breaks, and how moments of crisis reveal the raw, unfiltered truths of who we are. With themes of familial bonds, the longing for acceptance, and the recklessness of youth, Barry Pearce's story collection captures the tender, often tumultuous journey of growing up and growing wise.

—ACHY OBEJAS
author of *Boomerang / Bumerán* and *Days of Awe*

THE PLAN OF CHICAGO

a city in stories

BARRY PEARCE

CORNERSTONE PRESS
UNIVERSITY OF WISCONSIN-STEVENS POINT

Cornerstone Press, Stevens Point, Wisconsin 54481
Copyright © 2025 Barry Pearce
www.uwsp.edu/cornerstone

Printed in the United States of America by
Point Print and Design Studio, Stevens Point, Wisconsin

Library of Congress Control Number: 2025943469
ISBN: 978-1-968148-11-9

Cover photo © Joeff Davis, www.joeff.com

Cornerstone Press titles are produced in courses and internships offered by the
Department of English at the University of Wisconsin–Stevens Point.

DIRECTOR & PUBLISHER
Dr. Ross K. Tangedal

EXECUTIVE EDITORS
Jeff Snowbarger, Freesia McKee

EDITORIAL DIRECTOR
Brett Hill

SENIOR EDITORS
Paige Biever, Eva Nielsen, Reilly Crous

PRESS STAFF
Alex Diaz, Lilly Kulbeck, Josh Paulson, Sam Zajkowski, Samantha Bjork, Sophie
McPherson, Madison Schultz, Autumn Vine

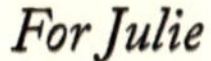

For Julie

Contents

Chicago, on becoming a city, chose for its motto Urbs in Horto—*a city set in a garden. Such indeed it then was, with the opalescent waters of the lake at its front, and on its three sides the boundless prairie carpeted with waving grass bedecked with brilliant wildflowers.*

—Daniel H. Burnham and Edward H. Bennett
The Plan of Chicago (1909)

Enumerator

In Chicago we rented an apartment in a squat brick build-ing on North Kilbourn, detached from its neighbors in a square ground. The apartment was large but old and poorly maintained. Jason arranged the lease with Mr. Castillo, who had crossed the border from Mexico illegally with one hun-dred dollars hidden in the heel of his shoe (the neatness of that number made me question his account later but at the time, seemed to add authenticity). Now, he owned eight buildings, our twelve-flat the smallest and seediest of them all. He drove a royal-blue Mercedes. He lived on the North Shore. Our landlord seemed like a living endorsement of the illicit plan I had made to leave Poland: look what was possible in Chicago! How you got there didn't matter.

I should have paid more attention to his daughter's story. Sarita lived alone in the apartment below ours. She was Castillo's only child, American-born, the old man's great hope and joy. He set aside money for college and medical school before she turned five, plans that had no effect on her actual life. She was thirty, seven years older than me, but like a lazy teen, had never held a job. Sarita dressed like a teenager too, tiny tops, short shorts, dresses with key parts missing—so skimpy I had to look away. She was attractive, not beautiful, but had the largest brown eyes I'd ever seen, hair and nails clipped from the glossy pictures in magazines.

We heard her fighting, watching TV, making love—all so loudly I stuffed cotton in my ears—yet she complained of our heavy footfalls, felt through her ceiling more than heard, she said, as if we should tiptoe around our apartment or adopt her schedule and sleep until noon. Like the male satellites that circled her, everyone and everything should orbit Sarita. I quickly lost count of them, the anonymous men spinning in and out of her place, though I recognized the trails they left in warm weather: beer bottles, cigarette butts, occasionally a hat or pair of underwear lingering where lovers sat with her on the back porch.

"I am Sa-ri-ta," she announced the first time we met.

"Margaret Cieslak–Jablonski," I corrected. I had been married two months, and taking Jason's name still felt literal, as if I was stealing a piece of his life when I used it. "How are you?"

"Very good," she said loudly, watching my mouth. I could not tell if she was answering my question or complimenting me on uttering a simple sentence in English.

My complaints about Sarita made Jason nervous. She was the landlord's daughter. He did not want trouble.

"People live all around us," he said. "Thin walls, awful separation—that's city life. Can't you be a little patient?"

"She should be patient," I said. "In hospital for crazy drunk people."

He could not suppress a laugh, never sure if my sentences were meant or accidents of the language I was still learning to live in. I struggled for English words when I thought of Sarita and her untouched tuition fund, which was enormous, according to Mr. Aegeis, the old Greek next door. I would have given my firstborn to attend American university, and she threw the chance away to have fun like a child. When her noise or beer bottles became unbearable, Jason went downstairs so that I would not. He wandered endlessly before coming to the point, often gone fifteen minutes or more, but his indirect approach worked. Music was lowered, bottles thrown out, the porch cleaned. When he was not home, though, I sometimes stomped on the floor in a fit of annoyance. Sarita banged back on her ceiling. I stomped harder. She pounded harder again, each of us counting the other's knocks and adding more. We could go on this way for ten minutes, like prisoners in adjoining cells forced to invent a new language.

Sarita's father had raised a MAP, Mr. Aegeis explained. Now, old Castillo was trying to undo the damage by exiling her to a shabby apartment in a desolate neighborhood. He hoped that a little suffering would motivate her to find her calling or at least a job, a husband, something worthwhile. Two years later, nothing had changed.

I looked at Mr. Aegeis in confusion. "A map?"

"Mexican-American Princess," he said. "By the way, do you know the difference between a MAP and a JAP? That's a Jewish-American Princess." Aegeis leaned forward, leering on the stairs, and I breathed through my mouth to avoid the sickly-sweet smell of liquor. He tugged at the goatish tuft of gray hair on his chin. "With a MAP, the jewelry's fake and the orgasms are real." His laugh rose like a revved engine, then sputtered and stalled in a wet cough. I escaped as he doubled over, clutching the banister.

That week I began using the back stairwell. It was dark and narrow, and unless they had to do laundry, Sarita, Aegeis, and our other neighbors used the front stairs.

Mr. Aegeis called ours a desolate neighborhood, but it was not a neighborhood at all. When people asked where I lived, I said "in between." Our creaky flat sat at the point where two highways split, dense power lines on one side of the building, an abandoned mannequin factory on the other (lifeless dummies still perched in certain windows). We were on the edge of Portage Park and Old Irving but not quite in either. Hearing my address, people sometimes suggested Albany Park or the Villa. They were nearby, but we did not fit in their borders or in Jefferson Park's. Years after we moved in, when I worked for the Census, I saw a map of Chicago, with the neighborhoods shaded various colors. My spot was the white of the paper, part of a pale scar running parallel to the bright red arteries that marked the expressways. No one wanted to claim that swath of poor transients, weedy lots, and industrial waste.

Our location was not the only thing in between. I no longer felt completely Polish, yet no one accused me of being an American. In Gdansk, we lived with the War every day. "DP" stood for "displaced person," even my generation knew. I heard the letters muttered many times in Chicago before I learned that here, it meant "dumb Polack."

MAP, JAP, DP—what kind of place shortens even such insults, as if the full label might not dehumanize enough? On crowded buses and trains—terrifying, with their painted slogans, foul odors, strangers crammed shoulder to shoulder—people heard my accent, checked a box for nanny or maid, and discounted whatever I said.

"It's the greatest city in the greatest country in the world," Jason insisted, with a look that demanded gratitude. I did not always agree, but I left home and family for good when I chose him—displaced person, dumb Polack, in every sense a DP.

We met near Gdansk as Solidarity was gaining power. On every corner, it seemed, volunteers passed out pamphlets, workers staged strikes, crowds coalesced. The communists had turned us into numbers. Now the numbers had faces and names, needs that must be addressed. I hardly noticed. At the time, I saw only Jason—hapless, handsome, completely naïve. His father had sent him from Chicago to the family farm in Poland to learn independence and toughen up. His uncle, an alcoholic and a tyrant, happily obliged, working the soft American boy from dawn until after dark. To sharpen Jason's ear for orders, he had me out to tutor his nephew in Polish each week. I was an interpreter at *Instytut Miary*, with perfect German and Russian. I could read English but wanted to get fluent. A student from Chicago was for me a gift.

For Jason, the arrangement was one more chore. He sat down to our sessions dirty and disheveled, so exhausted that one day he did not realize he wore a single shoe. I pointed when I finally noticed, as I was leaving, and he waved dismissively, no idea why one foot was bare. He had a haughtiness that endured no matter how wretched his state—the cracked hands, sore muscles, clinging odors of earth and manure. Stunned and sunburned, with hooded green eyes and thick chestnut hair, he looked like a delicate ancient hero stuck in the wrong myth, unequal to the sentence some god imposed.

My impatience did not help his motivation. Overeager, I pushed on him vocabulary and complex constructions that would have emerged naturally in time. His beautiful eyes died a little during the lessons I planned so carefully but came alive in the times between them, when we chatted in English and I became the student. My imagination came alive too, as I learned something of his history and life in sprawling, crowded Chicago. He described Mexican bakeries, Irish taverns, and restaurants of all kinds—Italian, Indian, Greek, Chinese. Elevated trains wound through the city in midair, between low brick houses called "bungalows" and enormous towers of glass and steel. Snow amassed in thick white sheets, which life emerged from like a miracle each spring. Jason had held various positions there—line cook, landscaper, life model (terms I did not understand but quietly wrote down to explore). Nothing took. He mentioned few friends and blushed beautifully when I asked about girls.

"I always feel like I'm waiting for my life to start," he said.

"Maybe now you are in Poland, it comes better."

"I thought that too, then…" He frowned, overwhelmed by the brutal farm, but with no idea what to do next.

The less Jason knew what he wanted, the more intrigued I grew. My rough English and his trouble expressing himself, in any language, gave our exchanges an air of mystery. I filled in gaps where I struggled to understand, never sure how much I was inventing. I grasped enough to see that punishing labor and constant harassment would kill him if he stayed on the farm. I was not one of those sentimental girls drawn to the lost and neglected—just the opposite—but Jason's abject state made him more handsome, perhaps because he remained so aloof. In a farmhouse kitchen, I rubbed homemade balm into rough palms and, trying to articulate the difference between collective and substantive numbers in my native tongue, fell in love.

Eventually, I arranged for Jason a job painting with my brother Czeslaw and a temporary sofa—very temporary, my father insisted—in the backroom where my mother had mixed herbal remedies. She taught me the skills before she died, repeating the stories behind teas and tinctures—the tales of their creation and people they healed—until I could recite them. I understood only much later that the stories and salves were inseparable: in our ramshackle lab, one helped her remember the other. A woman's life is harder, she said, so hard each must find a way not to go mad, her own balm, a private sanctuary. This room was hers, ours for a time.

It was off limits to my father and brother, but I gladly let Jason inside.

At work, I was the blindest of interpreters when Jason first lived with us, so close to me yet as distant and unattainable as ever. I found myself ignoring the tone of speeches, confusing subjects, missing words and sometimes whole sentences, missing Jason so badly at the office, I barely could type. My work suffered. I suffered. Everyone around me suffered, not that I noticed. I was too centered on myself and the evening, when I would see him. After work, I rushed through flaring streets, jostled by drunken men and bargaining women, laborers protesting the state of our native land. They blurred into a single vague impression as I carried thoughts of Jason like treasure above the market crowd. The shop walls were blank as fresh paper in Gdansk then, lined with rows of empty white shelves. There were lines for everything. The way to get the goods was to sink into one and live in it, all day if necessary, but I hated waiting, and the makeup of those lines, so full of desperate people, the pain of each linked to distinct shortages, which could be tallied if you looked long enough—the pale woman's iron deficiency, the weathered old man's lack of heat, the scrawny child's want of protein.

I avoided their suffering but could not escape my own. Two things brought it on. The first was that my brother tried to fire Jason. Czeslaw mocked his pacing and rough brush strokes, but the teasing seemed good-natured until one day, he accused Jason of stealing from a job. When the outraged customer, a powerful party official, found the jewelry his wife had misplaced, Czeslaw had to apologize. Later, I overheard my father tell him not to worry, he would get rid of the lazy American soon. This threat was weighing on me when I discovered the second thing—I was three months pregnant. I had crawled onto Jason's sofa after dreaming of him night after night, the idea entirely mine. He lay there lifeless at first, terrified of being revealed, and even after coaxing, showed all the grace of a puppet with tangled strings. *Not here*, he whispered, *wait*. I would not. I nudged him to life nightly, made love, and awoke lost hours later, panicked in the dark until I could tell where I was.

Neither of us had any money. Poland was killing Jason, and I was afraid my father would speed the process when he found out what happened across the hall. My brother attacked Jason for the smallest mistakes. I had no idea what to do, and then, complaining about Czeslaw, Jason said he could have taken more than trinkets from that customer's house if he wanted to steal. He had stumbled onto hidden money—real money, German marks—while patching cracks in an upstairs closet.

He dropped this detail into the conversation like a pearl into mud and in my mind, a plan began to form. It was centered on his city, the place he described so vividly, I could see the landscape and even picture myself in it. I mapped his escape once again and this time, my own. Jason would need persuading, maybe coercing, but he was miserable and wanted to go home. I could get him to follow my plan. Going into this stranger's closet would make me a thief, but not the ordinary kind. He was a faceless *apparatchik* who had robbed the people for years. If I could make a life by plundering his, did he not owe me that?

Once I have a purpose, no obstacle stops me long. My father would never speak to me again. Czeslaw, my only brother, my brother who loved me as no one else had, might face arrest, certainly blame. I could never go back, never return home. I knew all of this and went on, determined. Jason would be mine.

When Tadeusz was six months old I brought him home from buying milk one afternoon to find Jason in bed. He told me that he had been "let go." It was an expression I did not know. Did that mean he had been fired, that there was no work for now, what?

"Yeah. Same thing." He waved me off.

I did not see how those could be the same thing and wanted to ask. His work shirt was covered with white paint, not just drips and drops but wide lines of it, as if someone tried to connect the usual specks. I wanted to ask about this, too, but I was learning when to leave him alone. I laid Tadeusz down and fixed an early dinner that I knew Jason would like—pork chops, new potatoes, cabbage, apple sauce. Usually, the smell of cooking brought him into the kitchen, where he hovered over the stove, sniffing and nibbling, adding butter to this and spice to that until, bit by bit, my dinner plans were revised beyond recognition. Jason put on weight after we had Tadeusz at about the same rate I worked it off, as if he was feeding on my loss. I did not mind. I wanted a substantial man and was glad he liked my cooking. On this night, though, he lingered in the bedroom. When finally he sat at the table, I was in the kitchen slicing bread.

"What is this, Marge?" he called.

It was not enough that I gave up *Cieslak* for *Jablonski*, Jason insisted on shortening *Margaret*, too. I hated Americans' lazy habit of "nicknames," *Marge* most of all, but I stopped and counted to ten. He had had a difficult day, I thought, trying to put myself in his place.

"What?" I asked, carrying in the bread.

He pointed at his plate.

"Is pork chop."

"*It* is a pork chop," he corrected. "I see that. What kind?"

I shrugged. "They are good. Try."

"These are butterfly chops!" He banged the table. The baby began to cry.

"*Gówno*! I will never get him back to sleep." I groaned.

"See, they're thicker, and there's no bone. You pay extra for that."

I hovered between table and crib, reluctant to pick the boy up. I was wonderful pregnant, full of energy and drive, but some part of me felt that Tadeusz—in the world and more or less complete—should now manage on his own.

"So, is no bone," I said, plunging a fork into the meat. It jiggled there like a flagpole. I plucked up the baby and rocked him. He continued to bawl.

"So these cost a fortune," Jason yelled. "We can't afford them."

Below us, Sarita banged twice on the ceiling. I stomped three times in response.

"Then find pork chop your own. I not care."

Shopping was a sensitive subject. I remembered my only orange in Poland, eaten when I was fifteen, like an epiphany. I had never seen asparagus, pineapples, pot roast, was over-whelmed by cases of glistening meat and shelves bursting with boxes at the supermarket. I needed all of it, I thought, worried that the shops would run out. Eventually, I learned to take only what I could use, to weigh and compare, and if I did not see just the right ingredient, to wait, confident it would appear. Jason thought I could economize even more.

I brought the baby into the bedroom and slammed the door. Twice I rocked him to sleep, only to wake him, trembling with hatred. I would leave Jason. I spent all my time alone in this spacious cell, feeding and changing the baby, cleaning, cooking. At midday, I listened to Sarita waking to couple with her latest lover. Sometimes I passed her in the evening in my sour-smelling robe stained with spit-up at the collar, as I dashed down for the mail I dreaded checking (I had written to Czeslaw and months later, had no reply). Going out in one of her tight, expensive dresses as I prepared for bed, Sarita narrowed her enormous eyes and looked down, as if just seeing me too closely could ruin her plans.

She went out nearly every night, while I stayed in for days at a time that winter, imprisoned by wind that cut like barbed wire. I felt naked outside, no matter what I wore. When I did venture out to a store—my big treat—Jason found the receipt and checked every line. Well, he could do his own shopping from now on, cleaning too. He was happy at home, better with the baby than I was. He loved getting groceries, cooking, and, as demonstrated by the crater his growing *dupa* left in the couch, watching TV. He would have liked staying with Tadeusz while I worked, if not for his pride. I missed working. I missed the colorful gables and dirty medieval lanes of Gdansk, too, the Green Gate and the legless violinist who played Wieniawski inside it, the scent of factory smoke mingled with sea air. I missed Czeslaw and my father most of all. To endure the pain, I had to think of her as someone else, the selfish girl who treated them with indifference when she fled with her lover. That myth soothed like salve, helping me to live when I believed it. I didn't always. Some mornings I woke up crying and left the bed only when Tadeusz began to sob, too.

An hour after I slammed the bedroom door, Jason opened it gently. The pork chops were good, he said—he had eaten mine as well as his own. I wanted to get angry about this, but a little laugh gurgled in my throat. He apologized. Thoughts of leaving him instantly seemed childish. Jason was a part of me. I could not decide to leave him any more than I could leave my heart or liver. In seconds, we pulled off the necessary clothes—no more—and rolled like one body on the floor.

Quietly, I searched for things to translate while Jason was idle, but the people hiring wanted credentials I did not have. I made a little money selling my herbal remedies through a Polish shop on Milwaukee Avenue. Without the proper space to grow or mix ingredients, though, it never amounted to much. Eventually Jason found a job at a company on the South Side. A year later, he again was "let go." He found another job, just after Emma, our second, was born, and lost it before she turned one. I had pushed this work on him out of convenience or lack of imagination and had to admit that it was not sticking. Czeslaw had not been hard on my lover in Gdansk, I began to think, but kind to keep him on so long.

Painting was all Jason knew. What else could he do? I weighed the options until I could not sleep, and then an idea struck: he needed to be in charge. Jason's sizeable ego—the thing that first drew me to him—had never waned, not through hair loss (those chestnut locks were thinning) or weight gain or firings. Running things would feed his pride. As an owner, he would guard material fiercely, check each detail, count every cent. He could not ply the trade himself, but placed in charge, would get good work out of even the most uninspired hack. I approached the subject at an angle rather than putting words in his mouth, as I often had. I simply made space for the idea to grow, and it did, as if he had thought of it himself. Gently, I addressed his objections—no shop (Castillo would let him use the garage if he painted it), no equipment (he could rent sprayers and scaffolding to start), no money (little was needed). Once he agreed to open up, I defined myself as a kind of secretary—typing up estimates and translating what people wanted (many of his customers were Poles and Lithuanians on the South Side). Jason and I acted as if this was all I did, a necessary illusion, though behind the scenes, I quietly steered the business. We operated on narrow margins at first, but work appeared in regular bursts, and just as I thought, he came alive once he was, at least on paper, in charge.

The business was fifteen years old and we had been together nineteen when Jason did something I thought he no longer could: he surprised me. I knew him better than myself, could finish his sentences, predict what he would do before he moved. Both of the children had left the apart-ment by then (Jason refused to pay a mortgage long after we could have afforded a house). Tadeusz moved out before he turned eighteen, with hardly a word. He was smart and a talented artist. He could have gone to university. Instead, he lived with friends in a hovel and worked in a print shop—a non-union place that paid poorly—as if taking revenge. Ink dotted his face and grained the lines of his palms, defining him as paint did his father, faded layers obscuring where it stopped and skin began. Emma was not as smart as her brother but worked twice as hard, so eager was she to get away from home. She had my sense of purpose and her father's practicality, but with a better facility for numbers. She studied accounting at UIC, where she insisted on living in a dormitory, though campus was only half an hour away.

My children were Americans. Obvious, I know, and yet somehow, I never understood that they would be. Until they started school, they spoke Polish and even when talking English, sounded like me. They ate *pierogi* and *krupnik* as fast as I cooked them and on Christmas, made a grand ceremony of setting an extra place at table and breaking *oplatki*—both favoring the wafers that displayed the nativity scene. In Poland I ignored the tradition of the extra setting, but here, laying a plate for anonymous strangers at Christmas, the homeless and missing, made me think of my father, or the way he might think of me. I wrote letters home every Christmas, and my grief at the holidays deepened each year they went unanswered. The children felt it as their own. They were a part of me one day, and the next, without warning, little mysteries. They stopped talking in Polish and to muffle my accent in public, spoke over me. I felt more invisible and alone than when I first arrived, as absent as the stranger not sitting in that extra chair at Christmastime.

The day Emma returned to college after Christmas break her first year, I found Jason's note taped to the fridge. He had scribbled it on the back of the bill for an account I had figured wrong (Mr. Juozas Vidas of Marquette Park owed $1,700 with the detail work I'd missed and not $1,150).

The choice of stationery felt like a criticism and added to the sting.

Dear Marge,

I am sorry but I am leaving. There is someone else. Nevermind who, that does not matter. I know you will be very upset. That is the only reason I am telling it this way, to give you a chance to think about it and calm down. When we met I was flattened out, like these creatures I saw in a movie once that were trapped in two dimensions. I was lost and you were lonely. That is what tied us together. Since then I have grown and got successful, and you got to come to America. We have both changed and it is time to cut the line. A better situation has come up that I will take and once you calm down I think you will see it is not so bad. I will be able to help the kids more now with money, and I will help you to, as much as I can. You probably feel lost right now but believe me you are better off then if you were still stuck in Gdansk. When you calm down I hope you will see that and realize this can be a good thing in a way.

Love,
Jason

I was being "let go." I thought of the vague phrase Jason taught me years ago and smiled bitterly. A blue pen sat on the kitchen table. I picked it up and on his note, drew a line through *nevermind* to make it two words. I added a second *o* to the word *to* in *I will help you to* and turned *then* into *than* where he had written, *better off then if you were still stuck in Gdansk.* I shaded the *L* and then the *O* in *love*, all four letters, until they swelled and connected, more painting than word, like the fat graffiti gangs scrawled on el cars and billboards, turning the city into their personal notebooks. I went over and over it until the paper disappeared under my pen. I screamed myself breathless and tore it in pieces.

In the lull that followed, I listened for Sarita's knock through the floor, wanting a ready target for my anger, or maybe just the knock itself, that universal sign of another life across the divide. She was usually up by now, but no knock came. After living above her for nearly two decades, I knew her tastes, habits, history. She and Mr. Aegeis had remained on the creaky premises year after year, a part of the landscape, as familiar as the figures still perched in the windows of the mannequin factory next door. Alone and in his eighties now, Mr. Aegeis would depart only for embalming, I felt sure, and lately, wondered if the same might be true of her.

I sat on the linoleum's pattern of intersecting circles—the floor I had cleaned for twenty years—and sobbed among the fragments. How could he do this in writing? I gathered the biggest pieces and tried to reassemble them. The meaning shifted but was no clearer. A *better situation*? Only Jason could label another woman this way. Who was she, this *dziwka* he was trading me for? Some drunk girl he met in a bar? And what was this about more for the kids? Was she rich? Of course, she would be younger, some child he could order around. A young American with blonde hair, bouncing breasts, creamy white skin. *Time to cut the line*, he wrote, as if we were fishing partners.

Showering was an effort, but I dressed most days, usually from the laundry basket. I forced myself to take walks. On one, I saw a sign in a shop window:

> Work for the 2010 U.S. Census
> $12 / hour minimum
> Part-time
> Flexible hours
> Other language desired

I was running out of money. The business, the bank statements, everything but our personal checking account was in

Jason's name, and anyway, I wouldn't have taken cash from him no matter how much of it was actually mine. I applied for the job mostly, though, because I felt so lonely I thought I might go insane. No one knocked on my door and after avoiding my neighbors for years, I did not know how to knock on theirs. I lingered in our hall, hoping to see Mr. Aegeis, the friendly nuisance I used to avoid, but he now watched me with distant sadness, as if there was something he wanted to say but could not put in words. He made excuses when we met and scurried off. Now that I wanted to hear Sarita downstairs, her clatter disappeared. She finally had gotten a job. I had seen her only once lately, struggling out the front door with a year's worth of dry cleaning. Like Mr. Aegeis, she kept a safe distance and would not look me in the eye, as if loneliness was contagious and she was afraid of catching mine.

I knew nothing about Census work, but the other reason I applied was a vague idea that the job might help me get to Jason. I could start paying bills. I would appear more stable. The first messages I left probably scared him, but even after I made myself sound calm, he would not answer my calls. I still did not know who he had left me for. Tadeusz and Emma called dutifully each week but wary of getting stuck between us, would not discuss their father. I'd had two children with this man, left home and family for him, and did not know where he lived. I would find out. I would learn all about the happy couple, the smallest details of their life together, and find a way to render him and his *dziwka* so pathetic, their worst enemies would be moved to empathy.

The Census Bureau had a temporary office at the Coperni-cus Center, a Polish institution in Jefferson Park. It had been built over many years, without much planning. Sections were stolen from various places and times—the façade of a Polish castle, the gilt lobby of a 1930s theater, the exposed brick of an American factory. The center was always expanding, new rooms and revelations on every visit, but its strange parts somehow worked together. The grand clock out front was called "Solidarity Tower," and the twenty or so people who came to our trainings reminded me of the movement's earliest days. *Solidarność.* What a strange name, I used to think, for that disunited, disgruntled group of nobodies who related their stories of lack with such relish, savoring the meals they did without. *This* bunch of nobodies had a similar air. They were not all there, as Jason would have said—near-homeless, elderly, disabled, disturbed. Of the many foreigners, hardly any spoke fluent English. Even the few recent college graduates had a defeated look, as if already resigned to lives of underemployment. I thought about leaving, then remembered the empty apartment on Kilbourn.

Our job title was *Enumerator*, and we worked on NRFU, the "Nonresponse Followup," going door to door to count people who had not returned their Census forms. A retired Air Force colonel named, appropriately, Frank Hard led our crew. He was seventy-five, slow and stern, with a gaunt face that, like the fighter jets he had flown, tapered to a severe point. We called him the Colonel, and he did not seem to mind, oblivious to the fried-chicken jokes that attached to his title. Frank Hard had a love of regulations and procedures found only in *apparatchiks* and career soldiers. Not only did he make us memorize the labels for Census forms—the D-1(E), D-308, D-225—we spent hours filling out samples and exchanging them with our neighbors to correct them. Ruth, a short fat woman, balding and heavily medicated, was always my neighbor. She wore the same oversized yellow print dress to every session. I hoped she had several, until a ketchup stain appeared, and then reappeared daily, on her chest.

"He's tougher than the last guy, right?" she said on our first day, each eye moving in a distinct orbit. "Here." She handed me one of the stale doughnuts provided at training. "It's good to see you, but you've gotten so thin!"

I did not know who she thought I was, but there was no point in correcting her.

My other neighbor, Jerzy, an unshaven man who smelled vaguely of urine, stroked his long gray ponytail like the owner of a precious new pet. Guarding two doughnuts wrapped in napkins, he looked around defensively, as if they had to see him through the week. He scooted his chair back when he finished one and breathed through a sugar-coated hand. Incredible. He smelled like an el stop but acted as if the odor of somebody nearby—why was he glaring at me?—offended him.

In Frank Hard's defense, Ruth, like most of my fellow Enumerators, needed the practice drills. She added incorrectly. She left out the Task Code or forgot to check "Occupied" under *Unit Status on April 1*, which was "Census Day." She neglected to use abbreviations from the official list: *CL* for *Crew Leader*, *OT* for *Other*, *EQ* for Enumerator Questionnaire.

"We use abbreviations for a reason!" the Colonel said in our second week, his outrage mingled with martial zeal. "The beauty of these forms is that they allow us to categorize everything, uniformly, in seconds. Communicate it to the Bureau. Communicate it to each other" (yes, "the Bureau," as if we worked for the FBI). "And if we're going to communicate effectively, we all got to…?" He paused to let the class deliver the refrain drilled into us.

"Speak the same language." We replied with one flat tone but half a dozen foreign accents, some so thick the words did not resemble English—an irony lost on Frank Hard.

The Enumerator Questionnaire broke a person's information into key parts—relationships, race, age, housing—each with a box to check or fill in. All sorts of contingencies were covered—exotic origins, boarders, vacationers, soldiers.

Boxes marked "other" took care of the rest. "The beauty of the forms" was not an idle phrase. For Frank Hard, an EQ interpreted the world more elegantly than anything hanging at the Art Institute.

Jerzy nodded vigorously, stroking his ponytail. In a moment, I knew, he would find a way to use an abbreviation. Sure enough, as Frank Hard finished, Jersey raised his hand with a question regarding "pay for OJT" (On-the-Job Training). Jerzy strafed Frank Hard with questions at every session, but he was not the one testing the Colonel's patience today. Column 3 on the Enumerator Questionnaire had only two boxes—*Male* and *Female,* without the usual catch-all, *Other.*

"What if homeboy's gay?" asked Sonny, a man so obese, I wondered how he would count people in buildings that didn't have elevators. He grinned widely at Chuy, on his left.

"Being gay doesn't make you a woman, *güey,*" Chuy said.

Frank Hard held his Enumerator Manual open like a priest citing scripture. "Respondent and household members' sex may seem obvious," he read, "but it needs to be asked or verified for everyone…"

"Verified?" Jerzy said in genuine alarm. The class giggled.

"Meaning, ask your Respondent to verify the sex of all Subjects in the household," the Colonel said. "No one needs to drop trow."

"What if the Subject is transgender?" asked Magda, a college girl.

"Well, use your judgement, but you know, just ask him. Or her. Them."

"But such a question, that itself could be offensive," said Ravi, Magda's friend.

During the next twenty minutes, the two college kids, posed a dozen more scenarios involving people who "identified" as male, female, both, or neither—transvestites, transgendered, transsexual, transitioning. I listened in fascination. I did not know the differences between many of these labels—some of the terms I had never even heard.

Frank Hard was not fascinated. These earnest students were undermining his beloved forms, going out of their way to find examples that did not fit the boxes. Under narrowed eyes, his pointy chin rose like a rifle, fixing the insurgents in its sights.

Ravi said, "Also, I know a transgender person who is now biologically female but gay and identifying as male, and if you asked him—"

"Look, just ask which bathroom do they use, okay?" the Colonel said, appearing flushed and less confident, clutching the lectern, as if to keep the room from spinning.

I started to write Jason several times but tore up the pages. The words did not make sense, and who besides me would read them? I still did not know where he lived. I kept calling but got no reply. After two months of dialing his number without hope, I heard his voice. I was so shocked, I could only listen while he talked about the business and the kids as if we had spoken yesterday. I interrupted finally to ask who she was. It did not matter, he said in the same casual tone. People change, plans change. That was life. I had to be open to it.

The English curses I yelled at him gradually became Polish.

"You're making this harder than it has to be, Marge. Okay, we didn't work out, but you wanted to leave Poland, and I helped you to live in America. You live in the greatest—"

"*You* helped *me?*" This from the man whose escape I planned twice, the man I stole for, dreamed up a business and gave birth for. Someone else seemed to utter what gushed from me then, as if I was an interpreter again, translating one of those speeches so complex the subject remained a mystery, though I supplied every word. He hung up on me in mid-sentence.

During the next month, I worked on my tone before every call, so calm and friendly, I barely knew my own voice. Jason finally agreed to meet me at the apartment.

He had gained twenty pounds. His head was not just bald now but shaved, the patches I used to trim gone (he hated to pay for haircuts). He wore a shirt I had never seen, fashionably loose, untucked, and pale blue, a shade carefully chosen to bring out his eyes. On the coffee table between us stood a cheap Greek vase, a gift from Mr. Aegeis, on which a boy pursued a girl, or vice versa. I imagined smashing it over his head. Instead, I smiled and offered homemade *pączki*, strawberry and custard, his favorites. I was glad he had got fatter but was angry too. What was she cooking him, the bitch who bought the perfect blue shirt?

I apologized for attacking him on the phone. He looked relieved. There would be no scene today. I told him about my new job, and he sat back on the couch, almost relaxed. He was glad I had found work and said, as I expected, that I should get a smaller place now. There was too much space here, and the landlord needed to collect the rent again. Old Castillo was selling his buildings, Jason said, and the bigger his receipts, the more he would get.

"But you paid the rent, yes?" I asked.

"Well, yeah, I mean he needs the full amount. He gave me a discount after..."

"You're right. Filling all this blank space on my own is no good." I tried my best to look contrite. I had laughed at my neighbors' lengthy tenure in the building, but I would be the last of the longtime renters to leave it. Sarita had finally moved on after getting a job, and paramedics had carried Aegeis out, black and bloated, after he stuck his head in the oven. No one had noticed his absence or bothered to check on him. Now, I kept thinking I heard his wet cough next door and caught glimpses of him and Sarita in the hall.

"In a smaller place, I won't have space for Emma over the summer. Can she stay with you?" I had steeled myself for the pause that I knew must follow but still had to press a nail into my thigh to keep from screaming.

"Well." A full minute passed while he chewed *pączki,* a drop of custard quivering in the corner of his mouth like a pimple. Oh, how I wanted to smash it. "I'll have to check." He muttered this and like an incantation, his sentence produced her, a vague form taking shape between us, thirty, with blonde hair and milky skin, a wide smile and tiny brain.

He considered a hug at the door, then changed his mind. At this retreat, I almost gave up. I wanted him inside me. I wanted our old life back. Also, I wanted him dead. Not just dead, but disappeared, all traces—memories, mementos, friends, our own children—erased.

Frank Hard fed me Enumerator Questionnaires labeled with addresses. I marked each on a map, planned a safe, logical route, then ordered my EQs accordingly. Some Enumerators did not do this. They completed the Questionnaires as they came, working in circles, retracing their steps, taking detours through dangerous places. Laughing, Ruth or Chuy would tell me how they revisited the same block three or four times in one day. When I suggested that they plot the addresses and plan their work, they shook their heads with pity, as if no one artless enough to suggest such an approach would understand its futility.

Feeling official—ID dangling, pencils sharpened, map in hand—I marched off in search of Subjects. My first batch included half a dozen EQs at Historia Commons, a tattered corridor building on North Knox that must have been a hotel a century ago. It was full of winding passages and grand common rooms whose purpose had become a mystery. I heard voices inside or sensed something moving at the first places I tried, but no one answered, not that night, or the next, when I returned to pound on apartment doors. Calling it a breakthrough will sound silly, but on my third visit, I found my knock, more forceful than my first tentative efforts and less aggressive than my last, the mix of humility and authority most likely to produce the person hiding inside. I felt energized but soon realized that knocking was the easy part. Questioning those first Subjects made me so self-conscious, my hand shook as I marked the page. My voice shook too. I groped for words, unable to access the language I had spoken daily for twenty years, though I followed a standard script: *Hello, I'm* (NAME) *from the U.S. Census Bureau.* (SHOW ID). *Is this* (ADDRESS)? *I'm here to complete a Census questionnaire for this address* (HAND RESPONDENT AN INFORMATION SHEET). *Please look at List A. It contains examples of people who should and should not be counted at this place…*

I returned to Historia Commons a fifth night to complete one last EQ. Outside the apartment, I crouched over my bag, groping for forms and noticed for the first time the motif I had walked on all week—a faded pattern of linked, ever-widening circles on the blue carpet. The door opened and jolted me out of myself. An elderly man with thick glasses thrust his head into mine as if surprising a burglar planning her next theft.

"What is it? I thought you were my son," he said. "Are you lost?"

"I work for the Census." I could feel my heart pumping, as if he switched it on when he opened the door. "We didn't get your form. I have to ask you some questions."

"Yes, yes," he said in Polish. "Come in. The kettle is on."

No Respondent yet had invited me into his home. As we stepped inside, I asked if he had lived at this address on April 1.

"Yes, yes, but sit," he said. "I must make the tea first."

I sat on a long vinyl couch with metal legs that looked like it belonged in an office waiting room. Next to the kitchen entrance, where he disappeared, a small table with two wooden chairs pressed against the wall. Two places were elaborately set—forks, knives, plates, bowls, red cloth napkins. It was late for dinner, but maybe the son was bringing it. I did not smell cooking.

"Hello?" I called. "Sorry, but I can't linger." The Colonel had given me a new stack of EQs that day, and I was anxious to start them. I would come back another day. Just as I had not possessed the stamina for impossible lines in Gdansk, I didn't have the patience to sit here waiting for who knew what. I made motions to leave but chewed my lip and continued sitting, from stubbornness more than anything, though maybe some slight curiosity, too. The phrase "God's waiting room"—I once heard a comedian describe Florida this way—came to me for some reason as I fidgeted on the uncomfortable couch.

"Yes, yes," he called back. "Soon."

The minute hand of a large black-and-white wall clock that might have come from the same office as the couch did not move steadily but sprang forward in surprising increments. There were no photos from the last forty years on the walls, but older pictures featured my host with, I guessed, his wife and son.

A kettle shrieked, and a long while later, he teetered in with a tray conveying cups, sugar, milk, a teapot, and a box of fig cookies. I almost leaped up to take it but stopped myself, sensing that interference could create a disaster.

He set the tray on the coffee table with surprising grace.

"Thank you." I sipped my tea and businesslike, took out a pencil. "Does someone usually live at this address, or is it a seasonal residence or vacation home?"

He gestured with uplifted hands at the small, cluttered room.

"Sorry, they make us…" I started to take out the list of who should be counted, a sheet all Subjects were supposed to get, but then put it away. "How many people lived here on April 1?"

"Only me. And my son."

"No other relatives, roommates, foster children, others without a permanent place?" I abandoned the script, partly because we spoke in Polish, but sped through a version of the standard question, scribbling in a 2 before he answered.

"He's all the people I have."

"You are the renter here? What is your name?"

"You are from Gdansk," he said.

"How could you tell?" I did not want to get lost in a rambling dialogue with the old man, but he surprised me. Poland is not like America—there isn't really a Gdansk accent.

"I lived there after the War. My wife was from Gdansk. I worked in scavenging, scrap metal, a big business then."

I nodded, losing my place on the form. "Sorry, I need your name."

"Arvad," he said, pointing impatiently at the page in my lap, as if it should be there. "Arvad Nauczycielwitz." I printed carefully as he spelled it. Frank Hard complained about my handwriting, which spilled out of boxes and took serious work to interpret.

"What was your age on April 1?"

"You know the Green Gate? I met her there. Well, stole her."

"Who?"

"My wife. Her husband—the first one, not me—was a violinist, but he was blinded in the War. He couldn't work, so he played outside the Green Gate for coins. Always *The Grand Caprice Fantastique*. Why that piece, I don't know, the same every time. His playing was perfect, technically, but he only played the notes, if you follow, no feeling in between. Great artists love the spaces too. They live in between. Strange that he played that piece because caprice was just what he lacked. Well, maybe the War did that to him, too. She brought him bread and tea most afternoons, my wife. His wife—she was his wife then. I used to wait around just to see her, but we never spoke. I didn't have the nerve. He cursed her if she was late, something awful, right there in the street. Even when she was on time, he found things to complain about. *Bitch* this and *whore* that. Such language! Well, he'd been blinded, but still. She never said much. Sometimes when he was at her, she made faces or flapped her tongue, mocking him when she thought no one could see. I saw. You know those big doorways in the Green Gate? I used to read or sketch in a notebook just inside one of them, waiting for her to arrive—an hour, two, sometimes more. I felt guilty, spying like that, but what a thrill to watch her, unseen. When she made those faces—it felt so intimate, like watching the woman in the next apartment undress on nights she forgets to draw the blinds."

I sighed as he pointed at the window where a neighbor apparently disrobed in plain view. "I need to know your age on April 1," I said.

"You think I'm crazy? You're right. She made me that way. I haven't told you how beautiful she was. Then maybe you would understand. You know Audrey Hepburn? That kind of beauty, but with better proportions." He described her voluptuous form with his hands.

"When were you born?"

"Grace, intelligence—well, you could see it a mile away. And beauty itself. Imagine this woman, his muse when he played for the symphony, bringing him bread most days, still full of love, still showing up, and he curses her in the streets. Because he's blind? So what. Lots of musicians are blind, and don't they say some even play better for it? He could still see her in his mind—young, beautiful, and sure, naked if he wanted. I would have traded sight for such an image.

He might have seen her unhappiness if he tried, all that she lacked. I mean, he couldn't see, obviously, but he might have sensed it. Well, and maybe it's easy for me to say. I watched her every move, hidden in that doorway."

"But you never spoke?"

"I followed her one day. I didn't plan to, but when she left, I found myself trailing her home, three kilometers, maybe more. Down Chlebnicka, past St. Mary of the Assumption, onto Piwna. On a bench outside a small nameless church, she sat and cried. I almost went to her, but how could I, a stranger? Even if I'd known her, interrupting would have felt like a violation. Crying only made her more beautiful. There was something sacred about it. Watching her, I began to tear up myself, I admit, a grown man crying in the street. I followed her the next day from the Green Gate, and the next, every day she showed up after that. I don't know when she discovered me, but she began taking tortuous detours through the city center, lingering in the Long Market, strolling out the channels, weaving through the maze of narrow lanes. Some days she took me up and down the same roads, looping back as if she'd lost something valuable and was determined to find it. On others, she circled her destination for hours, testing how long or how well I could follow. I'd come to Gdansk for the first time from Bergen-Belsen, the displaced persons camp the British wanted us to call Hohn—we refused—because a man I knew had work in the city. I got lost every day. After a while, though, I knew I could find my way back to the center from almost anywhere."

"But when did you talk to her?"

"She sat one day, on the same bench outside that church, St. Nobody's, where I'd seen her cry. She looked at me and smiled. We'd exchanged glances, even brushed sleeves once or twice when she turned and passed close, leading me back the way we came. This was different, such a look, I felt like her eyes were inside of mine. I was ecstatic and terrified. I couldn't move, and then she waved."

He waved as he said this and his sleeve flapped open, exposing the numbers on his arm. The blue ink blurred into his wrinkled skin, but I could make out vague figures, hand-printed, crude, slightly larger toward his elbow.

"We were strangers but intimate, knew each other well, yet not at all. It felt like…"

"Tell me," I said, aiming for the same mix of humility and authority I used knocking on doors.

"You'll laugh. I felt like I'd been trailing my soul through the city and finally found it. Or was found by it." He grew shy. "You see, I told you. Like a bad movie."

"No. That is a beautiful way to think of it."

We sat in silence.

"Eighty-six," he said.

"Excuse me?"

"March 7, 1924 I was born. I'm eighty-six."

"What about her husband? You came to Chicago with her after that?"

"What?" He no longer seemed interested in his own story. "No, Haifa. She left him, and we went to Haifa in 1947. She was Catholic, I was Jewish, not an easy thing in Gdansk. Going there wasn't my smartest plan, though I wouldn't have met her otherwise. Americans don't know, there were pogroms in Poland after the War also. A beautiful city, Gdansk—in a way, my life started there—but full of death and division too. Most Jews had already left. So did we, once we saved a little. I had enough of war and death. Of course, fighting broke out in Israel, well, Palestine then, as soon as we arrived. We tried to arrange our next move better, the trip here, but there was so much we didn't know. Some things you can't plan."

His story finished, he looked drained of life. He glanced at the big clock on the wall.

"Where was your son born?"

"In Chicago. He would be fifty-three. My wife would be ninety-one if she was alive."

"But your son lives here with you?" I glanced at the table, set for two.

"What? Yes, yes, he's with me."

He looked at the clock again. I completed the EQ and thanked him. I wanted to ask more, about the concentration camp (why tell so much but not that?), the move to Chicago, his wife's death, his son. Also, I wanted to leave. There was something unhealthy about the place. The air felt thick and stale, as if windows had not been opened in a long time. Gathering my things, I noticed a fine layer of dust on one of the plates set for dinner. Had he invented the son's imminent arrival? Was his child estranged or gone? A sense of anticipation permeated the room, and I imagined Arvad Nauczycielwitz waiting here day after day, as patiently as he had for his wife at the Green Gate, only for a child who would never return.

I took an apartment a few blocks south of our old place, on Kilbourn. It was only one big room but with a dining area, where I could mix my herbal remedies. No one used the backyard, so I took it over, planting mint, basil, foxgloves, lavender. I had not had a real garden or my own room since leaving Gdansk and did not realize how much I missed them. Women's lives are so hard. Each must find a way not to go mad, my mother said, a sanctuary, a private escape. I had our place to myself when Jason left, but it was not private. He lingered there like the ghostly guests at that grand hotel in *The Shining*, the first American film I ever saw. I thought of that movie often, sitting alone in our apartment, going slowly insane like Jack Nicholson in that big empty room, typing the same sentence again and again. I could breathe in the new place. I had to dip into dwindling savings to pay rent, but it was worth whatever I spent.

I changed my name back to Cieslak and after a day of knocking on strangers' doors, it felt good to come home and see it printed on my buzzer. Certain windows I could not completely close. Depending on the weather, doors stuck shut or sprung open of their own accord. Winter would bring terrible drafts, I knew, but within those walls I could pursue anything I wanted. The apartment was as old and shabby as the one where I'd waited out Arvad Nauczyciel-witz's ramblings and learned the value of patience while enumerating, but it was mine. I loved sitting at the window in my only comfortable chair, which I'd found at Goodwill. Sifted through the catalpas out front, the last of the day's light seemed to bring the street inside as the air cooled. I could sit for an hour, watching shadows lengthen and colors change in the fading sun. Neighbors returning from work laughed and complained under my window, swapping news. The smell of chiles and frying pork rose from downstairs. Children played on the street until an older sister shouted a dinner call.

The loneliness was hard, especially at night. I considered asking Emma to live with me for the summer, when she was off school. Forced into the same room, our sightlines would change, I thought, and we might even begin to understand each other. I did not ask because, for reasons I could not explain, I needed to be on my own. I also needed Emma to live with Jason. I still did not know anything about his girl, where they lived, what they did, or planned to do. I knew that I could learn this from Emma if she stayed with Jason, though I had no idea it would be so easy. She gave me his address on the phone when I offered to take her shopping the week she moved in with him. He lived in a small apartment complex in Edgebrook, a pricey neighborhood that felt like a suburb, though it was only a couple miles away.

She was waiting in the lobby when I pulled up. All this time, he was right here, I thought, anger rising like bile in my throat. I let it settle, composing myself while Emma walked to the car. Mechanically, she gave me a half-hug.

"How is school?" I asked, pulling into traffic.

She shrugged and stared out the window. Fine, she said after a few minutes, and then gradually, maybe from boredom, offered details. She had a B average, but As in her math and accounting classes. The student union was hiring (coffee and games, not workers' rights, she explained with a smirk, when I looked confused). A roommate had started calling her Dil-Emma, a name that, unfortunately, was catching on.

"It's no worse than *Marge*," I said, patting her leg, and she actually laughed. She knew how much I hated nicknames, especially the unwanted ones, especially mine.

She told me about a boy, just someone she had met, not a boy*friend*, she said, though I could tell the rest of her narrative was a mere shell built to house this pearl. Such revelations, like her spontaneous laugh, had little precedent in the history of Emma and me. Excited by her openness, I asked about him—his age, what he studied, how they met— perhaps in tones too eager or teasing. Her lips folded under, and the old Emma, moody and cynical, returned.

I drove in silence for five minutes and then, as if groping for a topic, asked, "So how are they treating you up there? What do you think of your father's girlfriend?"

"She's as messy as ever. Clothes don't make it into drawers—they dress out of the laundry basket. Drink milk from the carton. Dad eats from the pots. All very primal, like the dorm freshman year. She's still loud, but more settled maybe? I mostly ignore her. She's kissing my ass, for sure—little gifts, lunch invites, unwanted advice. All pretty weird."

Signaling, I pulled into a parking lot under a sign that said only *Korean Restaurant*. I pressed my forehead against the steering wheel, then banged it there once, hard. "Sarita?"

"Oh shit," Emma said. "Seriously? Are you that blind, Mom? It went on for like years under your nose. Literally."

"You not tell me?" I screamed, the language I had worked so hard to master getting the better of me. "Sarita? And you knew?"

"I thought you did too," she yelled and then said softly, "I thought you knew."

I faced rejection of many kinds as an Enumerator. Some doors closed on my first words.

Others never opened, though at windows, vague figures hovered behind blinds or stood still as mannequins, outlined in wispy material. I was called an asshole, thief, bitch, and double agent, but Evelyn Toomey was the only Subject to hiss at me. She lived in the basement unit—probably illegal—of a decrepit three-flat on Keeler. I knocked and Evelyn appeared, silent, wide-eyed, almost cartoonish. Her pale skin drooped so much around her eyes and mouth, it looked like a mask whose openings did not quite match her own. Smears of blue eyeshadow and circles of rouge heightened the effect, making her features look flat and sketched, not human.

"Hello, I'm Margaret Cieslak," I said. "I work for the Census. Is this Apartment 1B?"

She leaned forward and made a sound, snake-like but louder and more expressive. I repeated the question. She hissed again, gestured in frustration, and shut the door.

I was not discouraged. I would try her twice a day all week, and the next if I had to. Frank Hard no longer criticized when my writing burst from the boxes on EQs or took work to decipher. After a few weeks of enumerating, I completed nine questionnaires in a single day. When he heard, Jerzy, who held the previous record with five, nearly ripped the ponytail he was petting from his head. We were not supposed to return to an address more than three times, but I would go back ten times, twenty, as many as I had to.

For the toughest Subjects, I waited in halls, often for hours, if I sensed someone moving inside. I left endless Notice of Visit forms, wrote personal notes beneath the printed text, squeezed pages under doors as if stuffing sausage.

Frank Hard would have fired me if he knew, but my persistence paid off. Over time, I learned things about the holdouts and used that insight to draw them out. Catherine Lessing's mail piled up—*Shape, Woman's World,* Victoria's Secret catalogues, bitter unanswered letters from her mother. She lacked self-esteem, I imagined, and invested too much in the boyfriend (smug and proprietary in his online photos) whose place she stayed at most nights. In my notes and calls to her, I took a nurturing, not quite maternal approach (like Emma, she had a difficult relationship with her mom). I was much tougher on Nick Levin, who had the opposite problem. Each morning I found my NVs shredded in his lobby, impaled like heads of foes on the iron fence out front, or stuffed into the empty chardonnay boxes he stacked in the alley. How dare I interrupt his day? The building's other tenants rolled their eyes at his name, tired of his rants about their noise and clutter. When had he lost all empathy for his neighbors, stopped seeing them, despite their deficits, or even because of them, as human?

My methods violated policy, and sometimes the law, so I was nervous when the Colonel said he wanted to see me. Ruth pressed her unwashed body against mine in a hug, beaming as if the handsomest boy at school finally asked me to dance. Jerzy's take was closer to my own. Grinning smugly, he hovered at the table outside the Colonel's office, pretending to stock up on D-1(F)s. It was my first time in the tiny space, separated from the rest of us by a moveable divider. It had no door and offered no peace or privacy, but the Colonel clung to the detached square like a tribesman holding ancestral land.

"Marge," the Colonel said, "the Bureau is highly impressed with your work. *Highly.*"

Something bumped against the flimsy partition, and I imagined Jerzy livid on the other side. I wanted to stab the Colonel in the eye for calling me Marge, but felt relief mingled with, I will admit, a certain pride.

He knew I spoke Polish, the Colonel said, but reviewing my file, he saw German and Russian too. The Bureau wanted to maximize my skillset with a new assignment. Flipping through a manila folder, he asked, "What about Spanish?"

"No."

"A little, though?"

"No. I can't speak it."

"But a working knowledge?" He nodded slowly as he spoke. "A few words?"

"Well, a few words," I finally agreed and the Colonel smiled, maybe for the first time in my presence.

"Good. In Chicago, they like language specialists who have at least a little Spanish."

I nodded, astonished. Frank Hard, the king of regulations, was helping me skirt a rule. I would stay at his office for this new work, he said, but he would feed me EQs from others if the Subjects required a language I spoke. Of course, several in the first batch called for Spanish. I tried to return them.

"Just do your best," the Colonel said. "You know, you listed Spanish proficiency in your skillset when you went after this position."

I learned as I went, watching Spanish TV, listening to a course on CD, and practicing with the Garcias, my downstairs neighbors, whose children were thoroughly entertained by my mistakes. The new assignment took me all over the city. Hermosa was just a few miles south of my place, but driving there felt like crossing a border. Neon signs for *taquerias, lavanderías,* and *cervezas* winked on at dusk. From passing cars, bass guitars pounded the count of Mexican songs, pushing speakers past distortion. I counted Russian Jews in Rogers Park and Poles in Garfield Ridge. I filled out questionnaires for Romanians in Ravenswood and Lithuanians in Marquette Park, though I did not speak their languages. They spoke others well enough that we could meet in between and understand. I went to Avondale, Craigin, East Chicago, Archer Heights—so many strange, scattered neighborhoods, I gave up planning efficient routes, just as I'd read the city gave up on Daniel Burnham's plan to force order on wild city streets a century ago. I accepted that I would spend half my time lost.

Counting foreigners, who were often without papers and wary of authorities, forced me to get even more creative and persistent. The Census Bureau did not pay me for the extra time I spent, but once I noted certain details—a mysterious accent muffled through a door, neighbors' contradictory comments, Christmas lights still hanging in July—I had to see the Subjects, a compulsion that had as much to do with curiosity as with the desire to do a good job. Why, for instance, had Evelyn Toomey hissed at me? I knocked on her door for a week before she opened it again, out of pure exasperation.

I greeted her as if it was my first visit: "Hi, I'm from the Census. Is this Unit 1B?"

She hissed in reply, but this time, I heard a "yes" in her strained rasp. Then I saw it. At the base of her throat gaped a hole perhaps an inch across, red and uncovered, so raw it looked as if she had come straight from surgery. How had I missed that last time?

"I am just going to show you these questions and let you fill in the boxes, okay?" I said, pointing at the first one. "You won't have to speak."

Evelyn flung the pencil I handed her to the ground and hissing like a radio stuck between stations, retreated inside.

I kept Emma at my place late, drinking wine. She slept on my couch, and before she woke the next morning, I copied her keys. On the Recorder of Deeds website, I learned that Jason's building, of course, belonged to Castillo, our old landlord, father of the Mexican-American Princess. Jason would inherit the kingdom with Sarita—Castillo's real estate empire—but I had the keys to the palace.

My Census ID gave me access to Jason's building and made me a peripheral presence. As I entered the lobby, a couple saw my ID dangling from its lanyard and held the door, continuing their argument without pause. They would not have known me an hour later, though I still remember what I overheard: his claim that her work was becoming more important than he was and beneath her weak denial, a dawning realization that he was right.

On the fourth floor, I found Jason and Sarita's door. I knew their schedules from Emma but tapped to make sure. No one answered. Still, I could not go in. This door led to a Jason who was real on his own, who lived a separate life, who touched someone else as he once touched only me. The third time I inserted the key, a lock clicked down the hall, as if I'd accidentally opened another door. Voices reached me, I turned the handle and slipped inside.

The apartment was just as Emma described, large and nicely renovated, but cluttered and dirty. Built-in mahogany bookshelves stood empty except for a thick layer of dust. The doors of kitchen cabinets gaped, and a pot of food hardened on the stove. Polished oak floors disappeared under piles of clothes, shoes, boxes, and books someone must have consumed like food. Their bright covers cluttered countertops and tables and lined the sill behind the kitchen sink, where at home I kept my jars of homemade salve. Jason and Emma were not readers. I do not know why it surprised, even angered me, that Sarita was. Most of her battered volumes did not fit neatly into the categories of crime or romance but some trashy space in between: *Seduction of a Thief, Clues to Love, A Spy's Heart*. She read some serious novels, too, and volumes of Spanish poetry: Neruda, Lorca, Octavio Paz. Why did she not put them in the bookcases? I snatched books up by the armful and set them on the shelves in neat rows. The living room remained a mess, but the satisfaction I felt at the apartment's chaos faded after I organized her books. I thought of my own orderly place—books confined to their cases, surfaces scrubbed, labels facing front. It seemed to reflect an empty existence. Jason and Sarita lacked nothing—money, comfort, companionship. My life did not contain enough material for a mess.

Before I left, I turned the air conditioning down from seventy-three degrees to sixty-eight. Like shifting her books, it was an impulse, not a part of some plan.

The next night, Emma stayed at my place to escape Jason and Sarita's fighting. He believed she had turned down the air conditioning, an expense that bothered him more than any other. Despite his denials, she thought he had put her books away and saw his tidying up as a criticism of her sloppy domestic habits.

It took a second week of visits before Evelyn Toomey again opened her door. I explained once more that she would not have to speak—she could write her information down. Her breathy reply sounded like *I have need*. I shook my head in confusion, but as she continued hissing, I understood that she was saying, *I can't read*. I felt so bad, I almost turned and left, but if I did not finish her form, another Enumerator would get it and bother her all over again.

"Can I come in?" I asked.

Reluctantly, she waved me through the door. The basement apartment was a single dark room with concrete walls. A thin band of windows topped the far wall at sidewalk-level, but they were barred and did not give much light. Tan spiral ducts coiled like worms across a low concrete ceiling. The closeness and dim light made me sleepy.

Next to the sink, an old writing desk served as a counter. It was cluttered with spices, potatoes, and onions. We sat knee-to-knee in front of it, on green plastic chairs. As I searched for Evelyn's form in my bag, something shrieked. I started, wide awake now, or dreaming.

She laughed silently and rasped, *Watch it, Hope! Hope, be nice.*

An enormous blue-gray parrot perched on a stand a few feet from my head. It shifted from claw to claw anxiously, glaring at me and puffing up to twice its normal size. *Hope, be nice! Watch it, Hope,* the bird repeated.

Evelyn raised her palms and frowned. Yes, she seemed to say, the mute lady has a talking bird. Isn't the universe funny? She patted my knee to indicate that the parrot would not hurt me, but my skin tingled as I turned to her with that thing swelling over my shoulder, watching me like a detective expecting a theft. I started with a few questions not on the form to get used to Evelyn's voice, or lack of one. In a hoarse whisper, she told me she had lived in Chicago for forty years. She and her boyfriend, Andy, came from a town called Fallsburg, in Eastern Kentucky. I watched her lips, focusing on words that were more air than sound, felt and seen at that close range as much as heard—smelled, too (she had eaten garlic today). If I stayed close and worked hard, I could understand her.

I was about to ask if she lived in the apartment on April 1 when she volunteered that Andy used to grow marijuana in Kentucky. He packed his van full of it when they left. They planned to sell it in the city, to finance their move. Evelyn had an aunt in Uptown who they could stay with, but Chicago was just a stop on the way to Paradise. California was the real plan—beaches, sun, money, and sure, even movie stars, why not? Andy had too much ambition for Eastern

Kentucky, which was why he dropped out of the animal science program at the Voc-tech and started growing weed in a hidden patch on the West Virginia border, out past Freewill Baptist. It was why he told her to *dummy up* sometimes too. He didn't mean it. He was just tired of working like a dog and desperate for a real life. He didn't order her around like her Daddy or threaten to shut her trap for her if she didn't shut it quick. She loved Andy but went with him mostly to get away from Daddy and home. She had three younger brothers and a dead mother and missed a lot of school, keeping house. When she did go to school, how could she focus, worrying about every little thing at home? Why I never learned to write proper, she said. The words got all jumbled when I tried.

Andy had a contact in Chicago, a guy called Rod. It was short for Rodney, but the way he acted, Evelyn thought it was a nickname he earned. Wouldn't have been bad looking, actually, except for the ZZ Top beard and x-ray eyes, smiling like they saw not just the parts under your clothes but everything those parts ever did too. He raised rabbits right in the city, and he had a serval, which is a cat that is more or less wild. He kept a giant snake in a tank, too, a boa constrictor or one of those, that he fed his live rabbits and chickens and things. All real biblical, lording it over his own little creation. My aunt who we stayed with read from her Old Testament every night in this strange voice that came out of nowhere, like someone started speaking through her or she turned into God. Rodney could have stepped off any page.

The weed was low-grade, Rod said. He called it Lowlife on the street and sold it for cheap but still more than Andy got at home. Unloading it would take time. That was fine. We planned to stay in Chicago a month. What we didn't know, Rod got arrested a few weeks after we met him and sacrificed Andy to cut a deal. Rod walked out of County three months later. The prosecutor offered Andy two years.

He'd serve one if he behaved and do one on parole. I said he better take it. Otherwise, he might have got six to ten.

They locked him up and there I was, alone, stuck between Kentucky and California in a big city I didn't know, without any friends or money. Wasn't official and no one wrote it down, but I got my own sentence the day Andy got his. Without him, my aunt's place felt like church, stone quiet except for her reading from that Bible and shushing me in case I'd wake Uncle Emory, who had diabetes and kidney disease and smelled like he died last week. It was the most miserable year of my life up to then and the first time I thought about death. I mean, I knew we all die, but it felt real all a sudden, like at eighteen, I had one foot in the grave. My first job, wheeling old people around Baum Assisted Living, didn't help. Residents died all the time. I hated going to work that winter. I piled on layers for the walk, but when that lake wind blew, I still felt like I was naked on the wrong side of a barbed-wire fence.

The week Andy got out, I rented an apartment on Broadway, next to the el. We had no money and leaving was tricky, with his parole. Paradise would have to wait. We must have looked like animals in a zoo to people rattling past our windows on trains, but the place was ours. Andy said I could have got a better one. He came out of prison pissed at the world but blaming me. He could have won at trial, he said. It was me talked him into a deal. A year of his life gone! Could have been six, but he didn't consider that.

He was scared to leave the apartment. When I tried to talk to him, he told me to save it. He shushed me if I spoke during a show. He told me, quit yapping to neighbors. Some days I didn't say ten words. Except for work, I hardly left home, and never at night. Broadway was the border between three gangs. Guns popped so often we didn't flinch. Our apartment was a cell, not much nicer than Andy's at Stateville, and the city felt like one big prison.

Once he got comfortable going out again, Andy stayed away for longer and longer spells. He had to get a job, I told him, he had to. My checks from Baum Assisted Living barely covered rent. He was looking for work, he said, but couldn't find a thing. Four hours, six, eight he'd be gone. Pretty soon, it was half the night. Sometimes he came home drunk or high. Where'd he get the money for that? I was crying hard enough to crack a rib one night—I cried all the time—when he came in high as almighty, carrying a big box. It was cardboard, with oil stains all over. You could smell it was oil. Holes big as nickels were cut into the top. Something moved inside. I leaned down to look, and it screeched so loud I almost fell over. Andy laughed like that was the funniest thing ever. I was mad. I ripped the top off, and out flew this giant bird, almost smacked me in the face. I never saw nothing like it. It was gray with blue and green, and eyes like a person's, that smart. It fluttered around the apartment, bouncing off surfaces like it wanted to touch every one, or else couldn't find a place to land. I shouted and laughed, and Andy never stopped laughing.

Andy was shy in the bedroom after prison. The rare times we did it, it had to be with the lights off. That night, though, we did it like we used to, right there in the living room, lights on, blinds up, no thinking or hesitating, like animals. Three trains went by and must have got quite a show. I cried afterwards, I was so happy. He told me to hush and get dressed for dinner. He could take me out, he said, cause he found a job, unloading freight on the West Side. What about the bird? I asked. Let her get her own job, he said. He wouldn't tell me where she came from, and I didn't care. We were never happier than the week that bird showed up. Why I called her Hope, ain't that right, Hope? We made new plans—one more winter in Chicago, then west to Paradise. No more snow, gunshots, gangs. No more living in cramped rooms or struggling just to eat.

The next week, Andy came home from work smelling like the van we drove up in. When I asked about it, he told me to mind my business. He was worried about something but wouldn't say what. I felt like an idiot when I found out he was back working for Rod. Yes, the guy who put him in prison. Of course, it was Rod gave him the bird. I should have known. I told Andy, calm as I could, why working for Rod, in my opinion, was a bad idea. Since when did my opinion count? he asked. Now, not another word, he said. I got exactly one out—*but*—before the flat of his hand hit my cheek. I couldn't believe he done it. Neither could he. He cried into my neck for an hour after, saying, sorry, I'm sorry, sorry, over and over.

We made Kenny that night. I got no doubt, just like I can name the day eleven months later that Bill got his start in this world. I swear, the less we did it, the more it counted. I left Andy when he kept moving weed after Bill was born, less than a year after Ken, Irish twins, as Daddy would say. I knew what was waiting for Andy, sure as I knew that the train snaking past our window would finish at Howard Street—and I knew he'd make it my fault all over. He's been inside twice since then, this last time with a sentence as good as life.

The boys got out of Chicago as soon as they could, Bill at eighteen, Ken not even that, and without a word, like he was taking revenge. It was only then I felt how much I must have hurt my Daddy, leaving home. For years, I wanted to call him but was too ashamed—of running off, of Andy doing time, of having the boys without being married, a crime in his eyes. I kept thinking I'd visit sometime. I had a friend write letters. He never answered, and then came word from my aunt, he was dead. He didn't even know where I was, like me with Ken today. He was always in trouble, Ken, same as Andy, but Bill is another story. He bounced around and where do you think he wound up? Paradise! That's right, California.

When I got the picture of him in a place called Arcata—he works on a farm near there—I didn't know whether to thank the lord or cry. It wasn't what Andy and me planned, him in prison and cancer eating my throat, but at least with Bill, our story had something good at the end. He says I should visit, but I never will. Bill lives in Paradise in my mind, and seeing California now would just spoil it. No, I'll stay here, in the City in a Garden. Did you know that's the nickname they got for Chicago? Funny, right? This dump, the City in a Garden!

I went into Jason and Sarita's place with tragedy at my fingertips. A powder I ground from poison sumac caused severe rashes if rubbed into clothes. I could have poisoned them slowly with oleander or narcissus, or blinded them with carefully placed hogweed sap. I meant to make use of the drama packed in my Census bag, but when I sank into their space, small problems—more insidious than anything I could have planned—appeared like gifts. With Jason's credit card, I got Sarita subscriptions to *US* and *People*, Indonesian coffee beans that cost fifty dollars a pound, and a beautiful Laura Ashley gown. I wrote a note from Jason to the young receptionist he liked at his shop and left it under Sarita's shoe. The note was innocent and awkward, but overly friendly, Jason's from the steeply slanted handwriting to the words he always misspelled (I had learned to imitate him so well in print, when reviewing accounts, he could not tell his notes from mine).

I scrubbed their floors and kitchen counters, alphabetized DVDs, filed papers, and organized cabinets. I wrapped food left lingering on the stove, and signing Jason's name to Sarita's checks, paid the overdue bills stuffed in her desk.

One day, I read the first page of a book Sarita left open on a table. An hour passed without my noticing. I took it home and finished it. The next week, I took another, and then another, a new book nearly every time.

Emma moved in with me when they blamed their fighting on her, though their arguments only worsened after she left. Every word Jason and Sarita said now seemed to have a second meaning, and those they did not say carried even more weight, resentment simmering between the lines.

Looking through Sarita's jewelry one day, I found a hearing aid in her drawer. It was one of those small ones colored like skin, invisible unless you know to look for it. I held it between my fingers to examine in the light, like a little pearl of flesh. She probably would have been loud anyway, but this explained at least some of the noise that had bothered me when she lived downstairs. She was seven years older than I was, young for hearing loss, but I supposed it could happen at any age. Sarita squinted when you spoke to her, a habit that annoyed me, but had I misinterpreted concentration as condescension? How had my own face looked while I strained to hear Evelyn Toomey's voice, so faint at times I thought I imagined it? I had followed as best I could, with that crazy bird puffed-up over my shoulder, as if supervising my work. Certain things stood out, but between those islands of clarity, understanding her required an act of faith that would have made her religious aunt proud.

The last time I stood in Jason and Sarita's place, I got bored waiting for the laundry to dry. At her dressing table, I applied makeup halfheartedly. I had sorted through their closets and tried on everything I could get into. I had read most of her books, including the Spanish poetry as my skills improved (some of it, like *The Book of Questions* and *Impressions and Landscapes,* so beautiful, I wrote in the margins and could not return them). On a high shelf, I spotted a book I had started and abandoned, *The Icarus Agenda* by Robert Ludlum. I liked another by him, *The Bourne Identity,* but this one was harder to follow. Reading on their bed, I laid the paperback on my chest and drifted off. In my dream, it was spring. Giant oaks and ash trees were budding. I heard the tap of rain dripping from gutters, smelled damp earth and new grass. I do not know how, since I sat in a small windowless room. There did not seem to be a way out. Dread slowly overtook the hopeful sense of spring, but as panic set in, I saw a door. I opened it and only then recognized the room I was leaving as the closet in Gdansk where I stole from a stranger to escape to another country. I felt relieved to enter the next room, which was bigger, but despair gradually overtook me there, too. I panicked and again discovered a door. It led to another, even bigger room, and so I went from one to the next, by turns hopeful and despondent, each room expanding off the last, as if I was lost in a telescope.

The door to the last room slammed, louder than the others. I heard voices. Where was I? I recognized mahogany dressers and a rumpled green chenille bedspread. The book spilling from my chest. Jason and Sarita's bedroom. Someone was home. I sprang from the bed and clutching my book, stepped into the closet. The door had slats. If I bent my head at a sharp angle, I could see the room through them, or strips of it, like a poem with alternate lines in another language.

Jason came in. He pulled up the sheets I had tangled and slid into them clothed. Sarita sat down a few minutes later and busied herself at her dressing table. She wore a frayed terrycloth robe, with a coffee-colored stain above the left breast. She seemed to transform while I watched, as makeup came off and worry lines emerged. She looked the way I felt, as if she had aged years in the last six months.

"Maybe seventy-six isn't so old, but he forgets things," she said. "He can't count. I deposit the rent checks, something's missing, the account's off. How? He can't say, it just is."

"I forget things," Jason said. "I miscount. He needs a bookkeeper."

"What?"

"A bookkeeper."

"It's not just the rents." She brushed out her long limp hair. I had never seen it unwashed or so overdue for a cut. "Someone breaks into the house to steal his razors is the new thing, takes food from the fridge. On the phone last week, he had no idea who I was."

Her father was the same age as mine. Hers seemed older, but maybe mine had grown just as frail. How would I know? Sarita's dress—short and black, with an Empire waist— began to feel tight, constricting my ribs. I sat on the hamper I had emptied earlier and tried to breathe. Was this real? My dream had started in a closet and now I sat in another, watching my husband and his lover in their bedroom. If they became intimate, I could disappear, I thought, find a way to kill myself right there.

"We have two empty bedrooms," Jason said.

"Are you going to stay with him all day? You got a good translator? Cause he only speaks Spanish now, like someone is stealing his words along with the razors and memories." She turned her enormous brown eyes on Jason, her best feature I always thought, but tired and swollen today, they looked froglike. "What happens when he leaves the door open or the tap running, or wanders off into a dangerous area?"

"He's not that bad."

"He will be," Sarita said. "Like a child. Some place with assisted living—not *just* that, but as an option—they're ready for whatever."

Bottles clinked as she shuffled them around her dressing table. Some days, I rearranged everything, organizing the makeup according to tone, cost, function. On others, I changed a single item, spending an hour or more sometimes deciding what to take, add, move.

"Have you seen my Désirer? The bottle shaped like a bird?"

"Those places are so sad."

"They have activities and events, someone always watching," Sarita said. "He sits there like a statue now, hardly leaves the TV—and we're not equipped to handle him."

"We're not equipped to handle anyone."

"What?"

He didn't respond.

"If you're bitching about Emma again, I tried."

"To kick her out."

"That is not what happened," Sarita said.

It was not. I knew from Emma that Sarita had tried, much too hard, in fact—planning outings, paying compliments, leaving cheerful little notes. Emma's reactions fell somewhere between indifference and derision, but Sarita's hurt rose out of all proportion to the slights of a moody teen. That overreaction reminded me of others, when Sarita had lived below us. She felt more than heard the thud of little feet upstairs, she used to say, as if the disturbance was personal. Tadeusz and Emma had tormented Sarita, I realized, because she believed children were the missing ingredient in her life. She wanted what I had. Well, she had it now—Jason and for a while, even Emma—but she was no happier. She remained lonely and dissatisfied because as Jason was finding out, what she really lacked was empathy.

"It has wings on the sides," Sarita said.

"Huh?"

"My perfume bottle. The Désirer?"

"Désirer?" Jason said. "Oh yeah, it's in my coat. Inside pocket."

"Smartass."

"I lost your perfume too? Really? And you think your father imagines things."

"I didn't say you lost it. I just know I left it right here."

"Sure, and you're not saying I killed your plants or cleaned your desk, and you're not saying I'm cheap. You never said I slept with Jean either, just badgered me until I fired her."

"I speak my mind. That's better than all your little passive-aggressive…stuff." She ground cold cream into her face, as if with enough pressure, she might erase the lines massing around her mouth.

Jason closed his eyes. I thought he was asleep until he spoke. "The halls smell like piss. The food sucks, even at the best ones. Your dad is full of life still. He doesn't belong in a box."

"There are some beautiful facilities, and they cost less than it would to hire caregivers. We'll save money."

"*Facilities*," Jason said with disgust.

"He'll get better care, and we'll spend less."

Sarita focused on cost because that often worked with him. She had his number, as Jason would say. I had done the same thing, twisting him into positions like a mannequin to suit my plans and eroding what we had in the process (though I was the dummy now, a silent spectator under their control, contorted in a borrowed dress). Jason was attracted to assertive women. Indecisive and aimless, he needed a strong hand, but he resented it, too, eventually. Sarita's back was to him. She did not see the horror on his face when he described urine-scented halls or said the word *facilities*. It was not the money this time. He was more concerned than I would have guessed, genuinely worried about the old man he'd known for twenty years.

Jason and Sarita bickered on and off all evening, then made up grudgingly. They did not, thankfully, make love. I waited five hours, stiff and cramped in the closet, parts of me falling asleep so I might be sure that they were. I could not have managed it if not for spending so much time waiting outside strangers' doors, as if practicing for this all summer. When I finally left, I almost floated from the room. I was not happy—I barely kept from sobbing—and I did not forgive Jason. I still hated him. I simply knew I would never return to that place. I let go.

By summer's end, everyone I started with had disappeared. Our work with the Census wound down, and Frank Hard sent the others away—Sonny, Ravi, Magda, Chuy. Even Jerzy, the second-best Enumerator in the office, had to go. What happened to him, and to Ruth, who had such trouble counting, I could not imagine her in a real job? I was the only one the Colonel kept on for the next operation, counting the homeless and transient, "the uncountable," as he said. We looked for them in the places that addressed their needs—shelters, free clinics, soup kitchens—and would spend one final evening counting others on the street. TNSOL Night (Targeted Non-Sheltered Outdoor Locations), the Colonel announced, would mark the end of my tenure. I wished he had given more warning. Utilities were sending threatening letters. I was strangely calm about giving up power, prepared to live in the dark, but I was also a month behind on my rent. I cut all but the essentials—potatoes, bread, lentils—and still struggled to balance the books. The Bureau's checks were never enough, and I'd lost the small income I had earned selling home remedies. The new assignment left me with less and less energy to mix them, until counting the uncountable replaced the last of my balms.

TNSOL Night, which we pronounced *tinsel*, conjured images of a city strung with shiny gold strands, but there was nothing festive about it. The Bureau marked the colored neighborhood maps it gave us with white, not silver or gold, and these lines were not decorative—people lived in them. At first I thought white an odd choice to highlight the corridors where transients gathered, but it allowed us to write on the maps and as cartographer's code for the unknown, suited the sparse industrial strips and vacant blocks the homeless favored.

The Colonel sent my team to the center of the city. We followed the thickest of the scars on our map along the expressway. Beneath overpasses we stumbled onto shadowy figures guarding carts stuffed with rags, cans, bedding, and appliances. Some scaled sloping berms to sleep between massive concrete columns or the highway's steel ribs. Like Athena from the head of Zeus, they emerged from the structure as if part of it, born when I shined my light on their huddled forms. Our maps highlighted el routes, drainage canals, and railroad tracks, which like the expressways, fell between neighborhoods or formed their borders. Why did transients sprout at the city's seams like grass in cracked sidewalks? They liked the shelter of viaducts and trestles and the lack of police in those barren areas, but I realized that whatever particulars they lacked—parents, employment, sobriety, sanity—they lived this life because they did not fit in one box or another. They had straddled borders before becoming homeless and used to the geography of gaps, continued to live in them after.

The lines on our maps cut through busy, expensive areas too—along Lower Wacker and underground sections of Hubbard, Illinois, Lake Shore. I had never explored the city's subterranean streets or the Pedway, a network of pedestrian tunnels that connected skyscrapers, shops, and train stops under the Loop. I forgot it was there, just as those who lived in its winding passages seemed to have forgotten the world above, inured to fetid air and fluorescent lights that over time, gave their eyes a dull cast and their skin a pallor almost blue.

By dark, I felt like Dante descending into Hell. Another, submerged city existed beneath the one people knew. I had glimpsed it, exiting expressways and cutting through alleys, but never realized how vast and connected it was. Thinner lines branched off the thick ones on our maps, and even narrower lines off these, snaking through downtown beaches, neighborhood parks, and the rubble of demolished projects on the South Side. They fell between Old Town mansions and the CHA towers of Cabrini-Green, ran from Austin on the West Side to Streeterville on the lake, touched

Oakland, Chinatown, and the South Loop in one nearly unbroken band.

Spotting the people that the lines led to demanded stamina. They camped under bridges and in doorways. They wore clothes the gray of the concrete they slept on or as black as the bags of possessions surrounding them like walls. I had a better eye than many Enumerators working on TNSOL Night, but for once, filled out the fewest questionnaires. If the Subjects were hostile or afraid, we were supposed to count them from a safe distance. Most Enumerators did as Frank Hard advised in that case and simply wrote *MALE 1, MALE 2, FEMALE 1*…on questionnaires, or if the sex was unclear, *PERSON 1, PERSON 2*…This took only a few seconds, but I always tried to speak to the Subjects, coaxing and chatting, groping for language that might close the distance. Usually, I got at least a name. If they refused to give it, I made one up. I made up their ages, races, and housing status too. Once I met people, writing *FEMALE 1* and *PERSON 3* on their forms did not feel right. I was breaking the rules again, but so many of the details the homeless gave seemed fabricated anyway, was it dishonest to make up a few more?

They came naturally, the details I invented. My imagination flared that night like the campfires we found along the Chicago River, fed by moving shadows, half-hidden figures, the secret places transients lived. I imagined whole people too. Beneath an overpass, I saw Ruth shuffle by in her usual yellow dress. When I squeezed her shoulder, thrilled to see her, a young girl turned. Under the el on Wabash, Jerzy stroked his silver ponytail, one of several men sharing a quart of beer. As I approached, his features grew sharp, no longer doughy and vague like those of the Jerzy I'd met in spring. Up close, the man was three inches too tall. I saw Chuy eating crackers on a bench, and Ravi and Magda, the college kids who fell into Census work, sleeping in a doorway of the Washington Library on Van Buren.

I saw what was not there because difficult work on a dark night awakened my imagination, because I encountered so many with so little between them and the street. It was hard to see them, and even harder to see how little now separated them from me.

Out of Egypt

Before his first blink, even before he began to wake, his brain registered the smell, a mix of sanitizers—pine, bleach, alcohol—with hardly a suggestion of the odors they covered—human waste, food, blood. Every hospital in Chicago had it, that powerful ammoniac scent Izzy loved. It was the smell of comfort, order, and care, a smell that said as long as you breathed it, nothing could harm you.

He had been waking up slowly, by dizzying increments, for what felt like years. No one noticed the first flutter of eyelids that revealed the hospital room to the thirteen-year-old boy, and his instinct was to shut them quickly. He did not want to talk to anyone. He didn't have the strength and after the accident, would not have known what to say. He pretended to sleep while he looked for a sign, some clue to his condition and circumstances and most important, how he should act. Until he had a plan, he decided, he would remain unconscious.

An image of the car came back to him, a gold Cadillac sedan, mint, with an inlaid hood and that boxy front end the new Caddies had, nineteen-inch aluminum wheels, the chrome grill that looked like an evil smile. In his mind, the car bore down on him, relentless as the future, and Izzy winced, remembering the impact. The trick was to approach from the side, never head-on but at an angle you could fake as head-on for the driver and potential witnesses, anyone paying attention. His Pop taught him that two years ago, when they practiced with his El Dorado on abandoned land next to Wolf Lake, a place that creeped Izzy out since he'd heard stories of the bodies mobsters dumped there. He'd faked falls for his Pop before the lessons, at restaurants and playgrounds, parking lots and stores, but that was chump change compared to a car accident. With vehicular, the settlements could be huge, depending, and the risk was small if you were careful and knew what to do. Izzy was and did, so what went wrong today—or was it yesterday? He didn't know. He'd been pumped full of something, was still half under, and would have to get his bearings to figure things out.

Squinting secretly, he collected fragments and attempted to put them together. A framed copy of the Lord's Prayer hung next to the door and in small type below the last line was the name of the hospital, something *Covenant*—he couldn't quite see. He had trouble seeing himself, too, because of the angle of his head, but straining, he discovered that his right arm and leg were wrapped in splints of a stiff white material. Under the narrow slit of his right eye was more white—gauze or a bandage—with a faint chemical smell, like vitamins or Vicks rub. He flexed his right cheek and the skin beneath the textured pad burned, then went cold. Or wet. He couldn't tell. He did not feel pain, not in his face or arm or leg, and this surprised him. He looked like something half formed, his left side complete, his right still drying in a mold.

He squinted out of one eye and then the other undetected, fooling his father, who said he could never be conned, and the doctor he spoke to, a few feet away. The room was dim, the lighting extra low, which made it easier to sneak peeks without being noticed. At first, Izzy thought he would have to give himself away just to take a drink. A plastic cup of water sat on the tray beside him along with a small brown pitcher. His throat was so dry it stuck closed, as if his body didn't want him to swallow anything. Instead of reaching for the cup, though, he thought of a hamburger cooked rare, juicy, with lots of salt and cheese. He pictured himself biting into it. His jaw moved imperceptibly, as if chewing, and his mouth watered. Groggy as he was, he could taste the rare meat and hot juice, could make himself believe he was eating. That was the trick, making yourself believe, and halfway through the imaginary meal, it worked. He created enough saliva to swallow. The dryness disappeared.

"I don't want to argue with you, Mr. Bram-ha…Brama—"

"Just Bram, please. People call me Bram." Izzy heard his Pop's solicitous voice interrupt. Sneaking a quick look, he glimpsed the doctor, a tall man with thick sandy hair and pale skin, the opposite of his father in every way. His Pop was short and fat and bald on top, where two swatches of hair floated like dark continents separated by an ocean of skin. A gap between his front teeth was centered under the gap in his hair, aligning an otherwise disparate collection of parts. Izzy had noticed his Pop's baldness last week, when he turned thirteen, as if for the first time. Everyone said he looked just like his father had as a kid, and on Izzy's birthday, he wondered if he, too, would go bald someday. His mother told him not to worry: her father had thick hair, and for baldness, it was your mother's side that mattered. In biology class, his teacher explained how if one parent had brown eyes and one had blue and you looked at your grandparents, you could figure the exact odds you'd get blue or brown. It was like throwing dice, and that made sense. What his mother said, that you inherited certain things from only one parent, didn't.

Would his Mom come to the hospital? She worked two jobs, one as a housecleaner and the other as a phlebotomist, a word Izzy had practiced, impressed until he learned it paid minimum wage. You could call her at the houses she cleaned but never at the clinic where she drew blood. He hoped she didn't show up for a while. Izzy saw her every day but rarely saw his father alone. She would be pissed about his getting hit. She complained about the accidents he helped stage, but she never said no, not outright, and she was happy to cash the checks.

"We can talk about this when he wakes," the doctor said. "But he can't move now. We don't have solid casts on him yet. He can't get up, even for the toilet. Do you understand?"

"Of course, Dr. Burnham. Rick."

"Richard."

"I'll get yous the minute he wakes up, Richard."

"Why don't you go home. Sleep. Your pacing isn't helping him."

"I'll leave when he leaves, Rick. Richard. Look what this hillbilly did. You have kids? A son? Could you sleep with your kid like this? I'll sleep when I get him home."

"That could take a week. More. He is not going anywhere until he's ready."

A week? Izzy again tried to assess the damage, but again saw little beyond the flash of white on his right side. Judging by the way his head was spinning, something powerful masked the pain.

"You're the expert," his Pop said. "You didn't go to med school to hear advice from someone like me. I appreciate all you done here. Really. No one has more respect for doctors. I just think I can take care of my boy better in my own home. He needs family."

"He needs to be monitored in a controlled environment. If you—"

"When he's improved, I'm saying. I'm sorry I got excited earlier. I just feel sick about this. Christ, the poor kid. If he don't get better, I'll never forgive myself."

When did his father ever get excited? He remained cool through tense meetings with claims adjusters, doctors, even cops. He never lost control unless it was intentional, a part of some plan to gain advantage.

"It's hardly your fault," the doctor said.

Izzy sensed the shadow of his father's arms drop in dismissal. "Yeah, well, sometimes it's hard to say what is whose fault." There was a catch in his Pop's throat. Izzy's heart beat faster to hear it, and afraid they might notice, he tried to hide the change in himself. He slowed his breathing and squeezed his eyes tight, forced himself to lay still as a corpse.

"If this kid ain't okay…" his father began. "I mean, when's he going to wake up?"

"He's had a lot of trauma, heavy anesthesia. He'll wake up when he's ready."

Their words came to Izzy like voices in a dream, distant and warbled, but he heard something clearly in his father's speech. His Pop had a voice as smooth as waves rolling onto Rainbow Beach, a voice that could calm an irate cop in seconds, croon a gypsy ballad so beautifully women bawled. There was roughness in it, but that only disarmed people, making him seem plain-spoken, genuine, a regular guy. His voice also sounded hypnotic and musical and above all, sincere—whether or not he was. Izzy knew every nuance of his Pop's voice, but even in this woozy state, even though the room spun and his head throbbed and he felt sick and half-conscious at best, he heard something in it now that he'd never heard before. He did not dare peek or stretch or move any part of himself for fear he would ruin this new thing.

Izzy's Pop wanted him home. He said so to the doctor. Not in the messy apartment on the East Side, where Izzy lived with his mom, but in his father's own house, in Schorsch Village, with his newer wife, Till, and their kids. Izzy's mother spent all her time cleaning other people's homes but let theirs fall apart, dishes piled high, food left out, dust drifting thick as snow under chairs. Outside of work, she watched TV all the time, full of excuses for why she lay there like a rock. They always involved his Pop, as if he'd stuck her with this life, or lack of one, and she had no choice in the matter. Izzy had been to his Pop's house only briefly, but it was spotless. You could bury yourself in silk cushions on his big red couch. There was a giant plasma TV, an elaborate chandelier, and in the bathroom, a mirror with a gold frame so fancy you hardly saw what was in it. The fixtures, doorknobs, and sconces were gold, too, and the entire dining room ceiling. The neighborhood sat on the edge of Schiller Woods, between two malls—HIP and The Brickyard—with perfect lawns and houses laid out neat as the plastic ones on a Monopoly board. The air smelled clean, except on busy Harlem Avenue, where red sauce from the Italian restaurants fought with the stench of car exhaust.

Never before had his father mentioned the possibility of Izzy's moving in. For a year after his parents split, they argued whenever his Pop came by. During one of those fights, Izzy heard his Mom say that he "just happened" after Bram insisted Izzy was no mishap but part of a sinister plan on her part. He wondered if that was why his Pop stopped visiting. Maybe he blamed Izzy. Maybe his Pop didn't care, or maybe with some people it took a serious thing, like a disease or a wreck, to make them realize your worth. Then they'd want to spend time with you, to treat you better and make up for everything. Izzy felt sure that when all this was over, he would be closer to his father.

The doctor left and Bram sat in the bedside chair. Its metal legs scraped the tile floor until through closed eyes, Izzy sensed his Pop's shadow over him. He did not squint, not even for a second. He could feel his father's stare. After a minute, Bram cursed in a whisper and leaned back, the chair creaking under his weight.

The doctor hadn't said so, but maybe Izzy was permanently damaged, his leg or his arm, or some part he couldn't see. That might explain the catch in his Pop's voice. Izzy had been in plenty of accidents that weren't really accidents and always came out safe. Why did he get hurt this time? He wouldn't mind much if there was permanent damage. He pictured himself in a few years, leaning on his father's shoulder with one arm, a cane in the other, while they walked to Portage Park. They would stop in the Bucharest Tap, a place he knew all about, though he'd never been, and the bartender would pour Izzy a beer. They didn't bother about ID because of his bad leg.

"He's a tough kid," the bartender said.

"Just like his old man." His Pop gave his picks for Sportsman's Park that day. He clapped Izzy on the back when he agreed a certain horse was a sure thing because his father was teaching him about horses, how to pick winners and losers, the ones worth a shot and the ones good enough to risk your whole roll. The bartender said it was all chance, and his Pop insisted that chance was for fairytales and the backseats of cars. You had to know a horse's history and its lineage (a word he made one syllable), his Pop said, and where it was running and the weather and so on. You had to have a good eye and you had to listen. "You got to study the whole race, not the pieces you want to see."

He might sing then, after a few beers, vamping the beat-up accordion perched behind the bar. A voice like silver, Izzy's grandmother said, and he knew the old songs, though he was just a kid when she brought him to what she called, always and seriously, the Promised Land. Izzy couldn't quite get the lyrics, could barely tell Romanian from Romani, but the songs still gave him goosebumps. If he listened close to the melody and put himself in the right mind, he found a meaning of his own, which was better anyway. Sometimes words only got in the way. His Pop had so much talent. He could have been a great singer, with some training, everybody said. Or a salesman or an actor, given the right breaks. Sometimes he said he wished he'd gone to law school, then laughed 'til he had tears in his eyes.

Bram's phone beeped faintly as he dialed.

"It's me…New Covenant, where you think…No, he's out like a stone. It's bad, Milo, his whole right side, the leg and arm is broke."

Izzy squinted when he heard his uncle's name. His father was facing the door, worrying the gold chain, thick as rope, that he always wore.

"A burst artery," Bram said. "Blood was a big worry, but the doc says it should be controllable now…Well, he should be awake, that's what…I know that, Milo. Will you listen… No, they don't want him moved, because of the surgery. Nothing is set. Could go either way. The bones are—he's in these temporary splints can be taken off anytime."

The chair creaked as Bram sat down and then immediately stood again.

"On Belmont, under the el tracks, plenty of people around. He waited for the right car, old guy with Coke-bottle glasses driving slow, like we planned. Looked fine from where I stood…I don't know what happened."

There was a long pause and then Bram said, "It's watch and wait, but no, they don't seem too worried anymore." His voice grew thoughtful, as if he was talking to himself but with that coaxing tone strangers found so convincing. "I guess if they're not worried…It better work out. Christ, Milo, if this kid don't wake up soon."

The sound of his Pop's voice rose and fell, as if he was walking in a circle, close then distant. "Yeah, well maybe it ain't a good idea…I know what I said. Now I'm saying maybe it's a bad idea."

Izzy heard the crinkle of a cigarette pack and pictured his Pop catching a smoke between his lips. He heard him patting his pockets, searching for a light, but not the flick of a lighter.

"Carl says? Oh, fuck Carl. Christ, I can't believe you. Carl! You think I give a fuck about Carl right now, sitting here with my kid in pieces like Humpty Dumpty…Tell him to wait, that's what. Yeah, a cop makes it look legit, but when he's as big a screw-up as Carl…I could walk downstairs right now and find a hundred Carls."

As if tethered to a landline, he stomped back and forth in the cramped space near the head of Izzy's bed.

"I didn't say that…Milo, shut up and listen…I didn't say that. We'll have to see is all I'm saying…No, I ain't leaving. I want to be here when he wakes up…Yeah, but what if it ain't? What if it's worse?...I know, but…Yeah, okay…Yeah, I'll call."

His Pop hung up. He felt tortured, sick with worry—that was obvious—and meanwhile, Izzy was enjoying himself. The doctor said he would probably be okay. A couple breaks, but he was not in pain, and he liked being a patient. Part of him—the mature, guilty part—wanted to wake up right away, but another part couldn't. Not yet. His father was shaken worse than Izzy had ever seen him. He would be flooded with relief when Izzy stirred, and though he relished that thought, he wanted to remain in this odd space, a crack between waking and sleeping where he was helpless yet more in control than ever, a little longer.

Grow up! his mother would shout. *Can you not act like your father? It's bad enough you got Bramaciu blood in those veins, God help you.*

She waved his Pop's name like a knife, like everything he ever did was on Izzy. He imagined her fuming while his father brought him to the lobby in a wheelchair, lifted him gently into the back of his El Dorado, and drove him to Schorsch Village to recuperate. At his house, Bram would lay him on the couch like a present. He would buy sarma, wine, seasoned lamb—a real feast. Izzy imagined tears in his Pop's eyes as he made a toast, thanking God for sparing his son.

Maybe, Izzy thought, he was meant to get hurt. Maybe God was using this accident to change his Pop, which would mean that like the rest of his Pop's scams, it wasn't an accident at all. There were a thousand ways Izzy could have messed this one up—his timing might have been off by a second, his foot too close to the car, the driver too sleepy, the street too slick—but his instincts were too sharp for those mistakes, even the ones he couldn't control. Had he stepped into the car on purpose? In the neighborhood, kids said Heavy Garcia, who was in his forties and drooled all the time and delivered papers for a living, got that way because he fell in love with other fighters' hooks and jabs, so much that he looked for beatings outside the ring. Izzy thought the same kind of thing might have happened to his Uncle Milo, who'd leaned over and slammed on the accelerator when he thought his partner wasn't driving fast enough into the brick wall they planned to hit. The crash sent both of them through the windshield and for once, the medical expenses were real. Izzy remembered that accident the way some people remembered anniversaries and graduations. His family retold it every time they got together. Milo pulled his hair back to show the scar tissue and acted out the dive while they shook their heads in laughter. They hoarded the best accidents like heirlooms, to be brought out, polished and admired, treasured for their associations. The family history was a list of accidents, near misses and rough falls, bruises, scrapes and breaks, real or performed. Izzy's thirteenth birthday had passed last week nearly forgotten—a hug from his mother and a dumb kids' game called "Apples to Apples"—but this accident would be remembered. He had his own story now, one to rival Milo's best.

A hand brushed Izzy's hot forehead, sweeping his hair aside. A few strands stuck to his skin, pinching as his Pop moved them. His hand was as soft as a woman's, the scent of strong soap, with a hint of cigarettes and some food, onions or garlic, underneath. A nice smell.

"Come on, Iz. Why ain't you waking up?" His voice sounded natural, not smooth, as it had for the doctor. Urgent and low, almost a whisper. Izzy liked its sound and the attention. He liked that he could lie in the dim room and listen, risking glimpses that, so far, went unnoticed. He also could wake up at any moment, and he would, soon. He felt bad about making his father worry but was reluctant to open his eyes yet, as if to do so would break a spell.

His Pop went into the bathroom. He was gone a long time. The faucet ran. The toilet flushed, and then the faucet ran again. He returned with a damp cloth and a basin of water. He wiped Izzy's forehead, tracing his eyebrows, rubbing the dimpled towel across his temples. No one had washed Izzy since he was a little kid. The last time his mother bathed him, before his grandmother's wake, had been for her benefit more than his. She'd drawn a hot bath, washed his hair and back, rubbed olive oil into his skin before dressing him slowly. He enjoyed it so much he almost looked forward to the funeral.

Izzy didn't see that grandmother, his Puri, much after Bram moved out. His Pop sometimes brought her over, but his visits slowed, then stopped. Izzy's mother heard he bought a house with Till, who had babysat Izzy when she was in high school. His Pop hadn't been to the apartment on the East Side for at least a year when he showed up one day with no warning. He wanted Izzy to come to Disney World with Puri and Uncle Milo. His grandmother had lung cancer, and this was to be her last vacation. Izzy loved the rides and his Pop, who he felt like he was meeting for the first time, watching him interact with others. He made everyone laugh—people in lines, waitresses, taxi drivers. His Pop seemed to know them all. In one minute he would get the cashier's name and where he was from and how long he'd been in Florida, and soon they were sharing jokes like old friends.

Near the end of that trip, Puri fell in a hotel lobby and hurt her back. Milo was hit by a car in a restaurant parking lot, and Bram talked Izzy through a tumble on the people-mover to Tomorrowland. By vacation's end they had suffered two broken noses, a neck injury, and a blown-out back for a take of $80,000. His Pop used Izzy regularly after that. "The kid don't just look hurt," Bram told Milo. "He believes it—how could anyone doubt?"

Bram mumbled to himself as he bathed Izzy's face. "God, please. Please wake him," he said, each word a new stroke across his head. Bram patted Izzy's cheek with light taps that made it hard for him to keep his eyes closed.

"Iz," his Pop said. "Iz, don't let me down here. Come on, buddy."

His strokes grew mechanical as he forgot what he was doing. He was dreaming, the way he did at the track when he couldn't figure out where to place a bet, squinting at the sun glinting off the gold caps on the rail. He dipped the cloth in the basin absently, soaking and then wringing the material, water trickling like rain. Again and again he swirled it and squeezed, as if trying to wash clean a stain, mumbling to himself the whole time. The hollow splash of water in the basin made Izzy want to pee. He clenched his legs and told himself he didn't have to go. Just when he thought he could no longer hold it, his father stopped.

"You'll be okay." His Pop said this with finality, as if something had been decided. He seemed to perk up then and returned to washing Izzy with new energy. "What could go wrong? God, let him wake up okay, and I swear, never again."

His pats came harder, almost small slaps, the kind trainers used to bring fighters to in old movies. Izzy cringed, but his Pop didn't seem to notice.

"Wake up, son. Wake up wake up wake up." His father chanted the words softly and quickly the way he did at the track when the stakes were big. "Out of Egypt Out of Egypt Out of Egypt," he might mutter, oblivious to everything except the name of his horse and whether it could win, place, or show. He leaned forward with each word, the way he did now, as if his voice was a prod pushing the horse forward, his body rocking in rhythm with the jockey's while he clutched the seat before him. After the race he'd march past security onto the field and have his photo taken with the winner. People thought he was somebody, an owner or connected, and knew him to be one of the best handicappers at Sportsman's Park.

Someone came into the room. Izzy glimpsed a flash of white and then she was prodding his arm.

"How are we doing, Iz-zy?" The nurse pronounced his name like the kids at school who made stupid jokes—*Izzy? Don't know him, who iz he?*—and called him *Dizzy* after stories of a fall made the rounds.

A stethoscope pressed against his chest, its metal cold through the thin hospital gown. She leaned over as she listened in various spots, as if she couldn't find his heart. His father sat up. His startled eyes seemed to meet Izzy's— opened for an instant—and Izzy thought he was discovered. A moment later, he realized that his Pop was watching the nurse's cleavage as she leaned over the bed. She shifted and with his Pop distracted, Izzy could squint into the dark tent of her shirt. Her breasts were great white mounds that looked like they might melt without a bra to hold them. She was fat and smelled like flowers, not perfume but real flowers.

"How's he doing?" his Pop said. His voice was different when he spoke to women, quieter, gentler. He was a good-looking man in old pictures and still carried himself that way.

"Fine, considering," the nurse said.

"I appreciate you taking such good care of him."

"Why I'm here."

"I always say, the nurses are the ones I trust. Half of you, I think, know more than the doctors. I'd like to buy you a drink, Lisa, when he's better, to say thank you."

"That won't be necessary." The nurse laughed. She held Izzy's hand to check on his IV. Her breath was labored as she leaned in. He felt it on his cheek while she adjusted something. He had a hard-on and hoped no one would notice.

"I thought he'd be awake hours ago."

"Anesthesia affects people differently," she said. "Some wake up quickly, others stay in a fog for days."

"Days? He won't be asleep for days, will he?"

"I didn't mean that, just—he'll wake up when he's ready."

"The doctor says he shouldn't move, but they always exaggerate a little, huh? They like to keep you here just in case, play it safe?"

"Just the opposite, the way insurance works these days. No, if he moved too soon after that surgery it could sever the artery in his leg. The internal bleeding could kill him. The doctor must have explained…"

"Sure, but what are the odds?"

"The odds?"

Izzy heard his father stand and walk. He sneaked a peek. The nurse was staring at his Pop as she set Izzy's arm back on the bed.

"I'm just sick about this." His Pop's voice cracked again. Izzy took a bigger chance and opened his eyes halfway for a second. No one saw. The nurse touched his father's arm.

"He'll be fine," she said, her voice sympathetic now. She walked around the bed quickly, picked something up and went into the bathroom.

"Sir, have you been smoking in here?" Her voice echoed.

"No, ma'am."

The nurse stomped back. "It's a private room. Was someone else here?"

"The doctors, and another guy, janitor maybe. He was in the toilet a while."

"There is no smoking in this building."

"Yes, ma'am. Lisa. I wouldn't."

He raised a middle finger at her back as she left.

A few minutes later, his phone rang. The buzz jolted Izzy like an alarm. He thought his father would notice, but the noise startled him too, and he didn't see anything. Izzy counted four rings, six rings, eight before his Pop answered.

"Yeah, hi…Okay…Sarai…Sarai, don't start with me."

As soon as he heard her name, Izzy wished his mother was with him. When he awoke, he was glad she wasn't there, thrilled to see his Pop alone. Izzy had never had this chance before and would never have it again. Somehow he always understood that his father was never fully himself unless he was alone. He told Izzy that in life there were pros and cons. You can figure out a con's a con, he said, but a pro, you never know. His Pop was a pro. Confidence is not what Bram Bramaciu inspires, he told Milo, it's faith. Only he pronounced it "fate." Izzy thought for the longest time that they were the same word—what people got in life and what they believed, the same thing. As a rule, people believed his father. When they talked to him about an accident, most were happy to sign the claims. They wanted to believe, and they wanted to pay, the higher the price, the better. They knew they were guilty, if not for this, then for something.

"Sarai, he's fine." His Pop's voice went from annoyed to soothing. "It's a fracture in his wrist is all. A tiny one…I know I said sprain. It is a sprain. They think there might be a tiny fracture too now, but they're not sure. That's why they kept him so long. They're waiting on more pictures, playing it safe…You are not coming up here. Don't be stupid." His voice grew sharp again.

"We're leaving in an hour, maybe less…The doctor, that's who…Oh, you know more than the doctors now? Because you take blood from junkies at some clinic? He broke the fall awkward is all. The car didn't touch him… Fine, you want to get a bus up here from 109th to see an empty bed, go ahead. You're being an idiot…You don't have the money for a taxi…Sarai? Dammit."

He dropped his phone on the bed in disgust, and it bounced off Izzy's good knee. Izzy opened his eyes. He lay still, blinking at the ceiling while they adjusted to the light. Bram cursed a full minute before he noticed.

"Iz?" he said. "You're awake. Jesus Christ, thank God. I was starting to think you'd never wake up. How you feeling?"

His Pop patted Izzy's good arm and leg, as if making sure Izzy could feel them.

"Okay. Thirsty."

His Pop grabbed a plastic cup and jogged to the bathroom to fill it, though a pitcher of water sat on the table. He slipped a hand behind Izzy's neck and propped up his head while he tipped the glass to his lips. Izzy could sit by himself but let his Pop help him.

"How's that? Sure, you're dry. It's like they fill your mouth with sand, that shit. Here."

Izzy leaned forward and finished the water.

"What timing. I never seen a kid with such timing." Bram pressed his palms to Izzy's cheeks and kissed him on the forehead. He hurt the spot under the bandage, but Izzy didn't complain.

"I'm so sorry about this, Iz, but you're awake now, you're okay. Thank God. Thank God you're awake. Let me tell you,

I'd like to murder this idiot, a *beng* from Elmhurst driving his sister-in-law's Caddie. Only, she didn't give him permission. Can you imagine? He's uninsured, penniless. She'll probably fight it. Could be years tangled up. We'll work it out, though. Might even be better in the end. The main thing is you're all right. Have some more."

His Pop refilled the cup. Izzy had had enough but took a sip.

"What happened out there anyway, Iz? Was he dozing? It looked like a clean fall from the side."

Izzy said he didn't know. The driver might have been half asleep or too slow. Some couldn't react until catastrophe was in their faces, some not even then.

"Doesn't matter. The main thing is you're okay," Bram said. "Jeez, if anything'd happened to you, I'd have killed myself. I swear to God I would've. You look hot. Here." His Pop pulled the blankets down. Again he patted Izzy's good leg. "A couple of bruises, nothing major. How's this one?"

Izzy said his good leg felt fine. His Pop asked about the other one and the arm in the splint. He didn't feel pain there either, Izzy said, he was just tired. He smiled as Bram prodded and petted him. He couldn't remember the last time his Pop had touched him, other than a pat on the back after a good fall or a smack in the head when he was mad.

"That's good, Iz. God bless those painkillers, eh? I got my buddy Len working on some for you for home. At a discount. We're going to get you set up nice in the house—one of those Nintendos, movies. A movie every day 'til you're better. How's that sound?"

Izzy never played Nintendo, but he nodded. His father would check on him like this every day. He saw himself on the red couch in Schorsch Village with the remote control, his father squeezing Izzy's good leg, asking how he felt, monitoring his progress.

"Here's the thing, Iz," his Pop said, slowing down, tracing the gold chain under his chin with two fingers. "Are you awake now? You with me?"

Izzy nodded.

"Like I said, this carrot's a zero, but I got a way to fix it. This could be a big one, a hundred-fifty grand, maybe two, with no questions. It'd come in handy about now. Your Uncle Milo has a friend, Carl, a Chicago cop with—God bless him—more insurance than Lloyd's of London. Carl has some bad debt, though, he needs out of real quick. If we can get you down to Hyde Park, Garfield Boulevard, before they put solid casts on, we got a plan. The splints is perfect, easy to take off. We take you down there real gentle, and all you got to do is lay in the grass, on the median. In that neighborhood, the ambulance'll take you to U of C—a better hospital anyway. Than this dump. It's cake, Iz. All you gotta do is lie there, and we'll be real gentle. Two hours from now, you're back in the hospital, a better hospital, and Carl is shaking while he fills out a report. He'll say you came out of nowhere, but he should've seen you. He was adjusting the radio. He's a cop. No one's going to question. And we're golden with the injuries. Anyone can see they're real, we don't have to fake a thing. The best is, it's easy on you. Just switching hospitals really."

A sick feeling settled in Izzy's stomach. His Pop was way ahead of him, talking so fast Izzy couldn't see the whole plan. He struggled, groggy as he was, to order its parts. Had his Pop's only worry been that Izzy wouldn't wake up in time, before they put real casts on him or his mom arrived? Izzy's injuries would be wasted then, like meat left to spoil or coins dropped through a sewer grate.

"Deal?" His father leaned forward, squeezing Izzy's hand. "We understand each other, Iz? We're not even gonna go through the motions. It's dark out. Carl will squeal the brakes case anyone's around to hear, and you'll be lying there. You don't even got to stand up."

Had Izzy imagined his father's concern, or exaggerated it? He hadn't imagined the catch in his voice. That much was real, he knew. His Pop had definitely been worried, more worried than Izzy had ever heard him. He'd sounded like he might cry, and not just when the doctor was there—on his own too. He wanted Izzy's help to fix this accident, sure, but that didn't mean he was unconcerned. He wouldn't have mentioned Milo's plan if there was any real danger. There would be some risk, of course, but everything carried *some* risk. He understood what his Pop meant about odds. That was all life was in the end. The odds were better that you'd die in a car than in a plane, and quitting smoking didn't do anything but help your odds. Where you were born, or if you were, to who, with how much—it was all a gamble.

His Pop leaned close, his face inches from Izzy's. His breath was strong, coffee and cigarettes, but not sour.

"You feel well enough to get out of here?" his Pop said. "That doctor'll be back, and your mother's on her way. I could call her once we're down at U of C."

Izzy thought of his mother taking a cab all the way to the hospital, exhausted from work, only to find his bed empty. She would be sick when she saw that. She might even think for a minute that he was dead. She could have prevented this, she would think, as if it was her fault. How long ago had she called? Twenty minutes, forty? If Izzy refused to go, or said he didn't feel well enough, his father might argue, but she would arrive soon. There would be nothing his Pop could do. He would be mad, of course, if Izzy said no. He would try to sweet talk Izzy, mention the money and increase the amount without knowing he did it. The accident would be worth four or five hundred grand if he stalled long enough.

"What say?"

A sheen of sweat gleamed on his Pop's bald head. Izzy hadn't noticed the streetlights click on, but their fuzzy orange glow seeped into the room, diluting the already weak florescent light, dimming the stark hospital white, tinting everything with their dingy spray. In this softer light, the puffy moons beneath his Pop's eyes waxed purple. His face, normally so loose, was drawn. His eyes pleaded with Izzy. He did care about his son. The strain was obvious. It was there for anyone who wanted to see it, in his face. Izzy understood now what his Pop was pleading for, not for Izzy to agree, but to say no. His Pop saw an opportunity and worked out the details, sure, but he loved Izzy. His Pop stood to make a lot of money but wanted Izzy, the one who'd screwed up this fall, to turn him down. Why? There was a chance—probably one in a million, as likely as getting hit by lightning—that something could go wrong. Once Izzy saw what his Pop was willing to sacrifice, he knew what he would do.

"You ready, Iz?"

Izzy nodded. Expertly his father disconnected the IV and monitors. He slipped an arm under the back of Izzy's knees and another around his neck. He froze in this position for a moment, getting Izzy used to it, or gearing up to lift him.

"Ready? Up-we-go." His Pop hoisted him in one fluid movement. Izzy felt a stab of pain in his head, none in his arm or leg. His Pop staggered under the weight, righted himself. He paused at the doorway and turned sideways to ease through.

"We'll have to be quick in the hall, Iz. The elevator's right across the way. Once we get to the lobby, they got wheelchairs sitting around. I seen them."

His Pop crouched in the doorway, sagging under Izzy's weight until the elevator dinged. An old woman took her time getting out. His Pop whisked Izzy through the hall and past her. He was panting heavily when they leaned against the elevator's back wall. The doors glided shut, and he shifted awkwardly to press the lobby button. His arms shook. He lurched forward once and then taking a step back, regained his footing. Izzy's good arm shot out instinctively, groped for something to steady himself, and came to rest around his father's neck.

Izzy slowed his breathing and made himself relax. He imagined he was in the Schorsch Village house, his leg propped on a pillow whose silk he could already feel. His thumb twitched, as if clicking the remote for the plasma TV. He pictured himself playing Nintendo. It would be fun to check out those old-school games. The smell of roasting lamb drifted in from the enormous kitchen, making his mouth water as he settled on the red couch. The weather warmed, and he lay on the back deck, reading. His leg improved and to rebuild the muscle, he crossed Harlem Avenue to hike in Schiller Woods.

Izzy leaned into Bram's chest, a smell of aftershave and beneath it, cigarettes, holding tight as the elevator fell.

Chez Whatever

A Black girl walks through Lincoln Park in a blizzard.
It sounds like the start of an off-color joke, I know, but at some point, when she recalled that day, February 14, 1990, this was how she told it. *Girl* because, although the person in the story is twenty-one, it was hard for her, even a year later, to see that person as a woman. *Black* because *African American* is a new identity in 1990, one she test drives but cannot seem to buy.

I became *African American* more than twenty years ago.

She is Black, especially in Lincoln Park, a rich White neighborhood getting richer and Whiter by the hour, and especially today, when her dark face glares against a night white with snow, like a period on an empty page or a hole punched in the pale sky. Half a foot of snow has locked up the city. The airports are open only for departures, and the snow is falling faster now, an inch an hour, in angry swirls that make it tough to see more than ten feet ahead. She stomps over unshoveled walks, seething, each step an act of will, as she pulls one foot, then another from the wet mess. She might as well be swimming. Her face is wet with snow that melts on contact and leaks under her collar. An invisible opening in her right boot, probably no more than a pinhole, lets the slush in. The slow soaking makes her anxious and then so angry she wants to rip off the new perfect-looking boots—electric-blue Docs, a gift from Dot—throw them in the road, and continue barefoot.

As if she does not stand out enough in that sea of white— the snow and the people, who navigate hazardous streets in surprising numbers because it is Valentine's Day. Down Fullerton, she walks in their narrow, trampled wake, between walls of tall Victorians whose steep steps and smug facades are so imposing, their skinny windows seem to watch her pass. Jutting her chin, she does her best to act tough, but it's difficult to strut on ice. She turns onto Halsted, which is less oppressive, but feels no relief. The snow is slushier, and one block up, the Mexican valet she fought with hovers outside Dot's building. She can't see his face but knows him, even at this distance in heavy snow, by the cut of his coat. Maybe he won't recognize her, she thinks, but of course he will. Half an hour ago, she threatened to run him over, and she is wearing a pea coat identical to his—both threadbare and dark blue, hers adorned with patches for Public Enemy, Social Distortion, and Grandmaster Flash.

Finding a spot here is a challenge at the best of times—in this weather, impossible. She drove around for forty minutes before she fought with the valet, circling the same frozen streets over and over, afraid to go more than fifteen miles an hour. Her car, a 1975 Olds Delta 88, tan with a silver replacement door, has poor traction and a high idle. She hardly touched the gas as she looked for a space, her foot covering the brake like a finger on a trigger. On Lill Street, she got lucky—a spot two blocks from Dot's. Halfway in, she decided it was too small and could not get out. She punched the accelerator, though she knew her spinning tires only made the ruts deeper. A couple of passing frat boys in Dorothy Hamill haircuts and matching North Face gear—typical Lincoln Park—rocked her car back and forth until they pushed her out of the space.

"You're *welcome!*" one of them shouted as she pulled away, like he'd saved a baby drowning in a well and deserved her eternal gratitude. She raised her middle finger casually, driving off at a crawl.

She circled for ages without seeing a space she could get into. Around and around she went in the bleak landscape, heartburn raging from all the black coffee, brought on the drive from the South Side for heat more than caffeine. Her car is not much warmer than the street. The heater fan quit last month, and the wiper blades rotted long before that. She steered with her right hand as she looked for a spot and with her left, alternated between scraping ice from the inside of the windshield and snow from the outside. Even if everything worked perfectly, in this blinding mess, she could not have seen much beyond her front bumper.

She remembered a puddle-jumper she took once, visiting her auntie in Tennessee. The pilot had maintained a holding pattern over the tiny airport in the valley below, waiting for wind shears to subside, then announced in an indifferent tone that couldn't quite hide his fear that the plane was low on fuel and had to return to Memphis right away. She felt like that pilot tonight, as if she might die circling the neighborhood, or at least run out of gas. She did not have the money for more. There was enough in the tank to get her home to South Shore, but if she drove for another fifteen or twenty minutes, there would not be. She would be stuck. Dot would give her gas money, of course, but no, she could not ask for it after their argument, the only serious fight of their year together. Their petty dustups are usually her fault. She does not know why she starts them, except that Dot is so damn happy all the time. She has never met anyone happier or more secure, more present in the moment. She loves this about Dot and so it almost seems like someone else who starts the trouble, the bitch tossing rocks in that serene pool just to watch the ripples. Sometimes she thinks she does it for the makeup sex, so good it could be measured on the Richter scale. She never came with anyone before Dot. Now, it happens all the time, and occasionally, if they are making up, more than once.

She did not start this fight, however, Dot did, and there was no makeup sex after, no making up at all. They did not speak for three days, until Dot called this morning. It's always Dot who calls, though it has never taken her this long.

"You're not seriously leaving me alone on Valentine's Day?" she asked, and then, "Ya *do* know it's Valentine's, doncha?"

It was not an apology or an admission of guilt but enough to get her up to Lincoln Park for shrimp scampi—her favorite of Dot's culinary staples—enough to begin a thaw. She did not want a thaw. She wanted to stay mad. Before she even hung up, she was mad at herself for letting the anger fade, but what could she do? The mere sound of Dot's voice makes her instantly wet. No one has ever had this effect. The phone shook in her hand as she thought about reconciliation and what, after the worst fight yet, could be the greatest coupling ever. She shook with anger, too, at the mental space Dot takes, the control she effortlessly exerts over her schedule, moods, thoughts. Her body becomes Dot's when this short White girl is inside her. Time stops. At the touch of a single fingertip, her nerves light like fireflies. In a moment, she no longer knows who she is—no past, no future, only Dot.

The week before their big fight, they had gone to the Art Institute, where Dot dragged her away from Monet.

"Jeez, was he in love with that haystack or what?" Dot groaned. "How many times do we need to see it?"

She could have spent the rest of her day poring over his many versions of the haystack in question, but deferred to Dot, who had grown up with art and possessed an intimidating, effortless knowledge of it, careless with a commodity that the girl from South Shore treated as precious.

They drifted toward Modern American, but as they were leaving Impressionism, Dot stopped before a sketch called "Woman with a Muff."

"This is more like it, don't you think?" Dot whispered behind her. Hot moist breath caressed her ear. "Do you like her muff?" Arms encircled her. A hand slipped beneath the bag draped across her front, one finger grazing her, ever so lightly, there. In the black-and-white drawing, a vague faceless figure hunched as if against the cold, or from age, though her long, lean frame did not look especially old, or young. It was hard to tell. She stood in a blank landscape, feet hidden under an old-fashioned dress, the ground on the ivory page bleeding into air. The woman held out her hands, concealed in the muff, as if walking, but seemed to hover in place, ghost-like, too, maybe searching for something she'd dropped.

Staring at the sketch, her eyes watered. The dark figure seemed to dissolve and reform as Dot touched her. Her entire body tingled but remained as still as the cold marble statues they'd passed downstairs. She wanted to move but couldn't, held by Dot's touch, ecstatic and angry, turned-on and terrified. What if some guard or passing tourist saw? If she pushed Dot's hand away, she would be called a prude or, worse, Bettina, her churchy mother's name, so she pretended that Dot's touch wasn't a thing, that she didn't love it with every particle of her being, that it didn't mortify her to the point of physical pain.

"Amanda thinks you should pay some rent."

This was how their big fight started. Dot said it without looking up from the *Fit* magazine she thumbed on the couch, one of several vapid one-word titles she subscribes to, along with *People* and *Allure*. She makes fun of Dot's trashy reading but secretly likes her unabashed obsession with celebrity gossip, fashion, and fitness fads. There are no guilty pleasures for this girl, only pleasures.

"Even a hundred a month," Dot said, absorbed in a home workout plan that made use of tables, chairs, whatever was on hand.

She was warming her bare feet under Dot's thigh, still in the flannel pajamas Dot had given her. "Or she thought you could pay a utility bill—gas or the electric?"

Dot and Amanda, her roommate, grew up together in Lake Forest in homes as airy and bloated as beach balls. Dot's trust fund was worth more than her lover would earn during the next twenty years, and Amanda Hugankiss—her nickname for the gushing, love-obsessed roommate—had a similar stash. Did Dot really not understand what this would mean for her? It was as if Dot had been given a big present so early in life, she saw it as tiny, if at all, blind to the fact that most weren't so lucky. Her girlfriend certainly wasn't. After her freshman year at U of C, she moved back to her mother's cramped house at 79th and Stony Island, in South Shore, to stay in a converted pantry—her younger brother had taken over her old room—because she could not afford college *and* housing. Her scholarship covered only tuition, and in Hyde Park, she was learning how costly a free ride could be.

"You know what it costs me, coming up here every week? How hard it is just to find a spot in this yuppie hell?" She was furious that Dot not only asked her to pay rent for a place she didn't live but that she used Amanda to do it. She crashed at Dot's two or three nights a week, sometimes four, but that was rare. "Maybe I should just stop staying over. You need me, *Dorothy*, you can drive your skinny ass down to 79th Street."

It felt good to see Dot speechless, to sit in the driver's seat for a change, but the feeling didn't last. Dot's hurt expression grew cold and hardened, her pupils big and black as drains.

"I'm fine with going to your house," she said. "Is your mom? She won't mind us spooning in your little pantry?"

I came out in 1995.

She is figuratively and quite literally, as Dot loves to point out, in the closet, where she curls her nearly six-foot body in a strategic ball to sleep on a child-sized mattress. The pantry dig felt mean during their fight, but she laughed the first time Dot pointed out the absurdity—*you know that for most lesbians the closet is just a metaphor, right?* Dot's casual use of the word is both thrilling and panic-inducing. *Lesbian? Me?* She has never described herself this way, though she has known since before she could write her name that she liked girls. Dot has been out since she was fourteen. She brandishes this fact and her gold-star status—*no, never with a guy, gross!*—like a backstage pass. Good for you, she wants to say, try coming out on the South Side. Hold hands with a girl and walk down Stony Island past the Black P. Stones who own the street, past Maryam and all those Nation brothers in bowties and tight froes, huddled around the mosque like prim, angry penguins guarding a hole in the ice. Take your girlfriend to the annual family picnic in Jackson Park, where the preachers—your mother's brother Aaron and Uncle Shawn, who married Auntie Mae—offer terrifying visions of the eternal pain that can follow one moment of sin.

It was a little easier in your corner of the North Shore, where your lefty lawyer parents saw it as a bonus that your girlfriend was *African American*—savoring the term like the pricey Bordeaux they poured—and even your senile grandmother, stuck in 1971, the year she lost her husband, chatted with "Dot's special friend" as if they were kindred spirits. It was Granny she learned the old-timey nickname from, her eyes watering with suppressed laughter the first time she heard it. No one besides the grandmother—and now her—calls Dorothy "Dot." She said it in bed as joke the first time and it stuck. Now she uses "Dorothy" only when truly pissed.

"This isn't about my mom, *Dorothy*." She pulled her feet from under Dot's thighs and hid them under her own on the couch.

"What is it about?"

"It's about *this ain't my place*." She leaned into Dot's face to weight each word, and felt the urge to kiss her, a desire that only made her angrier.

"Are you sure? Cause you have a full drawer, clothes in my closet. Your name isn't on the lease, but you have the house keys."

Dot's expression remained colder and harder than she'd ever seen it, as if she had been practicing for this, though her voice cracked on the last words, a note of pleading or warning: *careful now, I'm not messing*. Her pupils, normally tiny specks, had become black holes that threatened to swallow anyone in their gravitational sway. Had she taken something? The idea that this drama might have been planned, cooked up with Valium and canned speech, angered her. In recent months, Dot had doled out spare keys, closet space, comfy pajamas, a drawer—practical little gifts that neither woman gave much thought, or so it had seemed. Now, those gestures looked like part of a carefully constructed plan to charge her rent. She said so, and next, Dot was ranting about love and commitment and time, stuff that had nothing to do with what she was asking for.

"How you going to put the squeeze on for a hundred bucks, then throw all this at me?"

"I feel like your hotel," Dot said, "not your lover."

This was infuriating, since Dot was the one acting like a hotel clerk, attaching a value to the nights she stayed over. Dot shifted focus so quick, it was tough to see the real story. And *lover*? Did anyone not working on a movie set call herself that?

Dot smeared tears across her cheeks. "Why are you always hiding?"

This from the girl who sheltered behind her roommate, nose in a magazine, to demand rent? Dot was swinging wild now, grasping at anything, like the drowning woman who, when Dot was a lifeguard, clawed her blindly during an attempted rescue. Dot's anger and fear, whatever their murky source, needed a target, and her girlfriend made for an easy bullseye.

She took the steps two at a time, ignoring the shrill cries from the apartment above. On Halsted, she leaned against the glass front of Chez whatever, the French place on the ground floor, and gulped cold air. A couple seated in the window froze but carefully avoided looking her way. She pressed her palms against the smooth surface and licked her lips, leering at their meals. The man instinctively encircled his with his forearms. Her disembodied smile flickered an instant on the glass, but she could not force a laugh as she turned to the sidewalk. What happened at Dot's tonight? She tried to make sense of it as she walked south, and three days later, walking north on the same street in what the radio called near-whiteout conditions, she still isn't sure. Dot does not need help with the rent, and she isn't cheap. This is about control, she thinks, not money. Asking her to pay is an assertion of power, a way for Dot to stay on top, to possess her fully, as if there is a corner of her that this girl does not already fill. How carefully she must have planned the demand for rent. *The bottom drawer is yours…Hold onto those keys, in case…Here, spare pajamas…Amanda thinks you should pay rent.*

A man carrying an unwrapped bouquet of flowers, bedraggled in the wind and snow, passes her, the tenth reminder on this short walk that she did not bring anything for Dot, who is slaving over dinner. Not even a rose or a little box of chocolates. If she'd had more time, she thinks, but even as she forms it, the argument sounds weak. This, too, makes her angry. It's all about money, anyway, Valentine's Day, thinly disguised capitalist BS. A holiday for suckers, and she is one of them, manipulated to feel guilty about not buying flowers, just as she was manipulated on the phone earlier today. Some flirting, a mention of Valentine's Day, and her favorite dish is all it takes. Next, she's driving through a blizzard for two hours in a car with bald tires and no defrost, literally risking her life. She could have driven to Michigan in the time it took her rusted heap to get here. The Vulva—she winces at Dot's nickname for her Volvo, but can't help using it—is just the opposite, a safe suburban mom-mobile, gifted, not surprisingly, by Dot's suburban mom. Any mention that she does all the driving even though Dot's car is much more roadworthy elicits offers from Dot to come south, disingenuous because where would they go? It is sad, Dot says, that she can't reveal her love to the mother she lives with, but Dot enjoys the leverage, playing the magnanimous wronged mistress while her girlfriend rushes around like a servant.

Her extremities are frozen numb even as her exertions and wool sweater send a trickle of sweat between her breasts. She wants to strip off winter's awkward gear and simultaneously wishes she had more of it. Half a block up, the valet she fought with steps out of Dot's doorway. He bounces on his toes to scan the street before dancing back out of the snow. The valets never stand at the entrance to the French restaurant. They shelter in the apartment entry to the south, where they can smoke, hidden from the weather and their bosses while watching for customers. The restaurant does not have a parking lot. Its valets patrol the surrounding blocks for open spaces and guard them while their coworkers ferry cars over. They take up half the spots on Halsted, which is annoying at the best of times and infuriating tonight. Earlier, she drove past the valet in the pea coat four or five times, holding the same spot, before she braked and began backing into it.

"Hey, stop," he yelled, arms flailing. "Lady, stop." A string of Spanish curses followed. He smacked her car's rusted trunk but was forced to retreat, her bumper at his knees. She reversed slowly, waving him out of the way. He inched backward but would not leave the space until, finally, she had to stop or crush him. She leaned out the window, and in two languages, they screamed past each other. Only a piece of the car's nose jutted into the street. She considered leaving it that way, but what would the valets do to it when she was gone? She couldn't win this. She pulled back into traffic and shouted—*God! Damn! It!*—punching up on each word. A flurry of dark flakes—dried foam exposed when she'd torn drooping fabric from the ceiling—swirled in her car.

The valet has not yet recognized her as she approaches. She tugs her collar high and hunches down. She feels like a bug for yelling at him and wishes she was, could scurry past unnoticed. The restaurant's parking scheme is outrageous, but it isn't his fault, some guy working the street in this weather for minimum wage, struggling to make it in a place where he can't speak the language. It wasn't her, all that yelling and cursing, backing into a person. If she could, she would turn around and go home just to avoid the valet. Part of her wants to avoid Dot, too, though another part aches to see her. Their fight was Dot's fault, but because she is nearly two hours late, she will be the one on the defensive, never mind the blizzard she drove through to get here or the hour it took her to park. Announcing that she has to leave after dinner won't help matters, but she has an 8 a.m. class and with this snow, can't chance morning rush hour. She can't storm out either because she does not have enough gas to get home. The needle on her Delta dipped below the point of no return before she circled back to the spot where she finally fit, the one on Lill Street that had seemed too tight. She would walk home rather than ask Dot for gas money if she didn't think someone would find her frozen in a drift at the next thaw. What choice does she have?

Fifty feet away now, the valet pops out of the doorway. He bounces on his toes once again, scanning the street right to left, then freezes. He sees her. He steps forward and raises an index finger, pointing not at her but upward, as if to say, *one moment*. She braces for the confrontation. He jogs toward her but when he's almost close enough to touch, veers between two parked cars, plowing through a mound of snow. A Jeep has stopped in the street. Its driver hands his keys to the valet and walks to the restaurant.

She stands outside Dot's entryway, which reeks of the restaurant workers' cigarettes. The valet does not glance at her as he drives off, not once, but her relief is tinged with dread. Maybe she inflated this conflict to distract from the real one, upstairs. She can't feel her fingers or toes but remains hunched in the cold while the jeep's taillights fade. A wet gust hits her like a fist. She shakes as snowflakes swarm in a shape that looks almost identifiable before dissolving into chaos once again.

When she told the story later, as she often did, she began here. She did not mention the restaurant, not right away, or standing outside Dot's door. She did not mention Dot at all, at least not by name. She said only that she was walking up Halsted to a friend's place.

A Black girl walks through Lincoln Park in a blizzard, she started, to general if uneasy laughter. Perhaps a year after it happened, she began with this line, in third-person, and part of her liked the effect. From the first sentence, no one could tell if it was an off-color joke or true story, about her or someone else, or all of these. The distant perspective brought the girl into focus, but it made her uncomfortable, as if she was watching herself, or someone else, through the wrong end of a telescope. She changed it up after the first sentence.

I'm trudging through the snow, pissed after spending an hour to park in the storm of a lifetime, when this house on wheels, huge red Cadillac, slows down. The driver, White guy in a black suit, maybe fifty, rolls out the door. He's fat but more than that, nearly round, like literally almost as wide as he is tall. This image elicited louder laughter, as her listeners felt themselves on firmer ground. She left out the fact that it is Valentine's Day in early versions, but this detail slipped in later and she used it to make the red Caddie more comical.

The driver brushes off the white stuff collecting on his shoulders, nervous, like it could ruin a good suit, but he's no match—a fresh dusting sits there before the last one's gone. He purses his lips and squints into the wind like he spotted someone he wants to kiss hiding in a drift. Dude is just standing there, exposed— this is Halsted, *no visibility—with that huge booty hanging in traffic.* There were groans and more laughs. *Finally, he gets a determined look, like, fuck it, I'ma take a chance, and waddles forth. He grabs at the roof and door like they're life buoys, getting leverage where he can to shift all that weight on the ice.*

Sometimes she did a duck walk here, which got a big laugh. Certain words always earned laughs, so she hit them hard: *booty, buoys, waddle.*

He's just ahead, in the street, as I'm walking up the sidewalk. We're about even when he turns in front of his car and throws something at me. My hand wheels around to grab it—lucky catch—but I can't tell what it is.

Be careful with that, boy, he says.

I open my palm: his keys. He waddles a little farther, then climbs the curb in front of a fancy French restaurant.

Her audience gasped. There were groans of horror, expectant laughs. Oh, uh UH, exclaimed a woman around her age.

I realize a few things at once, she said. *First, this cracker just called me* boy, *which would piss me off even if I was a boy. Since I'm not, it's like go-time. Second, he expects me to park his car cause, Black person in Lincoln Park? Got to be a maid or valet, right? Third, this restaurant, Chez whatever, and its idiot customers are the reason I spend an hour searching for a spot while Orson Welles here pulls up in front. Sure,* she sometimes said, depending on the crowd, *drive right up and throw your keys at the nearest nigger.* The angrier the audience got, the more they loved what happened next.

There is so much I want to say, so much I can do with those keys—keep them, dump them. A line-drive to the head is my first thought. I'm weighing them in my palm, like treasure or a bomb, but he's walking away. He's almost at the restaurant door. In a minute, he'll be gone.

I tug my collar around my face and put on a deep a voice: Yes suh! Enjoy y'all victuals suh!

I get in the car and start it.

This was the moment she built to, and the audience always exploded in laughter. There were hoots and hollers, often clapping.

I adjust the mirrors and the seat, crank the heat. I turn the radio to WGCI and can't believe it—Ice-T busting out "You Played Yourself," from an album I just bought, The Iceberg. *It's too perfect. I pull onto a street that looks like an iceberg tonight, spinning the tires a little and singing along. I crank it on these lines:*

Hype the snare, now I got a place to sit

And ride the track like a Black mack in his 'lac

She described a rich leather interior that smelled new, though it must have been twenty years old, the profile of that pricey red barge cruising up Halsted, herself leaning behind the wheel, hand dangling over it, pure O.G. Her audience couldn't get enough, interrupting because they had to know, what did she do with the car?

I drive it home to South Shore, park it on 79ᵗʰ, and walk to Stony Island. Just to be nice, I leave the keys. I leave the engine running too, heat on, passenger window half open. It's Black P. Stones turf over there. Night this cold, who knows, but I give it half an hour until the car's history.

Wow, someone said. Whoa! The audience had a new take on her. Who *was* this girl? Questions flew: What about the friend you were meeting? What about your own car? What if you got pulled over?

My plans no big thing, she said. *I know that my friend'll like the story so much, if she's upset, won't be for long. I can get my car in a few days.* She isn't sure she can get it out of the spot she struggled into, anyway, and she doesn't have enough gas to make it home.

Cops stop me, I'll say, wasn't no theft. This was a gift, pure and simple, and I don't know nothing about no valet. I never said who I was. Crazy person hands you their keys and tells you be careful, it's a present, right? Can I be arrested for holding onto a present? Be a sin not to. She shrugged then, as if her take was the reasonable one, the prospect of grand theft no big deal.

Amazed laughter rose, less hearty but laced with admiration. It was the response she wanted, but her story had problems, and in time, they bothered her. It was true, for instance, that loitering on Halsted, she never claims to be a valet, but she did not tell her audience that she is standing where the valets always stand. She did not say that she fought with one of them earlier or that she is wearing a pea coat identical to his. She is tall, and in a man's coat, with the collar tugged high and a wool hat pulled low, looks very much like a boy. This is her goal, though she won't acknowledge it for years to come. On another day, in another mood, being called a boy would please her, or at least a *young man,* which is what the owner of the car actually says.

Careful with that, young man. He smiles as he says it and tosses the keys cautiously—to her, not at her—his only option given the icy patch between them. She is outraged when she opens her palm but does not say a word (no *yes suh* or talk of *victuals*) before his silhouette disappears through the restaurant door. He is not nearly as fat as she let on. His shape gets distorted over the years, growing to grotesque proportions next to a car that might or might not be a Caddie. It is a classy ride, for sure, but she is so angry and cold, trudging through the snow, she glimpses only parts—a door, a panel, rims—and not the make, not even as she gets in. What is she doing? Where is she going? She pulls out without knowing she does it, propelled by a strange inertia. Something thrilling and terrifying is in motion, and she can't control it.

She is not cool and confident, cruising up Halsted, with tunes at full bore. She clutches the steering wheel like a lifeline, perched on the edge of a deep seat, accelerating and braking erratically, continually checking the rearview mirror. She is afraid to adjust the seat or the radio, tuned low to a classical station. Almost immediately, she wants to turn back, but some part of her resists the urge. I'll turn around at the Drive, she thinks, and then once she's on it, at North Avenue, at Michigan, Grand. Every minute makes her later, the trip back to Dot's farther, the consequences of what she is doing harder to face. The journey is slow, excruciating and yet seems to happen in a flash.

As she drives, panic rising, she tells herself the story of what just happened, is still happening, practicing how she will deliver it later. It has to redeem her, this story, to win over Dot, who no doubt is already livid. In her mind, she plays up the humor, makes the car's owner a little mean, a little fatter. She did not want to keep Dot waiting, she hears herself say, but once she caught those keys, it was as if she had no choice. The story becomes funnier and smaller, silly, outrageous, but not, after all, such a big thing. Telling it calms her, helps her to regain control. She will turn around and go back to Dot's, she thinks, as soon as she has it down. Already she can hear her girlfriend's musical laugh, grudging at first, then louder, then raucous, and finally, out of control.

She cannot get the story quite right, however, not now and not during the many years that she told and retold it. She tested it on coworkers, friends, strangers met at parties and bars. Details were added and altered, others cut. The narrative evolved until one day she realized she did not know the girl at its center. The story became whatever she needed it to be, an amusing anecdote, a joke, a way to break the ice or puff herself up, a loose accumulation of useful lies. I hated her, as much for the lies as for her behavior on that day. I hated her for telling it to every audience except the one that mattered, the one it was meant for. I hated her for making it about race and class, gender, sex, and economics, when really it was a story about love.

In her defense, most stories lie. Life doesn't fit neatly into beginning, middle, end, or past, present, future. Sometimes there is no middle. The end might happen during the beginning, or before it. The past can be present, and the present past, or completely absent. Tense itself is a lie. Putting her story in the past helped render it less significant with each telling, until her biggest moment, a disaster she is still living, became a comical speck on the vast surface of a life. She did not know she was lying or that the form of the story itself was false, only that she could not tell it right. After years of trying—every listener a stand-in for Dot—she stopped. In her thirties and forties she did not repeat the story, but the more she tried to contain it, the larger it grew, like a leak sealed with a plug so big it only makes the hole larger.

She could not tell the story, it turned out. I had to. Telling it required time and distance she did not possess. It required not so much understanding that girl on Halsted—in many ways, she remained a mystery—as seeing her clearly. It meant forgiving her after years of hating her. I finally understood, a quarter of a century later, that bad luck played as big a role in what happened as stupidity. She is stupid, but everyone is dumb at twenty-one. Your first relationship is supposed to be with the wrong person. It is supposed to crash in a tsunami of heartache and pain. You are supposed to see it as enormous when it ends, think that nothing will ever be the same, then watch its power diminish until, looking back, you feel no more than a bittersweet pang. Is it her fault that in this story the reverse is true?

Looking into Dot's eyes during a fight, she thinks *Valium*, not *fear*, although with distance, it became apparent—the consuming love and fear of losing it that turn Dot's pupils into wide black drains. Only later did she comprehend that asking for rent makes Dot vulnerable, is an attempt to cede not gain control. The little gifts—a drawer, some hangers, pajamas, keys—look coarse up close, like points in a petty plan, but from a wider vantage, they coalesced into something beautiful, the vision of a life shared. Dot is asking her— halfway to asking her, a quarter step from asking her—to move in.

She tells herself that standing Dot up on Valentine's Day is a minor mistake, another fight that will fade in time, and when Dot doesn't answer her phone, she tells herself that she simply needs to call more often—twice a day, then three times, four. When this fails, she tells herself that sitting outside Dot's building will work.

In early March, a tidy box of clothes and books appears on the porch in South Shore, tied up with a string and labelled with her name like a package at Christmastime. A note folded inside asks her not to call again. She smiles bitterly. The only time Dot has been to her home, and she wasn't there. No matter, she tells herself, and does her best to brush off this enormous love like a crumb. Easy come, easy go. Plenty more fish in the sea. She has no idea—how could she at twenty-one?—that this is a moment when her life permanently changes, that she will never love anyone this deeply again.

She does not know why she trudges back the next day to the spot on 79th where she abandoned the car. Criminals supposedly feel an urge to return to the scene of the crime, but surely for her that would be in Lincoln Park. Classes are cancelled at U of C, a first, and she has nothing else to do. Maybe she simply wants confirmation that the theft happened. Ten hours later, under a glaring winter sun, it does look like theft, though the trip last night was so quick, she was so furious and scattered, it almost seems as if someone else committed the crime. *Did that occur?* she thinks, and not, *Did I do that?* Already it has the feel of a dimly remembered event that took place so long ago, you wonder if it could be imagined.

The snow stopped in the night, and temperatures fell. Yesterday's soupy mix has become a solid crust that crunches underfoot as she walks down Stony Island. A numbing wind cuts through her mom's thick parka, the kind of cold that makes your eyes water. She wears her mother's enormous sunglasses and hat, too. It's not likely that someone saw her parking last night, or would remember her if they did, but why take a chance?

She turns onto 79th, where the drifts are deeper. She left the car about a mile down, on the edge of a patch so notorious, it's known in the neighborhood as "Terror Town." What does she intend to do, get gas and drive it back to the North Side? She could probably leave the car on a side street near the restaurant without arousing suspicion—the mistake of an incompetent valet on a chaotic night.

An idea occurs to her. The car had a full tank of gas when she left the North Side. Could it still be running? Is that even possible? Ten hours is a long time, but it's a big luxury car with, no doubt, a huge tank. How much fuel gets used idling in park? She isn't sure, but the possibility that it's still running makes her heart race. She imagines herself climbing inside it to get warm. Her pace quickens, though she is exhausted from lack of sleep and so cold she can't feel her feet.

At Yates, she does not wait for a signal to cross, but when she gets to Phillips, she can't find the car. She tromps two blocks east, backtracks, crosses 79th. From across the street then, she recognizes the two beaters that haven't moved since last night and between them, a hole where she left it. She stares, for a moment not believing what's plain as day at this distance, then turns to begin the cold walk home.

Creatures of a Day

The noise cuts through the night, steady as a heartbeat, shrill as an accusation. Paul Previdenza feels a stab of pain in his stomach and pictures a bird of prey diving to pierce his gut, then rooting around for the tastiest organ. The image is linked to a dream he can't remember, though it ended just seconds ago. He reaches over Iona to find the thing on the nightstand, but already she has it in hand. She turns it off, the silence a second jolt. He can sleep through his alarm for fifteen minutes, but the beeper instantly shocks him into consciousness. Each time he hears its penetrating tone will be the first.

Iona is calm, efficient, alert, with no sign of the panic building in him. She pulls on clothes in the dark—somehow able to find everything she needs—and gently closes the bedroom door behind her, giving him the option of remaining asleep.

"This is Iona Morrow. I was paged." Her voice fades to a murmur as she carries the phone into the kitchen to jot notes.

The bedroom is dark, its hardwood floor cold and creaky as new ice. Unable to face the glare of light yet, Paul searches on hands and knees for yesterday's randomly cast-off clothes, until he backs into a corner of the nightstand. The curse he tries to suppress escapes muffled and stretched, a prolonged, almost girlish whimper. He attempts to stand, but his body locks in a simian crouch, pain shooting from his tailbone to the tips of his fingers and toes. Three floors below, the waves of Lake Michigan growl against the rocks that keep the ancient apartment building from crumbling into the water. He feels as if they are battering him. He would like nothing more than to drag a blanket into the warmer living room and settle on the couch, but after a long pause, he resumes groping in the dark, half naked and shivering, until he locates clothes he dimly recognizes as his.

They had been astonished to discover this place, a lake-front condo renting at a price they could almost afford. Its owner would be traveling and, given the neighborhood, was happy to lower the rent for a couple of responsible North-western grads—if they signed a two-year lease. That wasn't the original plan, but they jumped at the tradeoff. Rogers Park came roughly at the price he wanted to pay, and she was intrigued by the neighborhood's secret side, the dark streets with odd storefronts under the el, the tattoos and piercings, faces so foreign you couldn't guess their origins, an edgy undercurrent absent from the safer places where they had lived separately during the four years since college. The condo oozed history. They fell in love with its concealed hutches, light leaking through stained-glass transoms, a clawfoot tub that Iona joked was big enough for three. On the edge of the city, their first place as a couple would be close to campus and familiar Evanston haunts, memories that were distinct (they had not known each other in school) but linked in palpable ways. Best of all, the building had a tiny beach of its own and lake views that stretched to eternity.

The building also has old casement windows, no match for storms that roar off the lake without warning, pounding their east-facing bedroom as if all heaven's fury has been directed at them. On the worst nights, they feel like they are camping on a clifftop. A layer of dampness covers their frozen bedroom furniture in the morning, as if the lake worked its way through the brick while they slept. Only months after moving in did they realize that the old building's biggest attraction—a lakefront location—makes it practically unlivable. They try to force radiator valves open wider, but the heat, like the lighting, electrical outlets, and water pressure, is wholly inadequate.

The neighborhood is no less distressing. The safest bar, a dive near Loyola, sits at an unlikely confluence of homeless men wallowing in old mistakes and thirsty undergrads forging new ones. Paul and Iona step over used needles and condoms in the alley as if over puddles and avoid the el stops and menacing streets after dark. Iona has never minded hardship and Paul suspects, perhaps even harbors a secret affinity for it. She adopts her mother's impenetrable Irish accent and a faith evolved over centuries of suffering when insisting that their "desperate accommodations" surely will have an upside. Determined to make the most of a disaster, she scavenges detritus on the beach as if hunting treasure, transforming hunks of sun-bleached plastic into planters, torn tires into coasters, broken branches into lamps. (This is the stuff Paul pictures when people ask where they live. "Iona House," he replies, continuing the *who's-on-first* routine until she slugs him.) She paddles her feet at the pier on warm days and buys heavy curtains for their bedroom when the weather worsens.

Paul thinks of the lease as a prison sentence and whines accordingly. He has a talent for imagining the future and knows better than she does how long years can last.

"I have to go," Iona says, peeking in the bedroom, since the light is on. He is dressed except for his shoes. "It's Weiss Memorial again."

"I'll drive."

"You don't have to."

The exchange has become so familiar he does not respond. It's worse remaining behind on these nights, trapped in his thoughts, time stuck, believing that morning will never come.

"Where in hell…are my goddamn shoes?" he says, to himself more than her.

She scans the floor and points to the toes of his shoes, peeking from under the bed. He gives her a guilty look and examines them suspiciously, as if they can't be his, before sliding them on.

Paul and Iona hardly speak on the ride to Weiss Memorial, a silence less awkward than it might be. It's easy to blame the hour, their sleepiness, the gravity of the task at hand. Both know there is more to it. Iona lay still as ice in bed tonight, not so much as an encouraging grunt, until Paul, feeling as if he was coupling with a ghost, quietly gave up. She snuggled into him then, affectionate in a way that seemed patronizing, leaving him too tormented to doze off. Now, forced from sleep but not fully awake, language fails them yet again. He does not ask why she is less comfortable than ever in bed, and she does not wonder aloud why he is so moody. Neither asks whether they can endure, but the possibility that they won't rides in the dark car with them like a sullen passenger.

Eventually, Paul asks about the call, and Iona relates what little she knows. A taxi delivered the girl: nineteen, terrified, intoxicated. The police were called. She has not said a word, so no one knows the particulars. This isn't always the case. Some speak up right away—a full accounting—and according to Iona, heal faster for it. Others let events trickle out, denying what happened at first, releasing an irrelevant detail here, an obscured memory there, until a narrative begins to construct itself. Their recoveries tend to take longer. And some never tell their stories, living with secrets that consume them like ulcers, tethered forever to the pain of a single endless day.

Paul drops Iona at the emergency room and makes a U-turn to park illegally across the street. The car is freezing, but he suffers through it, sitting on his hands rather than running the engine. His breath turns the windows silver, the unreflective complexion of old mirrors. He rubs a porthole clear but barely glimpses the hospital before the glass fogs once more.

Alone in the dark confines of the car, he once again finds himself the reluctant author of a story of his own, coloring the facts he knows, creating others to fill in the gaps. The exercise horrifies him, but this is what he does, isolated down here, no idea what's going on up there. They paged Iona at two thirty, so he imagines it happening as the bars let out, drunks clustered like islands on sidewalks, retailing various versions of the night, reluctant to let the party end. The girl separated from her friends at a corner and emboldened by beer and a full moon, took an alley shortcut. She didn't notice the older man following. Paul knows it is probably racist, but he pictures him as Black. He grabbed her from behind, dragging her half a block, forcing her down among the weedy flotsam and jetsam of an empty lot. Pebbles of broken glass pressed into her back like coarse sand as waves of pain washed over her, her muffled screams indecipherable to all but her and the person who will inhabit her nightmares for the rest of her life.

He tries to force the thought from his mind, the way he tries to forget about the beeper sitting in their bedroom like a ticking bomb on the nights Iona volunteers, but both are beyond his control. She has been working for REAP, the Rape Education, Advocacy, and Prevention project, since before he met her, two years ago. One night a week she is on call from six in the evening until six the next morning. Sometimes nothing happens. The beeper sits between them, an anonymous, anachronistic third wheel, silent but demanding, impossible to appease. It dictates their plans, shapes their conversations, and, like a terrible memory, weighs on them even when they think they have forgotten it. It would be natural, given her history, for Iona to panic when the beeper sounds, but she is as sober as a surgeon on call. Paul is the one who finds himself frantic and dazed, struggling to complete a sentence. When it's silent, the anticipation is almost as bad. Why a beeper? Paul has asked, surprised that anyone still made them. Calls are too easy to miss, Iona explained, because someone turns off a ringer or can't end a conversation. The beeper is always on, dedicated to one thing, its extra weight the reminder of a unique responsibility.

He checks his watch, four o'clock, and tugs the collar of his coat higher. Sleep is not a possibility. Work will be miserable tomorrow—*today*, he thinks, time a muddle in his bleary head—but sitting here alone in the freezing car, he almost looks forward to it. He finds himself thinking, as he sometimes does on these nights, of Cate Hecht, a girl he knew in college. Where would he be now, at 4 a.m. on a Wednesday in March four years after graduation if he and Cate had stayed together?

He senses more than sees flashing lights through the scrim of his side window and rolls it down. An ambulance speeds into the hospital drive, siren silent, lights whirring. A gurney is lowered to the pavement quickly and efficiently, disappearing behind automatic doors before Paul can see who is strapped to it.

Cate had been as bright as she was adventurous, pre-med with a double major in biology and history, or maybe one was a minor, he couldn't recall. The attraction began as simple longing for that athletic body, nothing like the emotional undertow that first pulled him toward Iona. Beneath her tough, sarcastic exterior, though, Cate also had a sweet nature and quick sense of humor. The similarities are striking because, on the surface, Cate appeared the polar opposite of Iona, who favors earth tones, flowing skirts, minimal makeup. Apart from jeans, which she wore tattered and skintight, Paul never saw Cate in anything but black—black shirts, shoes, coats, eyeliner. Her hair, too, was dyed black, short and choppy, not overtly Goth but close enough to draw looks in the small Iowa town where she grew up. He noticed her cropped, almost boyish hair from behind in his Intro to Greek Drama class, startled when she turned, to see how pretty she was: the surprise of pale blue eyes and a fair complexion under dark hair, that midnight smile rendering anyone who suffered its wry, delayed judgment painfully self-conscious. The prof droned on—dates and places, names impossible to pronounce—and they bonded over material that could have been compelling but drowned in a sea of history. Paul gave her notes over coffee when she missed class, a frequent occurrence. He wished he'd known her better, but she left school abruptly after sophomore year. He wrote her at the address her roommate gave (hesitant to call, not wanting to intrude) but never heard back. The roommate was a flake. Who knew if it was even the right address.

He checks his watch again, four thirty, and wonders what time the sun will rise, hoping he isn't here to find out. Back home, Iona will sleep soundly, exhausted and emotionally drained. Paul will lie awake in bed, horrors real and imagined filling his head as he listens to her breath and the rhythm of the lake beating endlessly against the rocks below their bedroom.

That day, Paul struggles through eight hours at his job as a claims adjuster for Mutual Security, "short-term" work he has done for three years. This morning, he was supposed to interview an off-duty cop who accidentally killed a boy with his car in Hyde Park, but something about the story is amiss. Paul's boss yanked the claim from him as soon as he sniffed fraud. Instead, Paul is losing patience with a man named Ptak, a giant Polish immigrant from the Southwest Side who fills his small office. Liability is clear in the three-car accident that stranded Ptak on Lake Shore, though at first, he blamed the erratic driving of the woman in front of him. It was her car he slammed, sending her to the hospital and the Drive into turmoil for the day. The price Mutual Security set for his car—five hundred over Blue Book—might make Ptak think he's getting away with something, but he is ignoring his injuries and the fact that his car was a Honda (their street value lasts forever). In the end, he'll get screwed, but he doesn't know that, or care. Only with painful coaxing can Paul get the man to admit that he has been hurt—bruised ribs, sprained wrist, and oddly, a pulled groin muscle, maybe from the force of slamming on the brake. What else is there? What isn't Ptak saying? Paul tells him repeatedly, in portentous tones, that once he takes a check, he can't file a claim.

"If you thought you might have some trouble down the road, with your wrist, for instance, now would be the time to make things right," Paul says.

Ptak has had at least one drink this morning and seems impatient for the next. He insists Paul can't compensate him for his injuries. What injuries? They've healed already, Ptak says, his left hand looking useless as a flipper.

"I am fine. Only fag care about little bruise," Ptak says, staring pointedly at Paul, who is jarred by the colloquial slur asserting itself amid awkward English.

"Some injuries don't show up for months, even years," Paul says. "I see it all the time. Has nothing to do with who's at fault."

Ptak stares blankly. Paul scoots his chair forward. He can't find the words to make himself understood. It's the opposite of how these meetings usually go, as if today, Ptak should be on Paul's side of the desk. The guy is a jerk but also completely clueless, a fish so many miles from water, Paul can't help feeling for him. He makes yet another veiled attempt to nudge Ptak before finally spelling it out.

"Mr. Ptak, we pay ten thousand dollars for injuries smaller than yours every day, and feel lucky. If you were to suggest how much—"

"*How much, how much?*" He sneers, waves a hand dismissively. "Everything in America, *how much?* Only pay me for car. Let's go." He raps his knuckles on Paul's blotter as if to wake him.

When Ptak leaves, Paul leans his forehead on the cool desk, resting his swollen eyes. He's not sure what is more frustrating, listening to people equivocate to escape liability or trying to persuade this guy, too macho or inept or something, to take what he has coming. Sometimes Paul can't help nudging people in this direction—another sign that he's in the wrong job—but today, exhaustion has overcome all subtlety.

Iona did not finish until six this morning. She slept for a couple of hours before work while Paul drank coffee and watched bad TV. He attempted to fix the toilet, which lately runs nonstop unless the valve is closed after each flush. He would like to attach a value to the endless time he spends fixing things in the apartment and deduct it from what he pays each month, but Iona won't let him. Minor injustices don't bother her. Her outrage over the major ones, however, can get frightening. She was livid this morning after three hours at the bedside of a nineteen-year-old Mexican girl named Selena.

"It was her boyfriend," Iona said, as she opened the door and plopped down in the car. Paul gave a startled shout.

"Jesus, you're jumpy," she said, the well of sympathy dry, her patience for the pathetic ways of men spent. Lately, Paul wonders if he is taking after his grandmother, who suffered from "nerves," a condition that everyone knew and no one acknowledged was probably brought on by successive husbands, the second more violent than the first.

"Her boyfriend?" As soon as he said it, he wished he could remove the note of confusion. She squinted at him, mouth agape, wondering if he really could be as stupid as he seemed. "Oh." He nodded. It wasn't exactly the first scenario that sprang to mind, he wanted to say, but pointing that out, saying anything, would only make it worse.

"The cops were complete and utter assholes."

Iona's poor Spanish was better than the girl's English, so she interpreted for the two policemen. The girl was intermittently hysterical, the translation painful. Iona thought she understood the most important parts, though, and when she came to a sentence she couldn't comprehend, struggling to the point of tears, it only stirred greater feeling, as if the missing words signaled a suffering so deep, the language that could convey it had not yet evolved.

"How could it be the boyfriend?" one cop demanded.

The other shrugged. "Can't arrest someone for grand theft if it's his car."

Paul pictured Iona's response to this: formidable, menacing, jabbing at air with the silver pen she aims like an arrow when making a point. This is her role, the advocacy portion of REAP, an acronym that strikes Paul as odd, both for its biblical implications of divine retribution and because it's an anagram for "rape." He wants to ask if shuffling the letters to turn that word around was intentional and if so, what it means, but somehow feels he shouldn't. Iona sits with these women, comforting and consoling, coaxing them to talk. If they need places to stay, she finds them homes. Protecting them from the police is, perversely, often the biggest challenge. In a way, poor communication was an advantage this time. The girl did not know that the men supposedly on her side had a mindset frighteningly close to her rapist's.

"If they get the boyfriend's story and don't charge him, he'll kill her," Iona said of the cops, shaking her head. "Maybe himself too, which would be fine if he left her alone." A single sob burst from her like a hiccup and then was gone. "The fucker chained her to the headboard while she was sleeping. The handcuffs were lined with fur or something, but the bruises were so bad, her wrists looked like—"

He raised a hand.

"Sorry," she said. They have a deal. She can talk about these cases when she needs to but is not allowed to give physical details.

Here was one instance where speaking up could prove disastrous, Paul thought, though he would not say so to Iona. He censors himself constantly now that they live together. They are still on their best behavior, lovers auditioning as roommates, but his silence is often a function of these late-night missions. Their sex life, never robust, has lingered on life support since they moved in together. Iona's volunteering is partly to blame for this, too, though not completely. She has always had trouble in bed. Her Irish Catholic upbringing put her at an early disadvantage, and being raped when she was eighteen and still a virgin solidified it. She can talk about that trauma openly—her volunteer work and years of therapy have helped. She told Paul everything on their first date. They had ordered a second bottle of wine at Les Contraires, a bistro in Lincoln Park—the place and the wine both her ideas. Fancy restaurants make him uncomfortable, and he didn't like wine back then. He did not tell her that, smiling as he choked down the merlot she raved about. He does like wine now, thanks to Iona, just as, under her influence, he has learned to enjoy jazz and to care about politics. He helped with a letter-writing campaign she ran for Amnesty

International and her fundraiser for the Coalition to Abolish Capital Punishment, though he has mixed feelings about that one. Secretly, he believes most men on death row deserve to be there, but he has never argued the point with Iona, knowing he won't win.

She thrives on lost causes and pet projects, another, more positive product of her Irish Catholic roots. She explained on that first date that her name came from the island north of Ireland, off the Scottish coast, where St. Columcille established his monastery. Paul could see even then that there was something of the missionary about her, something of the Irish ascetic too. Iona loves him, but if she did not also feel the need to save him (from what, she probably couldn't say), they might not last.

The air at Les Contraires—all artful presentation and elaborate trompe l'oeil—was charged with attraction that night, couples in love with each other, tourists with the mysteries of a strange, sprawling city. Paul realized that the waiter, who sounded French at first, was Mexican, and for some reason, this put him at ease. The man poured more wine, and Iona joked that she'd been dying of thirst waiting for Paul to do it. She had been the one to taste and approve the merlot, refill their glasses, and pursue the flirtation, a reversal of roles that felt strange but right somehow, too.

They discovered that their years at Northwestern overlapped and traded college stories: old dorms and apartments, past boyfriends and girlfriends, memorable events, best classes. Paul didn't have much to contribute. He'd grown up on the Near West Side—the real Little Italy, not that touristy stuff on Taylor Street—as Blacks and Latinos replaced families like his, the last Italians tenaciously clinging to a neighborhood without much future. His older brother, Dope, was in Stateville, five years this time, and at sixteen, Paul had seemed destined to follow. People thought his brother's nickname came from his favorite pastime. In fact, a teacher had christened him "Dope" because the boy couldn't think five minutes ahead, never imagined he might be punished for throttling a playmate, flooding a bathroom, burning his civics book in the middle of Western Avenue. Paul had been frighteningly similar as a kid. It was a miracle he made it out of Juarez High, much less into Northwestern.

As he mentioned Northwestern, a homeless woman—young and Black in a ragged man's coat—leaned against the window next to their table. They ignored her. She pressed her hands against the glass to stare down at their meals. A stern-looking manager approached. She licked her lips and with a mocking smile, turned away.

Paul laughed nervously.

"Poor kid," Iona said, looking as if she might leave to see if the woman needed help.

Paul didn't date anyone seriously in college, too out of place to think beyond the next hour. Campus was an island with the fleeting quality of fantasy, his life there as tenuous as his family's hold on an aging house in a changing neighborhood. Any minute, he thought, he would be revealed as an imposter and asked to leave. As a freshman he got blind drunk and rolled around with girls he wouldn't recognize the next day. Everything changed sophomore year. Partying lost its appeal, though his grades continued to sink. He became a hermit. He hadn't gone out with many girls anyway. Cate Hecht was an exception, and apart from those couple of times, it never went beyond friendship.

He asked Cate out the night he bumped into her at a dive bar on Howard Street, that seamy border between chaste, dry Evanston and the roughest blocks of Rogers Park. Only the most daring NU students went to places like the Tallyho, where earlier that year a man had been stabbed. It was the perfect habitat, though, for what Paul used to call "creatures of a day," and he was hunting them that night. He'd learned in class that this was the name Greek gods gave to mere mortals, but it seemed fitting slang for a certain kind of girl: adventurous, sexy, easy, maybe for any girl. At the time, they all constituted for Paul a desirable but foreign species, one that spoke a different language and had a lifespan of twenty-four hours.

He did not recognize Cate through smoke that swirled like sediment, just sighted a looker in a corner of the murky bar and walked to the juke box for a better view. She waved.

"Don't I know you from somewhere?" he said, an index finger pressed to his lips.

"Yes, your worst nightmare. Hell, in fact. You read that next batch of stuff?"

"Some of it. The *Oedipus*."

"Ate a puss? Didn't care for it. What about the Euripides?"

"Why do I sense a horrible pun in the offing?"

They talked for an hour, then kissed until the bar closed. He told her about a pool party that Friday. There would be kegs, dancing, Marco Polo…He felt foolish after mentioning the last item, the thing he and his juvenile friends were most excited about, but Cate laughed.

"I didn't date anyone my freshman year," Iona said at Les Contraires. Paul's reserve seemed to draw her out, creating a space she was happy to fill. She took a long drink of wine, then related in an even, matter-of-fact voice how, shortly after arriving at college, she had gone out with an older guy from another school. "He took me sailing on our second date, on a boat his uncle or somebody kept at Belmont Harbor. While we were out, he attacked me. Raped me," she corrected, looking up deliberately, as if precise language was painful, but anything less would disallow what had happened, diminishing his guilt and her dignity. He was a nice guy on the first date, she said, and then turned into someone else.

"The worst was being stuck there with him, utterly dependent. I fantasized about the boat tipping over—him drowning while I made it back. As we sailed to shore, he pretended like nothing happened. He actually asked why I was so quiet. Like there was something wrong with *me*."

She threw up as they returned to land. Gripping a rail, swaying as if chained to the oars of a galley, she ignored his pleas to lean over the side, getting sick all over the deck.

"That story, 'The Open Boat,' popped into my head," she said. "Do you know it? Strangers trapped together at sea, butt of the universe's cruel joke. It would have been a better story with a woman on board." She finished her wine and poured more, topping off Paul's nearly full glass. "I couldn't go out with anyone after that, not for a year."

She began walking alone, sometimes for hours, wandering miles from campus. Her grades suffered, as did her appearance. "I turned into a total cow," she said. She avoided shop windows and mirrors, any glimpse of her new heft and sallow skin, the wild tufts of hair sprouting like horns. But she couldn't avoid the warnings that surfaced in therapy: this thing would imprison her if she didn't take control of her future. Some women never had sex again, her therapist said, remained nervous wrecks all their lives. Iona decided she couldn't let that happen. She had always had a social conscience, but this was when the volunteering and political activism began in earnest, the rallies and protests, her work at the Women's Center and Amnesty International. She wanted distraction, but she also felt forever changed and decided it would be for the better.

"I've never told anyone that so soon," she said.

Paul covered her hand with his. He loved her in that moment. He wanted to take care of her and to protect her. And he wanted, slowly and methodically, to kill the guy who had done it. Difficult as it was to hear, her story—her openness and trust, the plain language in which she described this ordeal—established an immediate connection.

Sexual intimacy proved more of a challenge. She would have slept with him that first night—tipsy and attracted, she hinted as much—but after hearing that story, how could he? They saw each other a dozen times over the next six weeks and, determined to take things slow, he did not attempt more than a kiss. He has been patient with her from the beginning, and when their lovemaking fizzles, as it has periodically from the start, he is sincere in his understanding. He means it when he tells her that everything is all right, that he is content just to hold her, though he suspects she does not believe him.

Iona feels the need to prove to him, or perhaps to herself, that she suffers no ill effects. She used to suggest in the most self-conscious and transparent way that they have sex in his car on empty side streets, in bathrooms at bars, and once, in the bedroom closet at a friend's house as they drunkenly fetched their coats after a party. Sometimes she lies in bed as still as a blowup doll, and at others, postures like a prostitute, forcing herself to be aggressive in a way that makes him feel pity more than lust. He does not bring it up, wary of making her more self-conscious, but when the subject becomes unavoidable, she pretends there is no problem, laughing off their disasters as flukes.

From their hallway, the smell of Iona's tomato sauce hits Paul with the distant force of a childhood memory. Her Italian dishes are nearly as good as his mother's—no small compliment—and this is her way of saying thank you for last night. And sorry if she took her anger out on him. Her lips are warm, spicy from tasting the sauce for stuffed shells, his favorite. Her right hand snakes behind his back, pulling him close, while the left holds a wooden spoon. He feels the start of an erection at the unexpectedly deep kiss. When the kiss ends, she continues the embrace, her breath garlicky, face glistening with sweat. Held in the hot kitchen, he grows irritated.

"Poor thing, you're exhausted, aren't you?" She kisses his forehead, maternally this time. "I don't know why you insist on going with me."

"It's worse being stuck here, in my head."

She drizzles olive oil on a plate of bruschetta and arranges the Waterford crystal he has never seen her use. "I bought that pinot noir we can't afford. I couldn't resist."

"Red wine. I'm afraid I'd black out. Maybe a beer." He turns to get one, but she has a bottle opened before he reaches the fridge.

Their conversation during dinner feels forced. Halfway through the meal, he cracks a window. The weather has warmed, air heavy with the promise of rain, adding to the stuffy atmosphere in the small kitchen, the only warm room in the condo. They discuss their days. He hardly remembers his and is depressed at the thought that tomorrow will be the same.

Iona goes into the living room. Subterranean strains of bossa nova filter into the kitchen as Paul drops silverware in soapy water. He does not recognize the singer, but a few years ago, he would not have known the style of music, much less its obscure practitioners. Iona has made his life better in innumerable ways. What does she see in Paul that makes her love him?

Drops of rain, sparse and loud, tap the kitchen window as he carries his second beer into the living room. Iona has changed into a lace nightie. She lies across the sofa, one leg lazily exposed, pretending to read a magazine. He heads for a chair, but she pats the couch, exposing panties as she bends her legs to make room. Still reading, she places her foot on his knee, rocking it as if for warmth, inching upward until it reaches his crotch. Both are excited by the game, the pretense that their contact is accidental. An erection makes Paul's position impossible, but he doesn't move. She sits up, her breath thick, audible. She holds the back of his neck with one hand and slides the other beneath his belt, kissing him hard. At first, she seems to be massaging his neck, but after a moment she is simply squeezing, her thumb stuck in tense muscle. He feels like a bad dog held by the scruff. She senses his pulling back and moves forward, accidentally pinching his thigh with her knee.

"Ow. Hang on."

"Ooh, sorry." She releases his leg and fumbles at his zipper.

"Wait a minute."

"Please, let's do it now," she says. "Right here. You're so hard."

She straddles him, grinding on his lap, clutching at the nightie with her free hand. She can't quite get the top off, but a breast falls free in the effort.

"Just slow down," he says. His shirt tangles as she pulls it off, binding his wrists for a moment above his head. Gently he slides her from his lap. She slumps.

"It's okay. Hey." He kisses her cheek.

"What is it, Paul? Do you not love me?"

"Yes, I love you, but can't we be ourselves? You don't have to do this."

"I have to do something. But what? I've tried everything I know—aggressive, kinky, shy, innocent. I've taken charge, and I've given you complete control. Exotic places don't work or sexy outfits. Half the time nothing works."

"You're trying too hard," he says.

"You're not trying at all. You are never here with me, Paul. You seem so troubled all the time. God, I sound like my mother—*sorry for your troubles*—but you do." She strokes his cheek with the back of her hand, her tormented look a mix of love, beneficence, purpose. The look of St. Columcille before a pagan.

"When we do manage, I feel like you're afraid of breaking me. I'm not a vase."

Does she really not understand that he takes things slow for her sake? He knows how tough this conversation must be for her, but she is not being fair.

"I'm trying to be sensitive," he says.

"Well, stop! Try being *insensitive*. Greedy. Take me. I want you to have me. I want you to do me. I want you to pretend I'm not uttering these horrible clichés." She smiles, he laughs, but a moment later, the tension returns. "I thought moving in together would help. Are you not attracted to me?"

"Of course I am. You're perfect. You're the perfect woman for me."

"You're the first guy I've been able to really trust." She leans into him, pressing her face to his chest. "What if we got married?" He can see she's been thinking about this for some time. "Maybe you would feel more secure."

"Me?"

"Well, me too," she says quickly. "We both would. Things feel so turbulent, like this could end tomorrow. I don't want to be with anyone else."

"I don't want to be with anyone else either." His eyes widen, but he smiles. "Ever. We'd have to talk about it, make a plan."

"Of course. You don't decide your whole life in a day. I just need an idea about the future."

Since the night will be bad—more rain or snow or some sloppy mix of the two—he covers Iona where she fell asleep on the couch. Paul has been awake exactly twenty-four hours, but the day that follows the beeper's signal always feels like a lifetime. He is tired to the point of sickness but can't sleep. He closes the kitchen door softly behind him, and on the twenty square feet of porch they euphemistically call "the deck," pulls up a plastic chair. The porch sits at a right angle to the lake, facing south, poorly sheltered by the porch above and, on its sides, by a shallow recess in the building. The water is right there, but they must lean over the rail and look left to see it. He does so now and gasps at the bite of rain-flecked wind. It looks like an ocean tonight, the lake, swells bursting like bombs on the rocks below, spraying shrapnel on the base of their building.

Is Iona right? Is he to blame for their problems in bed? It would be difficult for her to think it was all her fault, so naturally, she laid some blame on him, but does he bear more responsibility than he thinks? He has been slow with her, *sensitive*, the word she threw back at him. Has he been too sensitive, too concerned with a trauma from her past? Both of them have been more self-conscious since they moved in. That beeper sits next to their bed like a watching stranger, waiting for a quiet moment to signal catastrophe.

He thinks back to his one-night stands in college and the short bursts of dating after graduation. There was no one special until Iona. Despite his best efforts for a brief, immature time, he was never a ladies' man. He used to think this was the problem with Cate Hecht his sophomore year, clumsiness, a lack of grace. The night of their only real date, she arrived at the party early, and he was thrilled to have her to himself. In a two-person game of Marco Polo, he groped around the pool like some primordial sea creature, blind and mute, growling "Marco" in his monster voice as he lurched toward her "Polo," eliciting ripples of laughter.

Later, they commandeered the stereo, playing tunes, comparing notes on bands, making fun of McNaughton, the pretentious professor who taught Greek Drama. She raised her cup. "It is a sweet thing to draw out / A long, long life in cheerful hopes," she said in a nasal, wooden voice: the prof's rendering of a Greek chorus.

"But my heart is eaten away when I am aware of myself," he said, a line from some play or other that McNaughton kept coming back to.

"My heart is eaten away when I am out of beer." She turned her cup upside down, well beyond tipsy by then.

He poured another pitcher, and they headed to the basement, pretending to take a tour of the house. In a downstairs bedroom they drank cross-legged on a ratty alcohol-doused carpet and when the beer was finished, kissed. She was woozy and placed a palm on the floor carefully, as if the room listed away. Another hand on his chest. He pressed forward.

She never said no. She never screamed or hit him. They were drunk, perceptions cloudy, cues confused. Later, he did not have a single visible scratch or bruise. He could spend hours supplying exculpatory details, and did over the following years, claiming to himself he had done nothing wrong. No cop would have charged him, but he knows what he did. He knew when she grabbed his wrist, weakly because she was drunk and stunned and he was a friend. He knew what it meant when she said "please," though for years he imagined that word, the only one she uttered besides his name, was open to interpretation. He certainly knew the answer, though he pretended not to, when she lay curled on the floor crying and he asked what was wrong.

One of those things. A misunderstanding. That was how he used to think of it. But he knows how Iona would see it. No, that is a copout. He knows how it was. How it is. He thinks of Iona on their first night out, telling him that someone attacked her, then pausing to use honest language: *raped*.

The wind gusts and the tired porch sways slightly, its timbers creaking. Paul shivers, gripping the rail, watching the patient fury of waves breaking on the beach. The rain that hits his face is freezing. He gasps like a man drowning but doesn't move.

He imagines himself going inside to tell Iona all of it, every detail, without omitting or coloring a single fact. The shabby Victorian house with dingy yellow trim, the earthy smell of a backyard pool, the damp rust-colored carpet in a downstairs bedroom. He describes the pressure he ignored on his wrist before he held hers, the way the lust of his fantasy gave way to real terror on Cate Hecht's twenty-year-old face. The guilt mingled with relief when no one confronted him later, the idiotic letter he wrote her. All of it. However Iona reacts, he knows her, and Iona knows him, knows the person he has become, a conversion in which she played no small part. She eventually will forgive him, he thinks, but that does not matter because he has to tell her, whatever the outcome. She will be on call again tomorrow, and he cannot stare in silence at that beeper for one more night.

"You're troubled," she said, unaware that this is the quality she loves most in him. Even as he imagines telling her, he knows that he never will, not because he can't face her anger or own what he did—speaking out, paying finally, would be a relief. He cannot tell Iona because, with the mystery of his suffering solved, she would no longer have in him someone to save. She would love him less—how much less he doesn't know and does not want to find out.

They never discussed marriage before tonight, but already he knows a wedding will happen. The impulsive plan will be carried out. He will marry her. He will buy a home with her in this city, raise kids, advance in a dull, stable career. Their future is as clear as the past day.

Chief O'Neill's

Dress things up however you want, once you seen through the bullshit and know it, you got to go out on your own.

It's what I decided the day Jablonski inspected the house at Division and Wood, the day I quit taking orders from him or anyone. I'm on a ladder cutting in the dining room ceiling when our fat fearless leader starts hovering. I'm already pissed cause the Polish Prince, who couldn't estimate the size of his manhood, gave a five-week bid for a seven-week gig. His wife can call a job better, no joke. I seen her do it—and change his mind about an estimate so he don't even know it changed.

"O'Sullivan, you got a holiday over here," the Polish Prince says, but I didn't miss an inch of that wall. The flash he sees is a reflection off the antique mirror that hangs opposite. A minute later, Jabo plucks sandpaper off the drop, shocked like he discovered something that could change his life and pissed cause he missed it until now.

He slaps the square on top of my ladder. "Not even half used!" He slaps a dollar next to it. "Throw that away too. That's what you're doing, wasting good material."

I set my brush, dripping the cloudy shade of gray I just mixed, on the dollar.

"We saved that piece so you could remove the unsightly surface layer, like they say on that skin commercial. You want to look pretty in your new hat, don't you?" He's been wearing a black beret lately, like some Dago artist, to cover his bald spot.

"What did you say to me?"

"I said, putting something on the outside don't mean there's anything inside." I tap his forehead.

"Prick! That's it. You've gone too far."

I guess I did. I fought with Jabo plenty before but always left the door open a crack, wide enough to creep back the next week. Who knows why I closed it this time. Some lines you can't see even after you cross them.

Jablonski's got me by the wrist, and with my free hand, I'm twisting his collar when Jim, who'd hate to see a slave lose his job, gets between us.

"Son of a bitch! I'll have you cuffed and shipped!" Jablonski yells, his face red as the trim in the Lutzes' dining room.

"What are you doing here?" Jim hisses.

"That," I say, "is the best question you ever asked."

The second I got outside, I knew quitting was the right thing. The world felt bigger, brighter, warmer—and not just cause I started celebrating at noon. I'd been planning to go out on my own since trade school. Jim acted like it was any other day, too blind or dumb to see what a change this big could mean. He's maybe five-four and looks all of sixteen, Jim, no Michelangelo but a good egg and a solid painter.

"It ain't secure, Sully." Jim shook his blond head slow like he does. "You knew where you stood with Jabo. Established company, somewhere to go every day. He's got his ways, okay, but you overlook stuff, you got to. You don't walk out."

Jim'll go along with anything eventually, but sometimes I wanted to grab his chin and stop that head from sweeping around like it was attached to a lighthouse, like he was answering "no" before you even asked a question. I was tired of being told what I couldn't do. Even if I still lived at home, drove a beater more Bondo than steel, slept in the bunk bed I had since third grade, at twenty-five I was running my own shop. More than becoming a journeyman or dropping out of school, even more than losing it with Tracy Lynch behind the Independent Trading Company warehouse on 65th, opening the shop made me feel like a man, one of those things you can't know 'til it happens to you. No thanks to Jim, or anyone in the neighborhood. All of them, the Old Man included, wanted me to crawl back to Jabo, begging. Sure, and have the Polish Prince own my ass 'til kingdom come? No thanks. Ignoring them was easier than I thought, and knowing I was right made going it alone all the sweeter.

Not that opening the shop was easy. Things started off slow, and for a while, I thought maybe the know-nothings were right. Covering up years of cheap paint, coddling blind old ladies who agonized over colors, fighting Bohunks who thought, just for them, add-ons should be free—it was the reverse of what I always pictured. After a few months, though, I moved the line we bought in *The Southtown Economist* out of classifieds. The new ad brought in more people. Tradesmen at O'Neill's dumped stuff they couldn't handle on me, and every week brought a fresh estimate. Soon, Jim and me were working tens and twelves and talking about adding a third guy.

It got so we hardly had time for a beer at Chief O'Neill's. Conn Keehan owns the bar, but it's named for Francis O'Neill, who preserved all the old trad music. He was one of the city's first police chiefs back when the whole department was Irish. Jim and me been drinking there since we were kids. It's a small place—a high bar that could stop a tank, a long mirror behind it, a jukebox plays dated rock and rebel songs, *come-all-yas*, the Old Man calls them. The pub's in one of the oldest buildings in the Village (Chrysler Village, officially, after a plant that made bomber engines for the War, but that closed before I was born). Everyone drinks at Chief's—workers from the factories on 65ᵗʰ, tradesmen from the neighborhood, cops from 63ʳᵈ and Homan, the ward super, even the alderman sometimes.

I'd pour drinks for Conn when the place got busy, not that I ever felt at home on his side of the bar. Nothing's where I think it should be, and it feels weird back there, like you're watching yourself have a beer. Feels even weirder when Conn pulls me behind the bar one night a few months after I started the shop, cause I ain't done it in so long. I'm wrecked after work, but the place is slammed and he's a friend. You can't say no.

"Tomato juice?" I ask. Mark likes a red beer.

"We're out," Conn says in an accent thick as plaster. He's got a big red farmer's face, lines cutting into eyes that look older than the rest of him somehow. "Tell Mark to have a proper beer and not be a big girl's blouse."

I deliver the message, watered-down, and buy Mark a proper beer myself. When the crowd eases up, I ask a couple mailmen in the corner about getting a P.O. box for the shop. Conn interrupts, which is annoying, but they aren't much help anyway. I guess they don't want to talk shop after five, and who can blame them? Not me, pouring beers I should be drinking. There's work and after work. Life's easier if you draw that line.

"Fill the ice," Conn says. "I've got them."

Later, he tells me, always let him handle postal workers cause they pay a special price—twice the going rate. It's a shame, but you need a tan anymore to work in a Chicago post office. There's one on the corner, and if O'Neill's becomes their hangout, Conn's regulars are gone. I'd feel funny charging them more, but he wants to handle it himself, so fine—his business, not mine.

When I'm back on a barstool, Conn slides me another Guinness, my fourth or fifth on the house. He wants some work done, he says, a perfect job for New Look Painting & Decorating, which is what I call the shop. "The walls in here are like the wife's hair these times," he says, waving a hand, "so many layers, even she doesn't know what's underneath."

"Sure, we'll do it for free, or for beers."

"Ha, your kind of free I can't afford. No, you give me a price like anyone."

I get him an estimate a week later, and he warns it's too low. "You'll go out of business at that rate," Conn says, turning serious. "Make an exception for a friend, and pretty soon, they're all friends."

We got to work late so the pub can stay open—Conn can't afford to close, even for a day. Maeve, a beauty who I saw for a minute back when, is behind the bar, and Conn's on our side, drinking when we arrive at midnight. Everything's backwards tonight—our tools in the place we drink, a job starting when I usually knock off, Conn drinking in his pub while we work. I say hello to some regulars, tradesmen off the boat, who sit up front where they can watch who comes and goes. A couple of younger guys with girls are at tables, where anyone with a girl sits. A few occasionals—oddballs and loners, amateurs out to test their tolerance—take up the far end. Mark and Abel Grabowski, brothers banned from the Warsaw Inn for fighting, sit down there, as glum as if they're drinking in Siberia. They get along fine here, but if Krol lets them go home to the Warsaw, they'll tear each other apart inside a week.

"Maeve, drinks for the artistes," Conn says. "Don't be Polish all your life." He's friendly behind the bar, but in front of it, a whole other person, relaxed and more than decent.

I suspect he hired us just to give us the work, not that the walls aren't rough. I never knew how rough 'til I looked at the job, which I hope says more about my focus as a drinker than my eye as a painter.

Stone-faced, Maeve ignores Conn, keeps mixing sanitizer, then washing glasses. She delivers an order, forgets the change, goes back. Finally, she lets herself notice Jim and me, squinting down at us like a queen at peasants. Conn laughs. He couldn't run the place without her, Polish or not, and actually, there's Irish blood on her mom's side, where she got the name.

She sets down our beers, and Conn pays her out of pocket, not like some owners who forget the register when they're social. If the owner pays out of pocket on his twist, so will anyone in the round. Cross the bar for freebies, you pay forever.

"Bout ye?" Conn asks. "How's your father keeping?" I miss things here and there, but the Old Man comes from the same place, so I understand him pretty well even when, messing, I pretend not to. Conn and the Old Man left Derry (Londonderry, officially, since the Prods renamed everything) for the same reason: all the best jobs, blocks, houses went to the other side.

I tell him my folks are thinking of moving south, maybe Florida.

"Florida! If they move anywhere, it should be home."

Home means Derry. Conn pretends he'll return someday and everything'll be fine, *grand*, but he ain't been back in twenty years. The ones who go regular on holidays, who face the looks and get called *Yank*, stop pretending they still belong.

"I'm moving out either way."

"Ah, stay at home. Save your money," Conn says, same as everyone in the neighborhood. "Tell your father to come 'round for the All-Ireland Sunday. I'll set him straight." In the old country they wouldn't talk—Conn's a *Sinn Feiner* and the Old Man supports a party that broke with the IRA. Here, they're pals, as long as they avoid certain subjects.

The last customer leaves, and Maeve locks up. Conn checks her work—lines cleaned, doors locked, money counted—everything in its place. He gives us a hand spreading drops before he leaves.

"Help yourselves to the tappers," he says.

"Sure about that?" I ask.

He pauses at the door, with a worried look, like he's seeing what the old man calls *the full magnitude of his actions* too late, blesses himself, and leaves.

We patched the walls days ago, but some of the mud sank, so we skim a few spots. Waiting for them to dry, we have some beers. Once the patches are solid, we sand them, but breathing Durabond creates a real thirst. A couple of drinks clear the pipes. Pretty soon, it's break time, but instead of coffee, we have a few more. On the jukebox I play "Back Home in Derry," a song about rebels exiled to Australia, one of the Old Man's favorites.

> In 1803, we sailed out to sea
> Out from the sweet town of Derry
> For Australia bound if we didn't all drown
> The marks of our fetters we carried

The chorus comes around, and I belt it out with Christy Moore: *Oooh, oooh, I wish I was back home in Derry.* Weird how a song that beautiful can make you miss a place, especially, I'll admit, under the influence. Don't seem to matter that it's a place I never really saw.

"Jim, let me buy you a beer," I say, feeling warm, and top off the two pints I left to settle. When it's his turn, he pours a couple small ones. That gets me into the bar's stock of Powers whiskey, my downfall.

When Conn arrives the next morning I'm squeezed onto the bench by the door, and Jim is curled up in a dusty drop cloth like a baby.

"Will you look at them," Conn says. "Mouths like Drumnacraig cod waiting for the tide." He tugs on my cuffs 'til I move, drags the drop Jim's on across the floor. He didn't really care that we were asleep, though he wasn't too happy I drained his last bottle of Powers, an import. He loved the work, even made us breakfast in the bar's rickety kitchen. The old walls had more cracks than Humpty Dumpty but looked so good when we finished, I didn't know where I was when I woke up. I warned Conn about the way the cracks spread.

"You should have an engineer check the place out."

"Rasher?" He dropped a piece of Irish bacon on my plate.

"Could be something wrong with the building."

"Do you know what I'm going to tell you now? It never looked better. Worth every drop. Nearly." He tipped the bottle of Powers upside down.

When we decide to add a third painter, I call the local, and a rep reads off the list of men looking for work. I stop him at Patrick Gallagher. He's in the painters union ten years and an Eight-Thirty man, a finisher, before that. I'm trying to break out of the South Side—the real work's up north and downtown—and a guy who knows wood could pay the passage. I tell the rep to send him out to our job in Homewood in the morning.

Around noon the next day I get to the house, where Jim's showing the new guy the ropes. This shine comes out of the master bath folding a ruler, and I about fall over. While we figured things out, Jim should have had him taping or scraping, not papering, definitely not here. The wallpaper's custom, top-dollar, a garden design full of flowers, trees, vines—so cluttered it's hard to say what you're looking at. Ugly, you ask me, but what do I know? The powers that be buy it, we hang it. The rolls are numbered, and if something don't line up, it's all ruined. *This* is what Jim set some shine we don't even know at? If he's pissed that I hired the guy and making a point, could be a pricey one.

Gallagher grunts something, but I can't understand him. He's got his bottom lip pulled out and is stuffing tobacco in there. He's about sixty, with a gray-black beard and a fro high as a bishop's hat.

"You can't be chewing that stuff while you work," I say. God knows what brand he's got going, but it smells like a fruit-stand dumpster in July.

"Lunch." He taps his wrist. Great, a clock-watcher too. I'm afraid to go into the master bath, wondering why he was out of work in the first place. Maybe it's one of these affirmative action deals and the guy can't paint his nails. What happens then if I fire him? I can see him screaming it's cause he's Black and the shop sinking just when things were picking up.

He follows me into the master. It's half-finished, and I can't see any lines. Gallagher flicks on the overhead light. I check the seams up close, feel the overlap, look for glue. I'm good with paper—a lot of painters, Jim included, ain't—but I couldn't have done better. And the guy supposedly knows wood. That's what I need more than anything, what could get us out of South Side bungalows and into real coin.

"You did this on your own?"

Gallagher laughs. "All by my lonesome. Okay?"

"Aw-ight. Yeah, fine."

Jim is staring like he can't quite place me. Gallagher's sizing me up, too. Endless guys need work. I can cut this one loose and replace him tomorrow. I should—he wasn't part of the plan. I don't want to hire him, only I'm tempted. If he's as good with wood as he is with paper, dumping him is like throwing away money. I'm trying to see it from all angles, part of me wishing I still worked for the Polish Prince and didn't have to decide. I used to think being boss was like playing God—you were free to do what you wanted. Now, I know it just means you get to decide which way your hands are tied.

The longer Jim stares, the more it's like he's daring me to keep Gallagher. We're equals and all, fifty-fifty partners, but his look is pissing me off.

"Well, are we finishing this job or what?" I ask.

Jim shakes his head once, sharp, so pissed, he don't notice he's trying to hammer the wrong lid back onto a can of stain. His head swung back and forth, disgusted the rest of that week.

I say, if a guy knows what he's doing, who cares? It was simpler, sure, when they stayed the other side of Western Avenue, before they moved west and neighborhoods kept changing. When the Old Man had to get the hell out of Derry, South Shore was all White. That's where him and my mom bought their first house. Then the whole area changed on a dime. Realtors went door-to-door like the Black and Tans searching houses: *the neighborhood's turning, your block is next*. My folks' home lost its value overnight. The Old Man talks about South Shore like it was paradise: so clean, with the beach, parks, gardens, a fast train downtown. And then, in a flash, everything junked. They moved west to Roseland, and when that neighborhood changed, west again, to Marquette Park. Now they're in Chrysler Village, on the edge of the city. And how long 'til the same thing happens here? It's why they want to go South. They're afraid, but also tired of moving. They want to leave and they want to stay. I tell them stay—what the hell would they do in Florida?—but I understand, too. The older I get, the more I see where they're coming from.

I kept one eye on Patrick Gallagher at all times. His painting was fast and neat, but he drove me up the wall. Every two minutes he sent a jet of spit through a gap in his teeth into an old coffee cup. Tobacco stained them permanently brown. He chewed some off-brand apple shit. One whiff and you gagged. Jim never questioned me about jobs, but Patrick'd shoot me these looks like, don't you know nothing? Like, you ain't blind and you think *that* looks okay?

We had it out at a residential in Chicago Lawn, one of these Lugans so stingy you got to do the job in about an hour to see a profit. I didn't plan on this many South Side houses—the big money's up north—but Jim'd rather work close to home for Polacks counting out change to pay you than fight the current of rush hour traffic for real green. The ceilings in this place are a disaster. They piled on paint for years, endless coats and colors, never bothering to even things out. Pieces flaked off 'til every ceiling looked like an ocean of jagged islands. I set Jim and Patrick on window frames and start patching the kitchen ceiling myself. I'm stuck in a king-size bag of Durabond trying to see things even, layering on mud like a gardener, thinking I should've known upfront my costs would be higher, thinking every minute's costing me a buck, when I hear the spit.

Gallagher stands in the doorway, watching me, cup in hand.

"Finished?" I ask.

"No, but you could be, all the time you wasting up there." He spits again in that damn cup, and I almost feel it on my skin. The whole room stinks of his fruity tobacco. Jim slides in, quiet, pretending to look for something but smiling inside, I can tell.

"That ceiling ain't worth patching," Gallagher says.

"Tell that to Mr. Prunskis."

"What we'll do is put canvas on the worst ceilings," he says. "It costs, but you get a nice level surface. Whatever we lose on material, we'll save on time and aggravation."

Jim looks up, definitely grinning now but wincing too, like someone just got clocked.

I tell Gallagher, what *he'll* do is get the hell back to the windows, and what *I'll* do is finish the ceilings the right way. Ain't no *we*.

He looks surprised, almost hurt for a second, then it's back to raging smartass.

"Fine. My check the same no matter how much money you waste. Shit, I *like* this house," he says, walking off. "I'll stay here all year, you want."

"You are not keeping Melon John around after that?" Jim laughs but not like it's funny.

I go back to patching.

"You're as cracked as that ceiling. Look, I'll fire him, you don't want to," Jim says. "Right now. I'll enjoy it."

"Those frames ain't going to sand themselves," I say, finishing the last of our last bag of Durabond—another sawbuck sucked into the Prunskis ceiling.

"Fine. You're the one taking lip." Jim walks off, shaking his head slower than ever.

By the end of the day, I'm ready to flip. I'm bleeding money and would like to try the canvas, but I can't now, not if the job takes forever. I also want to tell Gallagher to get lost—I've seen enough of his smug black face—but can't give Jim the satisfaction. I don't know what to do. I skate early and stop at the Warsaw on my way home, in case Jim is at Chief O'Neill's.

The next morning Patrick Gallagher arrives early. He hustles around like we never argued and while he's getting ready, says the ceiling I worked on looks good.

"That one came out nice and even. Those bedrooms worse, though. Terrible." He waits a minute. "You want to try it, I can bring in some canvas I got sitting at home, for the back bedroom. Test it out on the small one, see how it goes. What you think?"

He sounds like the idea just came to him. I shrug, tell him to give the canvas a try. Jim watches him work, smirking, but slinks away once the surface comes even. It ain't as easy as Patrick made it sound, but the ceiling looks new when he's done. We save time and if you figure in labor, money. He never mentions it again, though, never rubs it in once.

"Maybe I won't get handed my ass here after all." I check Patrick's work while he's finishing the last room. "I'm pretty sure Mr. Prunskis just said he loves you in Lithuanian."

Patrick nods, hiding a smile.

I took his advice more than once after that, and he lost the preachy tone. He didn't complain about long hours, and when he needed time off to bail out his derelict nephew, I didn't blink. This kid, Dashante (where do they get the names?), stayed with Patrick until he prodded him about drugs and the punks he hung out with.

"I told him he was lying to himself, and he stormed out," Patrick says one day, staring at his hands. "He's basically on the streets, nowhere to go."

"Some kids don't learn 'til their faces get rubbed in it."

"I was too overbearing," he says, "a know-it-all, like my dad."

"Overbearing? You're a goddamned wallflower compared to my Old Man."

"Uh huh, and look how well that worked."

We laughed. That got me onto stories about the Old Man, and he told some about his, and then we really laughed. I don't know if I'd call it bonding exactly, but things add up on the job and if he ain't a complete prick, you get to know a guy, even one you couldn't see yourself hanging with off-site.

Tony Almos is leaving O'Neill's as I head in. I ain't seen him in forever—one kid, another on the way and on a dime, he's a whole new guy. I try but there's no way he'll stay. Inside, Conn's behind the bar and Maeve's holding court with a few boys near the jukebox. Jablonski's at the far end, casting his giant shadow in Siberia with Mark and Abel Grabowski.

Abel is married to Jabo's cousin. It pissed me off when the Polish Prince started meeting them at Chief's, but I felt sorry for him, too, in a way. He split with the wife, I heard, and the business tanked. She did the books, wrote the checks, kept his Polack customers calm. What did he know about how things ran? After a while, he half-waved. I sort of nodded, and it was like we agreed: space enough in the pub. Running my own shop, I could almost see Jabo's side of things. It is possible I wasn't the easiest employee.

"Tommy O'Sullivan, the prodigal son!" Conn says. "It must be a special holiday, St. Pat's, is it, or some pagan feast day?"

I explain how busy we been, tell him about adding a third guy.

"Why don't the lot of yous come in after work?" he says.

That's when I notice the cracks in the front wall, some thick as ropes and smaller ones branching off those like veins. It pisses me off that Conn never got the walls checked. I do good work, and this was like a sign saying I don't know my trade, hanging in my backyard.

I had Sean O'Donnell, a general who drinks at O'Neill's, check the foundation with me. We couldn't see a thing. A week later, I thought I'd have Patrick swing by for another look. I told Conn, the guy knows construction inside-out.

"Stop in before work tomorrow," he said. "I have inventory."

The door's open when we arrive. I give Patrick the quick tour while Conn is counting the last of something under the bar. When he's done, he shakes Patrick's hand.

"You oughta finish this bar top while you at it," Patrick tells him, feeling the rail. "Look good with a fresh coat of varnish."

"What sort of price would that be?" Conn asks.

"Free, you go with Sully here, but thirsty as he get, free turn expensive real quick." They laugh at Patrick's joke, the same one Conn made when he hired Jim and me. "As long as it comes out better than these walls." Patrick taps the plaster around cracks that snake toward the ceiling. He kneels, then stands slow, following a line to where it intersects another, whistling low.

"Not so bad, right?" Conn says, what he's been telling me, only less sure.

Patrick grunts.

"That masonry's a foot thick. The building has stood a hundred years."

"Might not make it to a hundred and one. Look." Patrick points at the front wall. "This whole wall is cockeyed."

When Conn doubts him, Patrick grabs a plumbline from his car. Once it's hanging, anyone can see the wall is bowed, so bad I can't believe it took a plumb bob to tell. (How did O'Donnell and me miss it? All those beers before the inspection probably didn't help.)

Short-term, Conn could anchor that wall to the floor joists and brace it with cross-rods, Patrick says. Long-term, he's got to open it up, probably rebuild.

He can't afford that, Conn says, squinting hard. He'd be out of business. Patrick tries again, but I know that look. He ain't converting anyone today.

While we're talking, bottles of cider appear. Even Conn has to admit it's a little early, but he won't let us go without tea and whatever he can scrounge—eggs and toast and black pudding, which is a kind of blood sausage. Most Americans can't stomach it. Patrick cleans his plate.

"Jeez, buoy, you're living up to the auld name today." I lay on a brogue.

Patrick laughs. "Sticks to the ribs."

"How'd you get a name like Patrick Gallagher anyway?"

"You don't know?" Patrick says, straight-faced. "Man, we from the same place. Top of the motherfucking morning."

"The Black Irish, is it?" Conn laughs, but I feel stupid. I can see what Patrick's thinking: my great-great-granddaddy probably owned his, that's how he got "Gallagher." But my great-great-grandfather didn't own a chicken. He died locked in an English workhouse. I want to say this, but it seems out of place, and I don't know enough of my own story to do it justice.

Six months later I'm bidding on a job that could open doors, the kind of work that might get me off the South Side for good—two full floors for The Altier Company, an accounting firm in the Loop. The offices are paintwork. I can do them eyes closed, but the common areas, I don't know—hidden costs could kill you. The hallways are lined with these rosewood panels: pristine, twelve feet tall, matched so well, it's like they were all cut from the same tree.

Jim's with me when I get my first look. I ask, "One week enough for the halls?"

He nods slow, doing the math, or pretending to. "A week should do it," he says, when I know a week ain't enough to strip, never mind finish, them. I've gotten better at estimating, but a job like this, you want a second opinion. Patrick comes with us for another look. Guy cracks me up, gawking at this wood like it's cut from the True Cross.

"Brazilian. You can't buy it anymore, or you ain't supposed to. Rosewood's what you call it—endangered." Patrick strokes a panel like it's the wood he woke up with.

He paces the halls, measuring and jotting notes, spitting tobacco juice like a sprinkler, then hides in a corner with loose-leaf to add it up. Same as me, or close enough, he figures the common space at 480 man-hours.

"Twelve weeks? I could paint the goddamned building," Jim says.

Patrick smiles and shrugs, not quite laughing. *Sure*, his look says, *try that.*

I can't help wondering then if I'd make more money with Patrick as a partner. Actually, it ain't a question so much as something I know. Once you know something like that, you can't go back and pretend you don't, but Jim's been a bud since grade school and I feel bad just for thinking it. He turns to me like he sees what I'm chewing over, and I look away, wishing I could hide under the nearest rug.

The company likes Patrick's sample panel and my estimate—a decent price for three guys working six weeks. We get the job, my first downtown. Jim and me start with the painting and set Patrick on the panels. The way he goes at it, I'm worried he'll push me over budget. Each panel he strips, washes, and sands twice—first with 80-grit, then 120. Down to bare wood, he uses water and hot knives to pull out dents. After that prep, it's sealer, another light sand, and two coats of varnish. Some ordeal, but you can see yourself in these things when he's done.

We work twelve-hour days our last week to make deadline. Everyone's at the end of his rope when we finish the last office Thursday night. Friday is what the Old Man calls Reflection Day, when the only thing left to do is walk around, reflecting on how good it looks before you go. The panels are shining, painting perfect, everything clean and neat. No walls have moved, no new furniture, but hard to believe it's the same place. One last time, we scan for stuff we might have missed, clean up, and pack the tools.

Patrick doesn't want to come out, but I insist. The last day of any job's a holiday. This one's a holy day of obligation.

Jim and me arrive at O'Neill's first and save Patrick a stool. It's crowded, even for a Friday. Maeve's off the clock but jumps behind the bar to help out. Jablonski's in back with Abel and Mark Grabowski, practically a regular these days. I smile and wave. What the hell. All my hard feelings disappeared when I figured my final bill for The Altier Company.

Maeve brings Jim and me our second beers, and I'm getting pissed, thinking Patrick bowed out, when he appears.

"We were starting to think you led us down the garden path," I say. "Miss the exit?"

"I got your exit, hanging." He grabs his crotch, laughs. "Had to take care of business first." He waves a pouch labeled *Blended Smokeless Tobacco: Apple.*

I groan. Jim gets up slow, tired after all those hours, and goes to bail the ship, stopping halfway to play the jukebox.

"Glad you made it," I say. "You stay pretty far east, huh?"

"Seventy-Third and Exchange."

"No shit? My parents lived on Kingston 'til—until…I don't know, like thirty years ago."

"It's okay. Good blocks and bad. About as far from down-town as this."

The rush has eased up. Maeve is back to tying one on, and Conn's talking to Sean O'Donnell at the end of the bar. I wave until he sees me.

He starts a Guinness, leaves it to settle, walks over. "Sully," he says and nods once at Patrick. He rags a mark on the bar, gives up, folds the towel in perfect thirds.

"Special occasion today, Conn. We finished that big job. Everything's on me."

Jim is back at the jukebox after the jacks.

"What'll it be?"

I order a High Life for Patrick and tap the twenty on the bar. Eyes on the bill, Conn scoops it up and disappears. Jim sits down, takes a long slug of beer. There's no music playing.

Mostly, I'm embarrassed, like when you bring a girl home for dinner and your old man makes fun of your clothes. I should've known, but I thought today would be different. Conn liked Patrick last time I brought him here. That was business, though, and this is something else. Or maybe it's the reverse.

"So, did the higher-ups see those panels?" Patrick asks.

"Yeah, said they weren't completely ruined, *salvageable* was the word."

"Salvage my ass." Patrick laughs. "The thanks I get for making you look good."

"Oughta look good," Jim says. "Three a day? Guy died on those panels."

I'm waving for Conn again, at the far end of the bar. Jim and me are ready for more beers, and Patrick hasn't gotten his first. I catch his eye, gesture to make it a full round. A few minutes later, Conn drops off Jim's Old Style, my Guinness, and the change.

"High Life?"

"Coming," he says, and wanders off.

Jim catches my eye in the mirror behind the bar, where I look like I aged ten years in the last six months, and it hits me. I count my change. Sure enough, Conn charged me double for Patrick's beer. I can't decide if I'm more pissed or shocked. In ten years, I never seen Conn make a mistake, but I want to believe it so bad I can't rule it out. I could overlook the whole thing, forget my change, and sit there drinking like a dummy. I think about that for a minute that lasts an hour, but much as I want to, I can't pretend.

Conn's talking to O'Donnell again when I walk to the far end.

"Your Miller," he says, and sets it on the bar, wearing a face looks like it came in a box. I almost laugh. I feel like I'm in some bad Western, the showdown at the old saloon. How'd everything get so turned around? This is me, that's Conn, but it's like when I wasn't looking, he turned into someone I don't know.

"You made a mistake on my change." I say it friendly enough, giving him a chance to claim he messed up at the register, but letting him know, too, I see what's going on. There's an awful pause. Jablonski and the guys nearby are watching me.

Finally, Conn makes a face like someone stepped on his toe, and I get it. It's him they're watching, not me.

"No. I counted your change," he says in a clear voice and then in a whisper, "Jesus, Sully, are you blind? You can't bring him here."

"I already did. He was here before, remember?"

"As a worker. The bar was empty."

"Look, this is different. He's like a friend. I owe half my business to this guy."

"So I should let him ruin mine? Do the math for Christ's sake. You're out of line. It's not personal, but friend or not, he can't drink here." Conn lifts his hands together, palms up, like *what can I do?*

As I turn to go, he says, "Your next drink is free—when you're alone."

I want to tell him go to hell, like I told Jablonski the day I quit. I want to tell him what he can do with his free drink, drag him across the bar and drop him on this side. Instead, I reach for the High Life and head back to my stool. I can't leave yet—that would look like running. I don't want to drink Conn's overpriced beer, but we're stuck here for one more.

Patrick asks about the job we're starting Monday, a duplex in Kane County, middle of nowhere. He doesn't like the rickety scaffold I borrowed, wants me to invest in something new. Sure, princess, I say. He laughs and then we're quiet. In the mirror, I watch Maeve play with a silver bracelet at the table behind me. As it spins on her wrist, a greenish-black ring peeks out like a tattoo. It reminds me of the necklace I gave Tracy Lynch the night we went to Wally C.'s Halloween party, before she decided on college. We left early and did it in my car, drunk and half in our costumes, parked behind the Independent Trading Company warehouse on 65th. She gave the necklace back a week later cause it left a green-black line on her neck. She needed the pricey kind, she said, the cheap stuff made her break out. I did okay with the ladies later, but that was my first time. I thought I was in love. We went through the motions for weeks, but I should've known it was over when she returned the necklace. She moved back to Clearing after school but only for a few months. People gave her the business—said she thought she was too good for them. I guess the neighborhood suited her about as well as cheap jewelry.

When we finish, I suggest one at the Warsaw Inn, where I'll be drinking from now on. Jim says he's staying put and looks at me like so should I. Patrick says he's got to head home, and I say, I will, too. I anchor my change, all of it, with an empty glass, cause it ain't about that. Everyone, from the clump of tradesmen upfront to the oddballs in back, stares at Patrick and me as we go, laughs trailing us like wake.

I stop a second to hold the door open for Patrick. The last I'll see of this place, I think, more sapped than pissed now, like all the blood drained out of me. I figured this would be what the Old Man calls a red-letter day, but cause it was the start of something, not the end.

It's dark outside and cold. I walk Patrick to his car, parked on Lockwood, squeezed between rowhouses on an empty block. I try but can't say a word, as awkward as if I left the bar naked.

"Don't come in all bleary-eyed and hung in a couple days," Patrick says at the car. "I ain't covering your ass in Kane County."

"Yeah, yeah. Cover this."

The usual jokes feel forced. Is this how it'll be from now on? He's bound to see things different after what happened.

"Don't forget that scaffold neither. I ain't taking a fall cause your cheap ass won't buy something solid."

"Yeah, I'm on it."

We shake, and I realize I'm the one acting different. Nothing about tonight surprised him.

Around the corner, my beater's the only one on 65th. I stomp through weeds growing in the line of dirt and broken glass between the sidewalk and street, not worried about bothering monarchs anymore. Most headed south by now. Swarms of the butterflies invade the neighborhood every year to lay eggs on the milkweed that grows wild around the factories, in empty lots, and cracked sidewalks, slips of dirt you don't notice 'til the plants sprout.

Your next drink is free, Conn said, a gesture, even though he was pissed. I'm glad now I didn't make a scene. We both got out of order, but no one crossed a line, nothing broken so bad it can't be fixed.

I slam the door to my rusted boat. There's too much history to finish like this, I think. Walking out the door, it was easy to say I ain't coming back, but already, the thought of passing O'Neill's to drink at the Warsaw hurts my gut. It's too high a price to pay, too big a trade. I'll go back next week or the one after at the latest, once we finish in Kane County. It might feel awkward at first—half the pub wanted to string us up—but what all's changed? Conn and me will have some beers and laugh and talk like always. Not about this, of course. This, we'll pretend never happened, I think, checking for cops before I swing out to make a U-turn and take the hard right at the intersection.

Swing Night

The girl paused at the stairs leading down to the dance floor at Green Dolphin Street, posed above the old dancers below like a shiny new doll set over shabby ones by some child playing a cruel game. At least this was how it seemed to Cynthia, sitting on the periphery of that dance floor in the ridiculously named Boom Boom Room. The girl looked out of place but familiar—mid-twenties, skin like fresh snow, honey-blonde hair up in a forties-style do. She wore a dress of white satin crepe, crossover V-neckline with gathers at an impressive chest. It was new but modeled on a past fashion, a touch of wedding gown, yet more revealing somehow than the skimpy outfits that would appear late that night when a DJ replaced the big band.

The girl scanned the crowd indifferently as she descended the steps, not looking for a friend so much as allowing one to see her.

"John, it's that girl," Cynthia said to her boyfriend.

"What girl?"

"What's-her-name. Bell, Bella, Diane…"

"Don't stare," he said—Cynthia's line, but tonight she was the one finding it hard not to look for a change. Secret lover of old movies, Cynthia recognized both the girl and her implausible likeness in the same instant: the moony face and girlish features, lethal cheekbones, eyes a man could vanish in. Cynthia hadn't seen it when they'd met her at the strip club months ago, but tonight, wearing a dress Donna Reed might have worn, dancing in a club that mimicked that era, the girl could have been her long-lost twin.

"I don't see anyone." John was horribly nearsighted and not wearing his glasses. "Who are you—"

"Facing the stage, end of the bar."

How had he not noticed her entrance? Everyone else seemed to, men and women alike turning to watch her cross the dance floor. Cynthia remembered that sort of adoration, similar rooms lit just for her, though never with an audience half that girl's. At thirty-nine, Cynthia was still pretty. Lately, though, admirers seemed to look not at but around her, perusing her fishnets or tattoos, a sexy starburst halter but never really *her*, and the rest only until something brighter caught their eye. Fortunately for Cynthia, once so easily riled, age also brought forbearance. She did her best to smile at the transformation, watching beauty fade the way she'd learned to endure life's other unpleasant developments.

Not that she and John led unpleasant lives—just the opposite. They had avoided the fantasyland of marriage for something more authentic and original. He worked from home, doing PR for The Allegro, Hebe's Cheek Spa, and The Friar's Lantern Restaurant—a schedule that gave him time to direct non-equity theater and write plays. She had moved on from painting to run a small gallery that also did framing or a frame shop that sold modern art, depending on your perspective. They lived behind Gallery Cynthia in one of those palatial Bucktown lofts with hardwood floors, dramatic ceilings, and a spaciousness (no interior walls, just a moveable screen concealing the bed) that reflected the relationship—still open and playful after a decade when so many friends' marriages died overnight. They went to openings and movies. They saw live theater every week, and on weekends, scoured the urban landscape for new restaurants, bars, and bands.

"What is she doing here?" Cynthia asked.

John squinted. "Drinking an old-fashioned?"

"Now you're staring."

It was a stupid question—the club was big and open to all, exotic dancers included—but Thursdays drew an older crowd, and the place was hard to find. It stood on the river in a neighborhood whose name no one seemed to agree on, between Bucktown and the Triangle. Over railroad tracks and abandoned factories, its romantic sign winked in lurid red and green neon, the sole constellation in a black city sky. The club's newest section, which contained the stage and dance floor, was made of cheap cinderblock. An older brick portion housed a somber Italian restaurant, which John obscurely mocked as *Il Penseroso,* so often Cynthia forgot its real name. They'd never eaten in the pretentious place, where even people with reservations seemed to wait a lifetime. Instead, for ten years now, they had turned left every Thursday in the lobby bar and taken ten shallow steps down to the Boom Boom Room.

"I have an eye for skin art," the girl said.

She had wandered toward John and Cynthia's table aimlessly, skirting the old-fashioned music stands that lined stage and the red velvet curtains that covered an entire wall, lingering at "Legends of the Swing Era," a series of black-and-white photos hanging in back. John thought the décor pure kitsch. Cynthia laughed when he made fun but genuinely loved it.

"I thought I recognized you," the girl said, "then I saw that tattoo, and I knew. What's it called again?"

"*Eye*," Cynthia said, pointing to her eye. "Or *I*." She pointed to herself. "That's how they pronounce it in China. I guess there's no right way to spell it here."

"Neat," the girl said, as if the retro dress came with matching vocabulary. She wore it without irony, that dress, strange given her age and situation, what she had on, or didn't, the last time Cynthia saw her.

With a fingertip she traced the red ink that formed the Chinese character for "love" on Cynthia's left arm. Cynthia's body tensed under her touch. She smiled, trying not to feel awkward, telling herself there was no reason she should. She liked the girl but hoped John wouldn't ask her to sit down, not here.

"Join us?" he said, with the timing of a bad Robbie O'Ryan joke, polite but less friendly than she might have expected. Captain Robbie O'Ryan led The Swing Shift Players on Thursday nights. The big band had some young fans—usually there to try out moves learned in a class—but most were in their seventies or eighties. The eight o'clock showtime reflected their sleeping habits. O'Ryan had been a star in his day, touring with Count Basie and Duke Ellington as a kid, but faded into obscurity in middle age. Now he charmed the oldsters at Green Dolphin Street with awful one-liners, arranged new versions of the old songs they loved, and as his powers waned, overplayed his trombone with a bluster born of panic.

The girl sat and smoothed her dress in one move, a dramatic gesture that again reminded Cynthia of Donna Reed, pushing resemblance into a caricature that seemed practiced, though the girl probably didn't know who the actress was. Cynthia hadn't at her age, or for years after. Everyone focused on Reed's mythic domesticity, but she had a seamy side, too, in certain roles.

"That was 'Stella by Starlight,' a new twist on an old Nelson Riddle arrangement," announced Robbie O'Ryan, blinder at eighty, groping for elusive notes on his trombone, but in appearance, oddly unchanged from the first time they saw him. Cynthia fell for him instantly, a giant of a man, half blind, with thick waves of white hair, making quaintly bawdy quips before launching tunes she recalled from her grandparents' LPs: "I Only Have Eyes for You," "Body and Soul," "We're the Couple in the Castle." The first time she heard him in that dim room—red velvet curtains, highball glasses, ancient couples cutting a rug—Cynthia imagined she'd stepped into one of the old movies she loved.

"Here's another number we didn't get a request for: some Pole Courter. "Where Is the Life that Late I Led?" by Mr. Pole Courter," Robbie announced. The piano player made a show of whispering in his ear. "Sorry, Cole Porter," Robbie deadpanned. Oldsters who had suffered the joke for years smiled yet again.

"It was a good time, hanging with you that night," the girl said.

"Thanks," Cynthia said doubtfully.

"Really. It's tough seeing people there if you're pretending to have fun. Gets old real quick. You look beautiful, by the way."

"That's some dress."

"This old thing?"The girl laughed. "Isn't it amazing? Cost everything but my firstborn. I shouldn't have, but you only live once, eh?

John and Cynthia had decided not to have kids. Who needed the heartache and hassle? She couldn't picture herself changing and nursing an infant—only sometimes, as forty approached, she did, the malaise she'd suffered since childhood making a whim feel like more. The urge was pure biology, she knew, an embarrassing cliché for someone who'd worked hard to avoid becoming one. She had dropped out of

The Art Institute because of the conventional crap everyone turned out, quit the punk band she sang with when they wanted to do covers, consumed enough psychedelics while her peers focused on jobs that entire years disappeared. Now she had a business she liked running, and she had fun. John was right about the regrets that could appear with a kid, she knew, the various ways one might come between them.

"Mine is off the rack," the girl was saying. "That looks like it was made for you. Awesome." She felt a piece of the shredded peasant skirt that hung over Cynthia's leggings, brushed the black camisole John had bought her as a top. Having a partner in theater gave her that edge: he had much better fashion suggestions than the average straight male.

"It's Diane," she said, taking Cynthia's hand. "Thea, right? I remember that, and…oh, shoot."

"John," John said. "And you're missing the sin."

"Huh?"

"CYN-thia," he said. "Important, because she really puts the sin in—"

"John, shut up, please." Cynthia laughed in spite of herself—he could always make her, whether she wanted to or not. "Nice to meet you, again," she said, her hand still in the girl's. "Bella" she'd said that night, revealing her real name only at the end of the evening.

"Sorry. I'm so bad, but what's in a name and all that, eh? You guys definitely stood out, though. Later, I said to my friend Crystal, what a fun couple."

At the next table, the old man John called Mr. Bickerson argued so steadily with his wife, the fight seemed a part of the music. *Zip it,* he said every few minutes, *Give it a rest,* keeping the beat while she grumbled a solo. From afar, the pear-shaped husband looked younger. Up close, brown spots on the crown of his head and a cardigan draped over a slumped back put him in his eighties. Mrs. Bickerson was wiry, with an ornate cane and metal-framed glasses that matched the metallic glint of her perm.

"Waiter disappeared again," John said, standing. "What will you have, Diane?"

She laughed. "You can call me Di. A cosmo, please." It was the first time she had looked directly at him. "Everyone does," she said, turning back to Cynthia.

"Just a beer for me this time," Cynthia called as he walked to the bar.

Diane-call-me-Di leaned in as if relieved and perhaps slightly nervous now that John was gone. Cynthia sensed the same air of collusion—*Us sisters look out for each other!*—as when they'd met her at Grin 'n Bare It a few months ago, on John's forty-fifth birthday. Probably she was uneasy, forced to face in the real world people who had seen her naked in the fantasy one she inhabited each week.

"Don't you just love this place?" Di said. "I'm here all the time."

"I'm surprised we haven't seen you. We've been coming for years."

In a way, their outings to Green Dolphin Street were the fixed points by which John and Cynthia mapped their lives, replaying each Thursday what had happened since the last, making plans for the week ahead and reliving swing nights from years past. There was only one that they never mentioned, that Thursday ten years ago when Cynthia proposed. A stupid move after barely six months together, but she was drunk and in love, and something about the club (and a third martini) had altered her perception in weird ways that night: colors seemed sharper, lights brighter. Surfaces glowed with possibility. John laughed about it afterward—once. She cut him off with uncharacteristic sternness, mortified to think of her drunken proposal and sharp mood swing, the ugly scene she made that night when he thought she was joking.

"I usually never make it on Thursday. If that's when you're here," Di said. "Work. I'm watching the clock while you're having fun. Someone wanted to swap tonight, so I was like, I am going *out*. I was supposed to meet a friend, but it's getting late…I hope she shows."

Something about the way Di lowered her eyes on the word "shows" made Cynthia think the friend was fabricated. Hard to believe this girl could be here alone, but she must have trouble finding a man who saw the person behind the persona (that dress meant to create a new one, ridiculously traditional but equally false, a cliché so pretty it was ugly). Most women would regard her with suspicion. Cynthia was sympathetic because, wild as she'd been at that age, she could see herself in Di's shoes, led into a precarious lifestyle that eventually would be no life at all. She'd had unprotected sex with boyfriends who turned out to be strangers, banged guys drunk in dive-bar bathrooms and tripping balls in concert parking lots. During one coke- and vodka-infused month, she had stepped out of the shower to notice a mark beneath the blue rose on her ass: someone had Sharpied *Stan was here* onto her left cheek, the type cleverly reversed to look normal in a mirror. She didn't recall meeting much less fucking a Stan, but someone took the time to tattoo her in this weird backwards script, and she'd been too out of it to notice.

She met John while waiting tables, and the wildness faded soon after. Corny as it sounded—not that she'd ever say it aloud—he became the anchor she didn't know she needed. If not for him, she might still be waiting and modeling for artists. He had practically forced her to open Gallery Cynthia, fighting her moodiness and a tendency to settle. After noting at an early exhibition that some creative frames sold better than the hackneyed art they enclosed, he also nudged her into framing, now a mainstay, though not, she insisted, the gallery's real focus.

Older and calmer, Cynthia still didn't mind a little vice—occasional visits to strip clubs, for instance. She had decided on the creative present years ago, when with his birthday approaching, John made a joke of what he wanted. She went along, kidding right back, but when he squinted at her, lips pursed, implying she wouldn't follow through, she had to. Like Grin 'n Bare It, that first place was comfortable: cool and sophisticated and safe, some women in the audience, a burly man in the shadows watching over dancers, who appeared in total control. It was only here in the real world, where Bella became Di, that the girl looked like a gorgeous tragedy. Stories of women fed intoxicants—and not just booze—manhandled and manipulated, swirled in Cynthia's head. Who knew what happened behind the scenes? Di said stripping was temporary, something about tuition, but wasn't it always? Until, years later, too old or worn-out to make what she needed, she accepted offers that would have disgusted her once upon a time, blind to better options because she'd worked at Grin 'n Bare It so long. *From Here to Eternity*, Cynthia thought. In that film, Donna Reed played an escort biding her time in Hawaii, trying to earn enough to return to mainland suburbia, marry Mr. Right, and lead a "proper life." Only shipping back to the mainland proved tougher than she thought. John wouldn't get the reference. He made fun of "Alternative Girl"—one of many pet names—for liking films he found sentimental, disdainfully watching her watching them, as if this interest just didn't fit her character.

The Bickersons continued to fight. An old couple John called the Chaplins—Charlie and Mrs. Charlie—sat at right angles nearby, comically looking past each other, completely silent as usual. Robbie O'Ryan descended the stage and danced to "I'll Buy that Dream" with a young woman Cynthia half-recognized. It was after ten. The club would be packed in a couple hours, when the big band stopped and a DJ turned up the volume.

"Here we go." John set a cosmo and two dirty martinis on the table.

"Where's my beer?" Cynthia asked.

Gingerly, the woman dancing with Robbie O'Ryan removed his hand from her rear. You had to laugh with an old man so blind, never quite sure what was meant.

"Sorry," John said. "Three-for-one special on martinis."

"Really?" Di asked.

"No. That's his idea of a joke," Cynthia said. "You'll get used to it." She felt protective, almost maternal toward Di, awash in white satin and blonde hair, glowing with gullibility. So young. At Grin 'n Bare It, her eyes got enormous when John said, "PR is how I pay the bills, but playwriting's my real work." Cynthia didn't let it show, but that line always grated. He'd had exactly one original play produced and some months, barely earned enough planning press events to pay the electric. She didn't mind supporting him—she believed in John, was dying to see his name in lights—but parts of the picture he painted made her uneasy, the way she'd felt recently discovering hair dye hidden in the back of the vanity. His not telling her didn't make it a lie, but she wished he'd talked about the onset of gray instead of treating it secretly behind a shower curtain. His aging didn't bother her—she looked forward to growing old with him.

"Mmm, delicious," Di said. She took a sip and ran the tip of her tongue across her upper lip, sexy and ridiculous, a gesture a high school girl learns from bad TV. She clinked Cynthia's glass with her own. "To new friends."

She had been sexy, genuinely so, writhing around that pole, twisted into impossible positions, her seductive smile waning only at the most extreme contortions. As always in those clubs, John engaged in what Cynthia called SMF (standard male fantasy), suggesting various ways she wanted a girl. She played along with the illusion, harmless within limits, though they never saw it quite the same way. He didn't understand that while she appreciated the girls' undeniable beauty, Cynthia mostly admired their ability to move, a sensuality so confident it bordered on indifference. Men shook, powerless with desire, and the girls didn't seem to care. Di had an amazing body. Cynthia couldn't have competed at eighteen, she certainly couldn't compete now. At least she had remained thin—she still fit into clothes bought in her twenties. The curves that had half the room salivating would transform into chunky, even matronly, in ten years, Cynthia thought without malice. That was simply how nature had made her.

Two of the younger dancers spun nearby, the woman pivoting before her partner launched her in the air. She hung suspended for a second that lasted forever.

"Know any of those fancy moves?" Di asked, touching Cynthia's knee.

"No," Cynthia said. She tired of the kids' flashy choreography. The old-timers weren't pretty, but even the ones at death's door had some beautiful, quirky routines. Di let her hand linger before withdrawing it. So odd seeing her now, *here*, Cynthia thought, feeling the effects of the drink she didn't want.

"Wow, look!" Di squealed, watching two dancers do an over-the-back flip.

Cynthia didn't respond. She didn't mean to be rude, but she felt a funk coming on. They swallowed her like deep space, these moods, always had (as early as third grade, a teacher told her she "projected a tragic air"). People hadn't minded Miss Melancholia (another of John's many names for her) when she was an artist because depression was part of a romantic package. Now, she was supposed to hide it.

"Should we trip the light fantastic?" John asked as the band started Glenn Miller's "Moonlight Serenade." He'd heard the question asked seriously here years ago and jokingly posed it to Cynthia every week since. Of course, he'd noticed her drifting into space and pursued, knowing a dance might rescue her mood. He was scary good at reading her, the only man ever who could pull her out of a funk.

They headed to the dance floor. John took his dancing as seriously as the invitation implied, performing the usual dips and twirls with such irony, from a distance he seemed to invent exotic new moves. It was fun until he spun off in his own orbit, leaving Cynthia hanging awkwardly in some corner of the dance floor.

"That number featured a solo by our very talented saxophone player, Jack Milton," Robbie O'Ryan announced. "It's been a tough time for Jack. He moved to California hoping to act in the adult film industry, but he only had small parts." The drummer played a rim-shot on cue. The most obscene jokes came late in the evening, when the easily upset were too drunk or tired to react. The oldsters were trickling out anyway, as John and Cynthia would before long. Di danced to "Wanderlust" with Robbie O'Ryan.

"That guy is a perv!" she said back at the table, exasperated.

"The jokes are painful," Cynthia said, "but he's harmless."

"He totally tried to make me on the dance floor. Kept boxing me in corners to say I was pretty. He'd admire my dress, pretend to rearrange a part, then grope me."

"He's half blind. It was probably an accident."

Di squeezed Cynthia's left breast. "Does this seem like an accident?"

"Hmm, my eyesight isn't so good either," John said. "Show me that again."

Di kissed Cynthia on the cheek. "Sorry," she said, and they laughed.

Cynthia finished her third martini feeling as if she'd crossed a border. The blues subsided a little, but she was drunk and mildly dizzy. *In*-toxicated.

"Apparently, old Bob's a perv from way back," Di said. "The bartender told me that when he was younger, he actually had to flee the country. The girl he'd mauled, I guess her father was attached to the Outfit, one of those old Grand Avenue gangsters."

Cynthia knew that for years Robbie had got stuck leading a house band at the only four-star hotel in Port-au-Prince, Haiti of all places, but she'd imagined a romantic scenario: a mysterious woman, frustrated desires, tragic scenes of love suspended.

"Robbie," Cynthia said.

"Huh?"

"His name's Robbie, not Bob."

"He's a perv, whatever it is."

Funny, Cynthia thought, that the stripper should act so proper while she gave Robbie O'Ryan latitude. Surely, Di encountered real pervs at Grin 'n Bare It.

"A guy would get his ass kicked if he tried that in the club," Di said matter-of-factly, as if she saw what Cynthia was thinking.

"Do a lot of guys push the limits?"

"Most of the ones over thirty know where to draw the line. Someone always goes overboard, but I won't have to deal with that much longer. I gave notice on Monday."

"What will you do?"

"The usual. Get a real job, get married, make babies—one boy and one girl, if I'm lucky. I'm moving back to Broadview, where I grew up. Dancing got me through school, so no regrets, but it was always temporary." Di fixed Cynthia's eyes in her own as she drained the remains of a cosmo. "It was an adventure. Isn't that what your twenties are for?"

Cynthia hadn't really wanted to get married at Di's age, certainly not after dating John for just six months. The proposal of ten years ago had more to do with vodka than vows, but she discovered, she actually did want the glimmer of that possibility in her life. Likewise, she couldn't imagine how she would play a mother's role, but sometimes a little girl in a frilly dress invaded her dreams, small hands holding hers and John's, swinging between them over curbs as they walked past the shops and cafes along Damen. John had apologized after mocking Cynthia's proposal but admitted that he thought of marriage as a joke, an anachronism that would deny its own decline until the lies supporting it wore so thin, the idea disappeared. He wanted beauty in his life and for most couples, marriage meant the death of beauty.

"Want your life to stay fun? Live with me," he said. "Let's untie the knot."

He wanted them to connect the dots in their own way, find a more natural arrangement that avoided all the traditional role-playing and clichés. Cynthia hesitated, but over the course of months, the "arrangement" that John outlined started to sound perfect—long-term, committed, honest. So what if they didn't name it marriage? She adored him, was intoxicated just by the way he looked at her. They moved in together temporarily, a tryout, but as one year faded into another and they watched so many friends divorce—lying, posturing, using children as pawns—Cynthia had few regrets.

Some club kids arrived early for the evening's next act: boys in colored tee shirts or untucked button-downs circling girls who posed in tiny skirts and skintight stirrups. Cynthia's ensemble blended in fine. She wondered if Di felt funny in her vintage getup.

The band played "Let's Face the Music and Dance," Robbie O'Ryan waving his trombone like a conductor to avoid a difficult passage. The DJ who would start spinning soon, a Brit with a goatee and sideburns so angular they looked drawn on, killed time in the wings, waiting to set up.

"That was a tough chart for so late in the evening." Robbie O'Ryan laughed at the tune's conclusion. "We'll have to play that one earlier in the future."

"Isn't it great here?" Di slurred. She claimed to be a regular but beamed as if new to the club, maybe because she never went on Thursdays. The Boom Boom Room became a different place on swing night.

"Look at those guys." Di pointed to the Bickersons, dancing with a flair that belied their endless fighting. "Old people have such, like, synchronism on the dance floor. Watching them makes me nostalgic."

"*Synchronism*? Great album. But I'm not sure you can be nostalgic for a past that didn't happen to you. Maybe not to anybody."

"Whatever, John." Di smacked his shoulder. "You know what I mean." His teasing and her response felt oddly familiar, Cynthia thought, perhaps because everyone was drunk, perhaps because exposing yourself to someone—even once, some time ago—breeds a lasting illusion of intimacy. She suggested they make a move—it was almost midnight.

"Oh, you guys have to dance to this," John said as the band started "Twin Sisters." Cynthia said she was too tired. "Come on, make a scene. It'll be hilarious. Scandalous."

All eyes seemed directed at Cynthia and Di as they took to the dance floor. Cynthia didn't mind the staring, so common here years ago, before her place in the club—tattoos, edgy outfits and all—became fixed. Di played to the crowd, or at least to John, nuzzling Cynthia's neck, holding her close, resting a dreamy head on her shoulder. They joked about who should lead while Di subtly guided them across the floor. As they turned near the stage, a window on the back wall lit up. He wasn't visible in that bright square, but Cynthia felt him watching them, the man who ran sound for the evening's second act.

"I really like you," Di said.

"We like you, too."

Di kissed her gently, tentatively, like a sensitive older lover pursuing a virgin. Time stopped, or rather, Cynthia became aware of herself as existing outside of it, immediately embarrassed to have framed the sensation as a cliché. She felt like a ridiculous old woman clutching that youthful beauty and, simultaneously, like a little girl flustered by her first kiss.

"He can't see us over here," Cynthia said, affecting a light tone.

"Who?"

"John."

"Who cares?" Di kissed her again, holding her closer this time, swaying unsteadily, her hand traveling across the small of Cynthia's back. Di's skin was soft as an infant's, so white it seemed lit from within. She had been flirting for hours, but Cynthia had believed it was all for show, a continuation of her performance at Grin 'n Bare It.

"We're friends, right?" Di said. She was openly intoxicated, a thought that sobered Cynthia. The dance floor was half empty—many of the old-timers gone—and the club was filling up with kids. She and John hadn't stayed this late since that night ten years ago when she'd made her drunken proposal. As the average age in the club plunged, Cynthia imagined time accelerating, weeks and months speeding past, one generation dying off, another replacing it while she watched, aging years without leaving the dance floor.

"Of course we're friends," Cynthia said, squeezing Di's hand. "Listen, Diane, you're gorgeous and a good kisser, and I would pay a fortune to have that body—"

"It's yours, for nothing."

Cynthia laughed. "I mean, instead of mine. The thing is, I've kissed girls drunk a few times, but it never crossed the line. It was never serious. The strip club is only a laugh for us. I'm just not made that way. I don't want to lead you on."

"It's okay. He knew you'd be shy." Di rested her head on Cynthia's shoulder. It seemed for a second as if she might fall asleep. "That's why we did it this way, to make it natural. We'll go slow. I can show you."

"What do you mean?"

"Don't worry, I'm not a lesbian or anything. I'm totally serious about getting married and having kids and all, but I'm really drawn to you. It's just a fun thing before I settle down. We had to wait until I knew I was moving on. I couldn't see someone from Grin 'n Bare It while I was stuck there, not even a regular like John."

Cynthia tried to step away and then, dazed, swung back into her embrace.

"Hey, you alright?" Di asked. The music stopped but they remained swaying on the empty floor as if dancing. Robbie O'Ryan said goodnight. The DJ began to set up. Looking down, Cynthia noticed a tear where her leggings had worn at the knee, not that it should have mattered under her scarified skirt.

"Oh shoot. Don't tell John I told, okay?" Di said. "He wanted the fantasy perfect for you. That's why I confused your name. He thought that would make it seem natural. Silly, right? You knew the second you saw me. I could tell you were playing along."

The house lights came on while the man in the booth made adjustments for the DJ. John looked small across the room but was plainly visible now that the dance floor had cleared. Cynthia's eyes followed Di's, and she wondered just how this girl saw him. Did she have some sort of daddy complex? He was still handsome, but his hair, unnaturally light and free of gray, was beginning to thin on top. He wore it longer to hide this development, just as his blousy shirt was calculated to cover a growing paunch. His gaze seemed to return theirs, but Cynthia knew he wasn't looking at them. He refused to wear glasses in public and at that distance, could formulate only vague figures in a landscape. She imagined him twenty years from now, touting a play in some small, anonymous house, as fatuous as the old men he mocked on swing night. Each year he would work harder to hide the signs of aging, just as Robbie O'Ryan did, waving his trombone. Would John's jokes take the same dark turn? Would he resort to copping feels on the dance floor? That would be less troubling than the charade he'd planned for tonight. A *regular*, Di said. How often had he returned to the strip club alone to arrange it? Had he slept with her already? Cynthia didn't think so. Di seemed to set her own strict limits there, and given everything she had so artlessly revealed, probably didn't have much to hide. She had come here to meet a friend alright: Cynthia. John must have told the girl that Cynthia would be a shy but willing participant in his tableau, that secretly she'd always wanted a ménage a trois and he was simply surprising her with one tonight, as another man might with flowers or jewelry.

On the empty dance floor, Cynthia felt awkward and exposed. She turned, and Di held her hand as they waded through a sea of dirty glasses and wadded napkins, edging around stray chairs floating between tables like abandoned dance partners. They passed the DJ, absorbed in his elaborate rig—turntables, two laptops, tangled wires. He had snagged a curtain searching for receptacles, and behind him, a swath of cinderblock showed though red velvet like clenched teeth through curving lips.

"Where did you kids get to?" John said suggestively. In the stark light, his face had a lifeless pallor.

The anger that had been rising in Cynthia shot to the surface, flushing her face. It floated there a moment, straining to break free, then swung back along the arc it had ascended. Once, she might have thrown a tantrum, lashed out or run off, as she had from this room ten years ago when her drunken proposal was mocked, but she had learned to control her passions. Oddly, her anger had as much to do with this place, with John's persuading her to wait *here* for his burlesque to unfold, as with the plan itself. She would never return to Green Dolphin Street. His lie tonight made a lie of every night they'd spent there.

"Who could stand one at the Riptide?" he said, right on cue. Cynthia had guessed both the late-night bar he would name and the breezy way he would propose a drink there. A perfectly reasonable plan. They were drunk. The Riptide was close. If Cynthia agreed, they would share a cab, which would leave them wrecked and carless at 4 a.m. Di would crash at their place. What happened after that would look like an accident, one more thing to laugh about later.

Behind John the Bickersons argued, Mr. Bickerson impatient to leave, his wife searching for something under the table. "Good lord, Mommy, you left it in the living room like always," he said.

"I'm telling you, I had it here," she hissed, and then mumbled, "I think."

The Chaplins left as they had arrived, completely silent, ignoring each other with the studied nonchalance of strangers naked in a dressing room.

Hungry for a husband, kids, a house in the 'burbs—*the usual*—Di couldn't wait to join the ranks of those cantankerous couples. Cynthia thought of Donna Reed's most inane role, in the show a producer named just for her. In pearls and high heels, she had cooked roasts, mended clothes, and tended children in *The Donna Reed Show*, a smile affixed to her heavily made-up face. Like this girl's dress, it was a ridiculous image—and probably just what Di had in mind.

"Well?" John said. "Riptide okay?"

"I'm game if you are," Di said to Cynthia, clasping her and John's hands, as if to be lifted from her seat.

"Can you stand a little more action?" he asked. "Should I get a cab?"

Cynthia imagined lying in bed next to Di behind the moveable screen in their loft. Against Di's canvas-white skin, Cynthia's aging tattooed body would look clothed even when she was naked. What would it feel like to have a girl's mouth on her breasts? Strange, unnerving, perhaps comforting in an odd way. Not arousing. She didn't think so, though apparently, Di wouldn't have to pretend. For her, tonight was a welcome adventure, a last hurrah before she pursued a TV marriage. So naïve. Cynthia pictured her ten years from now, thirty pounds heavier in a discolored robe dusted with cigarette ash, nursing an infant whose father was beginning to disappear. Di couldn't imagine the heartbreak that waited, the mistakes that would make a tragedy of her life.

Electronic music began to pound. In black jeans and a dark shirt, John's figure faded with the houselights. Under the pulsing points that replaced them, Di's white dress took on a celestial glow, seeming, like her skin earlier, to be lit from within, brighter somehow than the lights that illuminated it. No less foolish, but its charm was hard to deny. She was about to make terrible errors, marriage the biggest among them, and Cynthia wished she could trade places with her. Di's illusions were no worse than Cynthia's, and when her dream dissolved, she would be left with particular realities: children, memories, a house, possibly even a husband. If her marriage didn't end, it probably would turn bitter—the Bickersons were a best-case scenario—but when she died, it would be with regrets that came from living seriously, not floating around life's unsightly edges. Weight gain and wrinkles and childbirth would not detract from her beauty. In a way, the disappointments of motherhood and deceptions of marriage, the sacrifice and pain natural to both, even death, would be beautiful. John was wrong: You could be nostalgic for a past that hadn't happened. Cynthia felt intense nostalgia for a past she'd never had, the past that would be this girl's future.

From across the table John stared, eyes silently urging her, ready at a word to tip into adolescent glee or paternal disappointment. Seated between them, Di watched her, too, eager as a child begging permission to stay up late.

Cynthia felt tired, old and very tired, the evening finally overtaking her. She was too tired for the Riptide, but she was also too tired for a fight. It was too late for that, too late for a scene, too late to say how ridiculous it all appeared.

A tremor twisted her face before forming a grin. "Okay," she said. "The Riptide. Action."

Dibs

Hector Chavez watched the street from his window the morning after the blizzard, waiting for his chance. When a decent parking space opened up, he pounced. The tread on his boots was worn, but he practiced walking on the treacherous ice, head down, shoulders hunched, until he grew used to the slick surface and his own mincing steps. Along the gutter he started, hefting snow over the curb, well onto the verge, so it wouldn't drift back into his spot. He cleared a square the size of his boots, then expanded slowly into a space large enough for the family car. When he'd finished, he sprinkled salt and planted two beat-up chairs, which faced each other across the gap like open lips waiting for choice words.

He trudged to his old Chevy. It turned over endlessly, sputtered, finally started. Hector smiled, then recoiled as *norteño* blasted from the radio. He scrambled to turn it off, the sudden silence so deep he thought for a second he could hear his heart thud through coat, wool sweater, flannel—the protective layers a Chicago winter demanded. His wife's station—always the same ghetto music, always booming—made her think of home. It made him feel like a *cholo* in a low-rider every time he turned the key of their rusted Cavalier. Andrea insisted they couldn't afford a newer model, which made Hector want one all the more.

He'd repaired their ancient car piecemeal, practically living at the junkyard to beat others to fresh parts. A former boss had tossed him the keys one Friday after missing a month of checks, both of them knowing the beater didn't cover his lost wages. Hector had been famous for fighting as a kid in Guadalajara and considered taking what was owed. As he imagined the options open to him, though, close enough to see strands of meat in the man's yellowed teeth, he decided that on this side, fighting wasn't the way to get what he needed. He scooped the keys from the pavement and drove away, dodging potholes on streets that were starting to feel like home.

His feet argued over the right mix of brake and accelerator as he coaxed the Cavalier back and forth, finally bumping out of a spot buried in snow. He removed his chairs from the space he'd cleared and backed in. Along his block, kitchen chairs, card tables, and broken drawers saved spots people had shoveled—occasionally, recliners, coffee tables, and mattresses, too, the bigger pieces marked for garbage and maybe halfway there, sitting in backyards when drafted as placeholders. Putting dibs on parking spots was a winter tradition in Chicago, but something about the barricades made Hector self-conscious, as if he was peeking into actual kitchens and basements, his neighbors' homes exposed to the road as they claimed a piece of it.

Avoiding those trashy placeholders as he headed inside, he almost didn't notice his new neighbor's attempt to charge out of a parking spot. The door of the Escalade gaped, its driver swearing as he looked down at the street. If the spinning wheels caught and he didn't amputate a door, he would hit anything in front of him.

"Need some help?" Hector called. "Hey, hold up, guy."

The driver smiled, showing teeth that seemed too large for his mouth. His sandy brown hair was almost blond, tight on the sides and taller on top, like a helmet with a plume that waved when he nodded. "Appreciate it," he said.

Hector shoveled in front of the tires. His neighbor, who wore a thick red sweater and khakis but no coat, joined him. Uselessly he swept at snow with boots Hector recognized as snakeskin. He'd always wanted a pair. They would be ruined in the salt and snow, but his neighbor didn't seem to care. He was smiling. Then the sweeping turned to kicking, which led to an odd fit of condensed swearing: *Goddamn. Mother. Son of a.* He seemed to forget Hector was there.

The driver got back in the car, and Hector hitched himself to the rear bumper to push. Too late, he realized he was standing directly behind a tire. His neighbor hit the accelerator, hard despite Hector's advice, spraying his front with icy sludge as the car bumped out of the spot.

"Thomas Polk." The driver pumped Hector's hand. "Quick snort? Warm up?"

Hector was explaining that he couldn't—it was 10 a.m. and he had to work later—but Thomas had jogged up the walk and into his house, leaving his neighbor speaking, car running, front door bouncing. His house, the first in Colonial Mews, sat opposite Hector's, separated by an alley that became a river each spring as snow melted and sewers clogged. The Ricans who ran the neighborhood were up in arms over the new townhouses. *Gentrification,* they screamed, *displacement*—big words hiding something small: jealousy. Hector saw the development as a gift, boosting everyone's value. Now that the homes were completed, he hated to admit that they did have a hollow look, with fake columns wide as trees and showy eaves painted cherry-red or plum.

The end walls were windowless, a spiked wrought-iron fence too high to be friendly, but you couldn't blame bad design on the owners, and already, people were paying higher prices on the street. His wife would die for a peek behind that façade, which seemed to appear overnight, as if the houses were built elsewhere and hauled whole to the block. Hector supposed he wouldn't mind a look inside himself.

The home felt like a builder's model, pricey but sparse, its surfaces—oak floors, marble tiles, granite counters—so pristine, Hector wondered how anyone lived on them.

"Bitch to heat evenly. Feast or famine," Thomas said, as Hector gazed at a vaulted ceiling, ribbed and crazy high. "More comfortable in the kitchen." He guided Hector, moving in the same clipped way that he spoke, as if words were a waste of his time.

The kitchen was empty except for some boxes stacked in a corner and the dishes that filled the sink. A smell of burnt toast hung in the air. They stood on opposite sides of a granite slab—no stools—a bowl of fruit so perfect it might have been wax perched between them.

Thomas poured scotch into mugs. Two empty bedrooms and a useless family room, he said, but try fitting his SUV in the two-car garage—so-called—if Linda parked her little Saturn there. Musical chairs: someone always had to be on the street. Why he was dicking around on the ice today.

Hector shifted from side to side over some of that ice, quickly becoming a puddle beneath his boots.

"No worries: Corazon," Thomas said cryptically.

Hector took a taste. The whiskey went straight to his head. He enjoyed the morning drink precisely because it was something he would never do. Still, he felt guilty. And cold. Wet. He really should get home, he said, tugging on his splattered pants. Thomas didn't seem to hear but disappeared, returning a moment later with a pair of khakis.

He tossed them to Hector with a friendly nod. No, thanks, Hector said. His neighbor insisted. Embarrassed, Hector finally agreed. In a heavily mirrored bathroom, unflattering images wavering on both sides, he tried not to watch the chubby man changing.

Thomas was on the phone when he returned. He tore into boxes while he spoke, pulling out pans, glasses, and utensils to assess as if pricing them for a yard sale.

"No. Granting any easement," he said, not quite shouting. "Leaves *me* exposed…Look, forget about air rights. Sure, a great guy, but…Bottom line—who controls the option?" He held his cell like a microphone to finish. "Exactly. So, no. No way. Tell him."

He looked surprised to see Hector, then gave a high-pitched laugh, that plume rustling atop his head as he remembered the neighbor he'd sent to the john. Hector laughed with him. Thomas was high-strung, strange if not crazy, but he had *carisma* for sure.

He'd moved in six weeks ago, Thomas said, he and Linda, his girlfriend. No, definitely no kids, he laughed.

Hector and his wife, Andrea, had five, he said. They'd bought four years ago, just in time. They couldn't afford their own house today.

"Going to be a good block," Thomas said.

It was already pretty good, Hector thought, much better than when he moved in.

"I wait," Hector said when Thomas asked what he did, gesturing toward the window, or the world beyond it, with his mug.

"For?"

"I mean, I wait tables, in a restaurant."

"Got that." Thomas smiled. "Which?"

After stints collecting scrap metal in alleys, salvaging bricks for a builder, sorting clothes at a Salvation Army—countless terrible jobs—Hector had started as a dishwasher at Les Contraires, a middle-of-the-road French place in Lincoln Park. Another crummy job, yes, but after three years bouncing back and forth—valet, busser, expediter, whatever they threw his way—he caught a break. Mercier, a Parisian manager who lived up to his nickname, *Merciless,* fired a server mid-shift on a slow night. The slow night turned busy, and Hector volunteered to take her slot. That was six years ago. The guys in the kitchen still complained at his luck. Never mind how long he'd spent building his skills and waiting for that window to open, expanding it gradually into something permanent. Why should it matter that he'd practiced English until he dreamed in his second language or waited years to come here properly, while the illegals in the kitchen could be kicked out any day? Sure, luck.

A horn blared like a bugle on the street.

"Your car." Hector remembered the Escalade double-parked outside.

"Les Contraires. No kidding?" Thomas said. His mother knew the owners. Owned restaurants herself in the 'burbs. She was helping Thomas break into the city market. The Coach House, his first foray, sat in an actual coach house, one of those places built behind the mansions when Humboldt Park was wealthy. Next door, Wicker Park had plenty of nice restaurants, but until The Coach House, none had crossed Western Avenue into Humboldt.

A woman bustled into the room, stopping halfway to the sink when she saw them. "*Terminé todo lo demás. Puedo limpiar la cocina ahora?*" she asked, gesturing at the kitchen she wanted permission to clean. She was old and dark, Indian blood for sure.

"Thanks, Corazon," Thomas said.

She looked at the sink full of dishes, confused, and then, warily, at Hector. He turned to the window. Outside a horn sounded in short blasts. Angry shouts rang like shots.

"Could use you at The Coach House," Thomas said. "Still openings." He drained his mug and poured two more before Hector could refuse. "Come work for the other side?"

The old woman stared at Hector a moment, shrugged, then left.

"I'm pretty comfortable where I am," he said. A voice rose above the noise on the street, but he couldn't quite understand the words. "They probably can't get by out there."

"Come check the place out. You and the wife. Dinner. On the house."

"Well, I—"

"Hold those words." Thomas held up a hand. "Just chew on the possibility."

He nodded while Thomas described the menu. Hector felt as if he were waiting on the street, stuck behind the SUV outside at the same time that he drank scotch in his neighbor's kitchen, amazed, even giddy at the way Thomas talked over the clatter, so easily Hector wondered if he imagined it.

Warmed by whiskey, Hector laughed as he walked home, thinking how Thomas had ignored or maybe hadn't heard, those voices on the street below. His neighbor seemed insulated from the petty problems of the outside world, a choice, no doubt, to focus on holding his own in a competitive business. They looked like opposites, he and Thomas, but beneath the surface, Hector thought, they had the same drive, compadres already. Why else would Thomas have offered him a job on the spot? It would take a lot for Hector to leave Les Contraires, but he found himself, maybe because of the whiskey, considering The Coach House. The chance to get in on the ground floor, a new place in a changing neighborhood—his neighborhood, no less, barely a mile from his house—was tempting. He imagined himself helping with ordering, as he did at Les Contraires, and eventually, scheduling. With Thomas behind him, Hector might be assistant manager in a year. He had done nearly every job you could do in a restaurant. He would make a great manager. And if manager, why not, someday, owner of his own place? It was a familiar dream, but one he'd never spoken aloud, afraid how the words might sound, even to his wife. At least there was room for them here. In Mexico, someone like him, growing up as he did, would look a fool mentioning such possibilities.

In Guadalajara, he'd lived in a procession of ever-smaller shacks, more than one illegal and in danger of being bull-dozed. The worst sat opposite the dump, separated by a fence that couldn't keep out the stench or an army of *pepenadores* who would steal your eyes if you slept with them open. The scavengers on the other side of the chain-link lived on the garbage people tossed, in it too, tacking up sheets of plastic and cardboard, hammering bits of tin and discarded wood into homes as vulnerable to fellow *pepenadores* as to the rain and cold. Ragged animals—birds, rats, packs of dogs—competed for the same scraps, living off the dump as if it was their natural habitat. On some days, the human scavengers got ahead: decent clothes and fixable appliances came their way, small jobs, half-meals hardly touched. On others, they had nothing to digest but a mumbled *mañana* and the hope that something better would appear then.

Chicago was a paradise by comparison, a place where you could plan a future. Hector struggled here, too, but to enlarge his life, going from bad jobs to better, from a shared basement in Bridgeport to a bigger garden apartment in Armour Square to, finally, the comfortable wood frame he owned in Humboldt Park—or would in twenty-six years. It was the investment of his life, that house. He barely made the mortgage and if he hadn't waited a year for the right fore-closure, it would have been too much even then, back when the block scared buyers away. Now, because of the improve-ments, his house was worth more. And the Ricans thought he should fight that? Should he feel bad that his block was safer and cleaner, too, that his kids no longer had to avoid the frightening house on the corner where he himself had been offered a narcotic and then robbed, an eyesore cleared with the others to make way for clean new housing? True, property taxes were rising. He felt for families who might get forced out—he had a heart—but he hadn't heard of any and couldn't see sacrificing progress to that vague possibility.

The Ricans didn't want progress, though, or anything in the usual order. They got welfare before unpacking their bags. They came to *el otro lado* with no wait, got food stamps and Medicaid right away, could vote the day they arrived. They were born with the keys to the country and still they complained, marching in the streets over jobs, housing, crime. Their right to this and to that. Everything was political, and in case you forgot it, their flags waved all over, in tattoos and shop windows and endless murals. Their addresses said Chicago, but they never left the slums of San Juan. Colonial Mews wasn't promising or inspiring for the Ricans—*someday I'll own one*—but a threat to their neighborhood, *theirs*, as if Humboldt hadn't belonged to the Poles and the Swedes and the Jews before them, and to the Indians, Hector supposed, long before that. Maybe they thought the biggest PR flags of all, the steel ones arching over Division Street like gates in a town wall—one at Western Avenue, its twin at California, to mark *Paseo Boricua*—gave them the final claim. Hector lived "between the flags," a nickname spoken with pride, as if those blocks were home to heroes holding off an army of Anglos. But that area was changing faster than any. As Hector teased his neighbors, even steel markers could be tossed aside, flags painted new colors in a flash.

At work that day, he took his time settling in, learning the specials while waiting for his shift to begin. Hector loved the hopeful feel of the restaurant in late afternoon, bartenders cutting fruit into tiny wedges, servers sipping coffee as they claimed their sections, the kitchen crew prepping in a frenzy that would not turn violent for a while yet. In winter, an hour of weak sun threw softly shifting light onto the two murals, *Versailles* and *Les Enragés*, in a way that made one and then the other look more like a window than a painting.

He thought he knew everything on tonight's menu and then noticed a new entrée, an old one, actually, returning after years off the list: steak in a reduction with asparagus spears and *pommes de terre Lyonnaise*. He practiced the chef's language—half singing ingredients and preparations, the obvious pairings and the unlikely ones that were the restaurant's specialty—until he could repeat it without thinking, accent and all. Some servers read everything in flat Chicago drones. Hector liked to recite the dishes slowly, rolling the words on his tongue as if they were the meal. "Tonight, I also have a steak special, a petit filet in a vin rouge reduction made with garlic and shallots…" As a busboy, he'd been shocked to hear certain waiters list specials in this way—tonight *I have*, as if they planned the menu. It took him years to repeat, but he now loved the way that *I have* felt in his mouth.

He delivered salads to his first table of the night, a couple on an early date, too in love with the possibilities to see even obvious flaws. She kept overfilling his glass, nudging him to drink, though he didn't seem to like the wine. A four-top of French tourists were afraid they could not afford the meals they wanted and maybe not even the ones they'd ordered. The exchange rate was a problem, a fear that they'd miscalculated the dishes in their range and a bigger fear of showing it. They were all smiles and nods and pointing fingers, but Hector had done the math: foreigners plus ice water minus dessert equals bad tip. Why, he wondered in frustration, did they come all this way to eat the same stuff they had at home?

Standing at the kitchen door, Mercier raised an index finger, as if hailing a cab. Hector walked over.

"José called in."

He nodded.

"You can finish those tables."

Again, he nodded silently, but Mercier saw something. "I will make sure everyone tips you out well."

An hour later, Hector was up to his elbows in back, loading the dishwasher and stacking plates. He lugged a rack of clean glasses to the bar, refilled the ice, returned to the kitchen with a tub of dirty dishes.

"Where's José?" Luis asked.

"What's wrong with Hose B?" said Adder, the sous chef.

Hector's fists clenched automatically, but he smiled. Luis gave him a look.

It happened less than it used to, but Mercier still gave Hector's section away if he needed a quick replacement for one of the slots Hector used to fill. He hated going back to those jobs. It wasn't just the money. Getting pulled off the floor made him seem temporary in the dining room, always low-man, and he no longer fit in the kitchen. That side of the restaurant had its own order, language, even weather—unbearably hot and muggy. Luis was okay, but the others were cold, pretending not to understand his Spanish, calling him *jefe*, teasing him about slumming it. They were jealous of the money he made, and some blamed him for Vicky, a sweet girl with enormous doe eyes, though she'd moved less like a deer than a snail, one carrying an especially heavy home on its back. Was it Hector's fault Mercier had noticed him picking up her slack, or that he was ready to take her place when she got canned?

He carried two pans to the sink and blasted them with scalding water. Measuring his steps in steam so thick he couldn't see the floor, his hands rough and dry as hooves, his section split between two other servers, he thought about The Coach House. He thought about it again while unlocking the compactor in the alley. A dark ooze had frozen in front of the machine, and hefting a trash bag, he slipped on the ice. He grasped at air trying to stop the fall. The keys disappeared in the garbage. He got a flashlight but couldn't see them. He climbed in. Waist-deep in the freezing compactor, he sifted through boxes and putrid food for fifteen minutes before spotting the silver ring.

"Who mugged you?" Adder pointed to Hector's pants, smeared red with tomatoes or maybe wine at the knees, as he came through the kitchen door. His neighbor's pants. He'd meant to change earlier, but dozing, ran out of time.

"Ah, *caray*. You empty the garbage, *jefe*, or roll in it?" Carlos pinched his nose.

Hector checked the storage room. There was nothing decent for him to change into, so he did his best to clean up at the slop sink before going back to his station.

"Look at this!" Hector said to his wife before he'd taken off his coat. He'd walked with fifty less than he needed, waited a lifetime for a bus in bitter cold on Division Street, then arrived home to find Thomas's Escalade in his spot.

"Shh, you'll wake the kids," she hissed.

He was angry, but more than that, disappointed. In what, he couldn't exactly say. He'd been on edge since his fight with Andrea that morning. Hector had come home buzzing after his drink at Thomas's. His poorly insulated hall felt almost cozy as he closed the door on the harsh weather outside. The big-mouth DJ they called *El Pistolero* was up in arms about something, his fuzzy rant emerging from the music on *Que Buena* FM behind the kitchen door, more comical than annoying today. Hector floated upstairs. Unseen on the landing, he watched his daughters play in the bedroom they shared. Carmen, the oldest, had pulled empty toilet paper rolls from the wastebasket to make dolls with popsicle-stick arms and hair of old yarn. She was dressed. Giselle and Elodia still wore their nightgowns, originally bought for

Carmen, the cartoon Cinderellas on their fronts—Carmen's favorite—worn to flaking silhouettes.

Hector's mouth was dry. His mood shifted as his head throbbed from the whiskey. A bucket Andrea had set out before the rain became snow caught drips under a section of roof he'd replaced. He saved money using scrap lumber from one of the houses torn down to make way for Colonial Mews and now wondered if the old wood had warped. An icy draft penetrated the room's ancient window frames. Last week he noticed black spots in the basement, the return of mold he thought was gone forever (the previous owners had let pipes burst as the bank foreclosed). The first night Hector turned the key to this house was his proudest. Only then had it hit him, this was *his*, but the home he'd waited so long for now seemed like a dump. Andrea argued that it cost too much, the same thing she said about a new car, groceries, decent clothes for the kids—reining him in at every turn. Was she right? He thought of how little equity he'd built in four years, the balance that each month took all he had, and the walls seemed to close in.

"*Dios mio*, what are you doing in those boots?" His wife shouted behind him, sending his back, sore from shoveling, into a spasm. "Look what you dragged in here!" She pointed to the icy trail that ended where he wobbled slightly. Next, she smelled the liquor on his breath, and then she was screaming, and the kids were crying, and he had the thought he always regretted later: he would be living like a king by now if he'd never known her, had them, bought this.

"How do you know it was the neighbor who moved your chairs?" Andrea asked that night. She guided him from the window, coaxing him out of his winter coat.

"That's his truck. I know it."

Maybe so, but when she went for groceries, she said, anyone could have moved those chairs, parked, and then driven off. To their neighbor, it would have looked like just another space. Would anyone with a vehicle that nice risk taking someone's spot?

"I guess you're right," Hector said, relieved. He pulled her close, kissing her neck, ear, cheek. She was heavier than when he'd met her, with lately, a touch of gray in her thick black hair, but more beautiful than ever, his love, the foundation he needed to stand. He was gently sucking her lip when she pulled away.

"*Pappi,* you stink," she said.

He hurried in the shower, but by the time he finished she was asleep.

The hostess said the wait would be just a little longer. Andrea groaned.

"Fine." Hector smiled. "Is Thomas around?" He'd called the day before to let his neighbor know they were coming. No reservations, the girl who took the message said, but he'd seen two couples brought to tables held for them.

"Mr. Polk?" the hostess asked.

"Can you tell him Hector is here? Hector Chavez."

From a distance The Coach House looked like a smaller version of the mansion it sat opposite. Up close, it had vinyl siding, not cedar, and the façade was only painted face-brick red. A typical Humboldt Park home, gutted for a restaurant that sat fifty and a small bar, packed with people greedily eyeing tables. Candles cast expansive shadows on a low ceiling, flickering over rich wood and brass fixtures. Spurs and riding crops were mounted on the walls. A bridle dangled near the door as if waiting for a horse.

"Don't you want something?" Hector asked his wife. "Have a drink."

"Hector, it's too much," she whispered. "You sure this won't cost nothing?"

He shouldered up to the bar, practiced at edging around crowds without seeming pushy.

"Baby, you know your problem?" he said, returning with a beer for himself, for her a rum and Coke. "You need to stop thinking like a *mojado*. Think like an outsider, you end up outside, squinting in other people's windows."

She sucked a piece of ice. "So what, I should think like a *gringa*?"

"Sure."

She laughed.

"I'm serious. At least try to look comfortable. The longer that bartender made me wait, the wider I planted my elbows on his bar. You got to act like you own the place."

"Tough when you're waiting a hour for a table, no?"

"Laugh, but if you're patient, opportunities start dropping at your feet here. You got to scoop them up, at least chew on the possibilities, or someone else will. Like with this job."

"I wish I had something to chew besides ice. I'm starving, Hector." She bit loudly into an ice cube.

Hector was hungry, too, but refused to show it. He looked around. The hostess had disappeared. A short man in a dark suit waited at the window where food came out. He pounced on plates and shoved them at runners, mixing up where meals went, ignoring anyone who questioned an order he'd confused. Managers like this were their own enemies: *pendejos* with the people on their side, then surprised they couldn't get ahead when the house was slammed.

"What makes this such a great *opportunity* anyway, moving from a place where you know how you stand to one where you don't know nothing?" Andrea asked.

He knew plenty, Hector said. He didn't mean to snap, but having Andrea here made him nervous. He liked to keep home separate from work and the world outside, where he did whatever was needed to get by. He didn't work at The Coach House yet, but since he'd marched out of Les Contraires last week, it was his best option. Mercier had wanted to pull him off tables early that night to fill in as host for a few hours. Hector heard himself refuse. If he didn't want to wait for half a shift, Mercier said, he could stay home for a whole one. That sounds real good, Hector said, his heart drumming as he left. He'd been cut on every shift since, yesterday after just an hour. The manager would fire him as soon as it was convenient.

"I know this is a better place for waiters than Les Contraires," Hector said, taking a gentler tone with Andrea. He hadn't told her about his trouble at work or the mortgage payment they'd missed this week. From the crowd, he knew the money would be better, he said, and already he had ideas. For instance, the room was too small for runners. Thomas could save money and give better service if he got rid of them.

"So now you're telling him how to manage his restaurant?"

Sure, he'd make suggestions, Hector said, since Thomas hinted that if he started out as a server, he'd be a manager before long. Hector had imagined this possibility enough that the lie seemed true, and Andrea had goaded him into it in a way, nagging about a job he had to take. She looked so surprised that once he felt the next words on his lips, hanging there as sweet as ripe mangos, just waiting to be said, he couldn't stop what followed. After a few years as manager, he said, with some money and connections, he would be in a good spot to open his own restaurant. She stared, doubtful but impressed, and Hector felt suddenly naked.

Thomas was staring at him, too, from across the restaurant, that plume of hair bobbing as he spoke with the hostess. He saluted when Hector waved, but his expression looked as vacant as it had on the morning Hector met him. Sweat collected on Hector's back and rolled down his sides.

"How's it going? Gotten stuck in any spots lately?" Hector laughed as his neighbor approached. He hadn't seen Thomas since clearing a path for his Escalade two weeks earlier.

"Hey!" Thomas said. "Made it!"

Hector introduced his wife.

Thomas held her elbow with one hand and shook with the other. "Well?" He gestured.

"Real nice," Hector said.

"Lost someone Monday. Still want a job?"

"Like I said, I'm pretty comfortable where I am, but—"

"Hang on."

Thomas ordered drinks from a passing server. If they were going to eat here, they had to have a sloe gin fizz, he said, the house special.

"It's real nice," Hector repeated. "I been checking the place out like you asked."

The Coach House was about going back to basics, Thomas said—classic cocktails, old simple recipes, seasonal produce. He insisted his kitchen work with whatever the market dropped on them. "Keeps them on their toes. Could eat here years and never guess the menu."

Their drinks came. Thomas stopped the manager as he passed. The man spoke to him in an urgent whisper.

"Come on, Dan. A little turnover. Make it happen," Thomas said, loud enough that the nearest diners looked up. "You folks, how long you been waiting?"

An hour, Hector said, and Thomas made the manager seat them right away. Hector smiled at Andrea. Maybe he hadn't lied after all. This guy wouldn't last as manager. He sat them against the windowless far wall, but they didn't care, happy to sit anywhere by then. Hector had never seen a nice restaurant from the other side, as a customer—a guilty, god-like pleasure. Neither of them liked the drinks Thomas bought (a hint of apricot or plum and a bitter aftertaste), but the gesture reminded them of home. Their server was friendly, until they spoke. He sighed when they ordered entrées only, no drinks or appetizers because Hector didn't want to take advantage. If he did become manager someday, he'd put this guy in his place, though he would do the classy thing tonight and drop a big tip.

The food arrived. The presentation was dazzling but the portions were small, and they finished their meals still hungry. Hector flagged Thomas down to thank him.

Thomas nodded, distracted. The restaurant was slammed.

"I been thinking about what you said, about a job, and —"

"Under the gun," Thomas said, glancing at his watch. "Wait here? Show you back of the house in ten?" He gestured to a bartender and before Hector could stop him, produced two more cocktails made with sloe gin.

Twenty minutes later, a rangy Puerto Rican kid showed Hector the kitchen and back bar. The busboy took small, shuffling steps, stooped, as if embarrassed by his height under the low ceiling. In tortured English, he explained what he could about the restaurant. Frustrated as the kid foraged for words, Hector spoke to him in Spanish. The busboy looked away as if he didn't understand. The painful exchange reminded Hector of the neighborhood meetings he attended to keep an eye on the Ricans. Few Mexicans went. Once, an old woman came in late, looking confused.

"*Que ocupa?*" he asked, to see what she needed, instead of "*Que necesita?*" The Ricans knew what he meant but pretended not to, laughing at the colloquial expression, greeting him with "*Que ocupas?*" in a sing-song accent after that. He gave it right back, insisting that the Ricans didn't bring food to the meetings because they were full from swallowing their *R*s.

"So?" Andrea said when Hector returned.

"Nice place. What's this?" Les Contraires printed receipts for comped meals, too, so customers knew what to tip, but Hector was surprised to see the pricey drinks Thomas had ordered included on theirs. The mistake wouldn't change the amount Hector paid by much, but it was odd. He figured twenty-five percent and stuffed cash in the billfold. The waiter returned it a few minutes later. He apologized when Hector explained, but no one had told him to comp the meal. He would talk to the manager.

"Hector, you said this was free," his wife hissed. "We can't even afford that tip."

"Of course it's free. He just has a lot going on, Thomas. You should have seen him the morning I pushed his truck—off in his own world."

Mr. Polk had stepped out, the waiter said, and didn't leave instructions. They tried his cell, but he didn't answer. No one knew when he'd return.

"No problem," Hector said, and the waiter looked relieved. "You know, I think we will look at that dessert menu."

They took their time finishing the awful cocktails while deciding on a dessert to share. Dessert came, a glazed fruit tart with fresh cream, the cheapest thing on the menu, and they took their time eating it. They took their time over a second cup of coffee and then a third. One dinner rush ended and another began. The manager circled their table like a vulture flying over sick prey. Finally, he offered to buy them drinks at the bar.

Returning to the spot where he'd started his evening, Hector's dislike of the man hardened. It was rude, forcing them to move, and the bribe of free drinks only added to the insult. Hector wanted to pay and leave, but he barely had enough for the tip, and Andrea cut up their only credit card two years ago after he kept hitting its surprisingly low limit.

"These are on Dan," the bartender said, setting down two sloe gin fizzes.

Andrea glared. "Can we please leave?"

"You want to pay for all this?" Hector said through clenched teeth, which turned into a smile when their server looked over. "We have to wait for Thomas."

"I got to give you credit." She pushed her drink forward. "You sure look like you own the place. Who but the owner sits in a restaurant all night?"

She was the one who finally went to get cash. She couldn't sit there another second, she said, grabbing her purse.

Half an hour later, Hector held up his drink as the bartender wiped the bar. He wished he was on the other side of it, helping to close instead of sitting here, taking up space. He hated those last lingering customers who made it tough to get ahead at the end of the night. Now, he was one of them.

What was taking Andrea so long? The lights grew brighter, and the room seemed to shrink. The tall busboy who had given him the tour crouched on the other side of the bar, stocking beer. A wedge of light, blue and harsh, as if chilled by the cooler, leaked from the machine, illuminating his face. He was not a boy at all, Hector realized, closer to thirty than eighteen.

Hector asked how much he walked with on weeknights, in English this time, but the boy, the man—had he ever said his name?—was gone.

"Did you get the lay of the land?" the manager asked ten minutes later. "Good fit?"

He was interested, Hector said, not wanting to seem too eager with this guy. He and Thomas would settle things later.

"You'd be three to midnight most days. Everyone fights for weekends, but I can give you every other Friday to start. The longer you're here, the more you'll pick up. Waiters tip out ten percent, fifteen if you hustle. Villalobos, the one who showed you around, always makes fifteen. He's hungry for shifts, works his ass off—a good model."

"I'm a waiter," Hector said, "not a busboy."

"Oh." The manager squinted. "Thomas told me you were."

"You sure?" Hector smiled. "Maybe he just mentioned *a* job, and you thought—"

"No, he definitely said busser. Twice. He reminded me again before he left." The manager's eyes flashed down to Hector's shoes and back to his face. He shrugged, embarrassed. "Sorry, but we don't have an opening for a server now. Maybe down the road…"

"I could lose my home." The sentence, spoken aloud, seemed to come from someone else. Hector's family needed *more* space. How would they manage with less, an apartment maybe half the size of their house? He couldn't even afford a rental on his block. He pictured a man from the bank changing the locks on his house, his furniture tossed onto the frozen street, kitchen chairs tipped, couch perched at the curb as if for a parade, passing Ricans pretending not to notice. An old rage rose in his chest. His muscles, much smaller now, tensed. He thought of fights he'd had growing up and imagined a similar one here, saw himself knocking Thomas down, his fist grazing those big white teeth. It wasn't a fight he could win in the end. He was too drunk and tired anyway, and he couldn't leave his place at the bar now that the wheels were in motion. He had to wait for Andrea.

Thomas had not done it out of meanness, Hector knew. There was nothing personal in his treatment, which only made it worse.

Something moved in the mirror behind the bar. A flushed face. Hector realized it was his, flushed though the restaurant was freezing. They'd turned the heat down to push out the last customers, a trick Mercier taught him years ago. He felt exposed and uncomfortable, the only customer left at the bar. He'd drained Andrea's drink as well as his own and a "mistake" the bartender tossed him rather than dump. Hector had been swallowing Thomas's liquor for hours, not noticing his own intoxication until he tried to stand and slumped back on his stool. The problem was that dinner. He'd gone without lunch, planning on a big meal later, but dinner was surprisingly small.

Hands grabbed his shoulders and shook him roughly from behind.

"Hector! Are you a bum off the street, to fall asleep in public?"

"*Qué? Estoy bien. Yo, yo*—I was just resting my eyes."

Beneath Andrea's voice—maybe he dreamed it—a *corrido* played in his head, a song full of longing and pride, something about Villa seizing haciendas while Carranza unlocked the border for the Americans hunting him.

"Resting? You're drunk on that...stuff. *Estás completamente borracho!*"

"Where are the keys? Wait, I need—"

"Sure, you need the keys. Like you need a tombstone. Just wait. I have to pay." Andrea clucked her tongue as she counted money from her purse.

"Do you hear that song?" Hector asked.

"Song? *Ay, que está loco,*" she whispered fiercely. "All I hear is money draining out of our bank account. Do you know what this cost?"

He strained to hear the words in his head, buried under the endless back and forth, an accordion's stuttering rhythm. Something about *Carranza, Pershing's mule.* Hector laughed at that, *Pershing's mule,* and the bartender looked at him.

"I'm glad you think it's funny," Andrea said. "We'll go without for a month now."

"I'll find something tomorrow," he said. "Tomorrow." He didn't know what, but just saying the word was satisfying somehow.

"Sure, the big hero. I wish your kids could see you now. Come here." Softening a little, she straightened his collar and smoothed his hair.

They were on his tongue, almost, the words, but he couldn't quite grasp the lyrics. Not quite, but his heart beat louder, stirred by the music, thin and distant, as if the band stood on the icy street outside. Villalobos, the busboy, spun chairs, expertly upending them, to sweep up napkins and the stray food dropped from tables. Hector closed his eyes again. In the bright rich room, eyes shut, a corrido in his head, he imagined for a moment that he was home. But the swinging doors in back gaped wide, then closed, voices rose then fell, bouncing in the hollow space, and he realized the music came from whoever was cleaning the kitchen.

Clearing

After two sleepless nights in a row, Chuck Gwozdek stretched out on his couch to call his old friend Tony Almos. A bubble of unease had pressed below Chuck's ribs for so long, he accepted fatigued and slightly panicked as his natural state. He didn't mind being high-strung—nervous energy helped get him where he was—but every couple of months, for no apparent reason, the bubble threatened to burst. His usual five hours of sleep escaped him, and things began to look sharp, stark and hard-edged. A dull conversation with someone from the old neighborhood was the balm that lulled him back to dreamland.

"I thought you were dead," Tony said but sounded strangely pleased to hear from Chuck, who was slow to return his calls. Tony made the usual small talk: gossip about Clearing, where he still lived, and Chicago Mail & Label, Ltd., the plant where he'd worked since high school. By the time he gave an update on the brood—Tony had five kids—Chuck was drifting. Absently, he wiped crumbs from the place where he ate dinner, an antique chest that lately served as desk and coffee table, too. He'd spent half the night cleaning but somehow missed them. The rest of his condo, a garden unit with oak floors and exposed stone walls, was spotless, and looking around, he was pleased with the feeling of space, the openness of his living room and kitchen, even the smaller dining room, since he'd lost the bulky table.

"Couldn't Ann take care of that? She doesn't get up at five for work," Chuck said, latching onto a sliver of Tony's monologue. Teething and feverish, the one-year-old had been up all night, which meant Tony was up all night, taking care of her.

"We take turns. Anyways, I was too worried to sleep."

At once Chuck felt bored by the conversation, sorry for his friend, and better about his own sleepless night, which at least was his to clean or read. Tony went on about cutting teeth, the child's trauma at not understanding her own pain, until Chuck felt like he was the one who'd sat up all night with the sweaty one-year-old, mashing aspirin in a teaspoon of milk and stroking her clammy head. His eyelids drooped. The room grew fuzzy. He'd had his fix and was making an excuse to hang up when Tony asked if he'd heard from Tommy O'Sullivan.

"Sully? Not in two years," Chuck said. "Maybe three."

"No? I thought for sure...Damn, you're the only one he hasn't called."

Chuck had lost touch with most of his friends from the old neighborhood, abandoning Clearing just as they settled in for life. He bought a condo in East Ravenswood, a North Side neighborhood full of potential. It wasn't far, but the North Side felt like a foreign country, his place surrounded by Nigerians, Assyrians, Mexicans, Vietnamese...Every day he passed an exotic store, a promising new bar, a woman he could see himself with. He loved getting lost in the dense forest of high-rises on the lakefront, cheered by the rumors of people rushing half-glimpsed between them. South Siders complained that the North Side was crowded, but that, too, was an advantage in his eyes: he could decide who to see instead of always bumping into the same narrow people with the same narrow views. In East Ravenswood he was free to create the life he imagined for himself, something Clearing's constraints made impossible.

Chuck's visits to the old neighborhood dwindled over the years, but his friends and their plans changed so little, he still saw them clearly: Tony's startled, ineffectual eyes, now perplexed by a screaming child instead of a chalkboard; Al's talent for avoiding work; Sully's vanity, one eye always on the next girl and his own appearance. They lived in the past, retelling and embellishing the same tired stories until they no longer resembled the facts. Good guys, generous and loyal under a rough surface, but terrified of anything outside the tiny box where they lived and died. They bought cramped brick row-houses identical to their parents', married the sedate girls they'd dated at sixteen, made babies, and got jobs at Midway Airport or in the factories that lined 65th. Chuck was the rare exception and now, in a way, so was Sully.

Sully was a champion drinker. Last Chuck heard, the wife had tossed him out and he was living with some barfly. Apparently, he and the barfly got evicted. She had a son to fall back on, Tony said, but Tommy O'Sullivan was stranded at The Comfort Zone. *The Comfort Bone*, they'd called it, because of the shady motel's hourly rates. Sully had no cash and no plan, paid up for just one more night.

"I'd take him in myself, but the kids…He's in bad shape, man. If you heard him on the phone…" Tony's sentences faded like an old promise.

Chuck didn't mind that Sully hadn't called—if anything, he was relieved—but behind Tony's concern, perched something small and black and smug. Chuck was *the only one* Sully hadn't called. He also was the only one of his old friends who wore a suit to work, the only one who lived on the North Side, the only one still single. Chuck, Tony hinted, was the only one in a position to do something for Sully. When he didn't, his old friends could list one more reason he thought he was too good for them.

Sully had called the last time he was homeless, a year ago, after his wife kicked him out. Chuck had erased those messages without listening. He didn't want to face Sully at the best of times, and his crisis came during Lennie's weeklong departure. Each day, Chuck's girlfriend returned to the condo, clearing out her possessions an armful at a time, pleading with him not to sever a connection cultivated over two years. She loved him and planned on a future together. Chuck loved her, too, that was never a question, but he felt buried alive once she moved in, the arrangement instantly and insufferably domestic. Lennie insisted that they do laundry together, turning it into an all-day thing instead of having it done for a few dollars, as he used to. They had to cook every night—no more restaurants—and she got hurt if he wasn't a psychic at the grocery store, anticipating her every need. Entire weekends passed when they hardly left the condo, the constant, insipid drone of the TV a new soundtrack for their lives.

She'd been christened Lenore after her grandmother, and as if to signal her new housebound personality, switched to the more matronly name with everyone but him. The end came when she mentioned kids. Imagining the little spare time he had consumed by a child's constant need for attention, Chuck began to crave his old freedom.

A year later, they still hadn't run into each other, not once. Odd, since he had dinner at Up Down Cafe on Wilson— an old favorite—once a week and had become a regular at Gemeüthlichkeit, a German tavern in Lincoln Square, one of the few bars Lennie liked. Sometimes he thought he glimpsed her on the el or in traffic—amazing how many short brunettes in Chicago owned blue Preludes—but the sightings never panned out. He hoped she was doing well. They had gained enough distance that when they finally bumped into each other, as they must eventually, it would be good to catch up.

Chuck couldn't sleep, with Tony's dig spinning in his head—the opposite of what he'd planned. Always this pettiness with his old friends, often disguised as a friendly gesture, cutting him down because he didn't live as they did. At his office the next morning, he decided to make some calls. He would find a few places where Sully could get help and phone him. Sully would be surprised to hear from Chuck. Tony would be even more surprised when he found out, as he inevitably would, what Chuck had done. Let him spread that news all over Clearing.

Chuck dialed Irene's extension in the next cube. "Lookout?" he asked.

"I gotcha."

He knocked thanks on the fabric panel that separated them. She would keep watch and give three short raps if their boss appeared in the stand of cubicles that gave them cover but made it tough to see people coming on their half of the fourteenth floor.

After an hour on the phone, Chuck had a list of halfway houses for the indigent, as well as endless unsolicited advice about tough love. He hated this twelve-step babble— talk of owning problems, staging interventions, taking a moral inventory.

"This must be very difficult for you," said a man at the United Way hotline.

"Not really."

"I hear the hopelessness in your voice," he persisted. "Don't give up. For years, I woke up half dead every morning and didn't know why. I thought a twelve-pack a night was normal.

Then one day—I won't go into the reasons—the fog lifted. I had what we call a moment of clarity. Last week I celebrated my fourth anniversary."

"Congratulations," Chuck said. "I hope you took your liver somewhere nice for dinner, but look, I don't have a lot of time here." Sleepless and frustrated, he realized during the first call that these people would excuse rudeness as the strain of a worried friend.

"If he can't admit the problem, don't cut him a break. Leave him on the street if you have to." The man ignored Chuck's sigh. This was half of why he couldn't sleep. He spent his whole day dealing with idiots who wouldn't listen. Clients were bad enough, but he had to talk to them.

"Otherwise, *you* are the problem. A lot of us need to live at rock bottom to see the truth. Some can't see it even then."

After the last cliché-laden pep talk, Chuck slammed the receiver. Irene peeked around the divider. Her hair fell in a perfect bob. She had a slight lisp, which he found sexy. He'd thought about asking her out, but her desk almost touched his—probably a bad idea.

"You okay?" she asked

"Sure," he said. "Just finding a home for my derelict friend. Hey, you have an extra bedroom, don't you?"

She smiled and laid a hand on Chuck's shoulder. Her skin was warm through the thin cotton of his shirt. He started to make another joke, then stopped himself. He liked the way she was looking at him. He lowered his eyes and considered a stain on the carpet, a dark jagged leaf on a smooth beige lawn.

"You're a good guy," she said.

At 63rd Street, inexplicably, Chuck almost passed Mythos Gyros, the Greek joint where he'd sheltered half his life, waiting for the bus. It looked different today, but he couldn't say why. The red brick facade hadn't changed as far as he could see. Neither had the striped red-and-white awnings or the wooden benches chained to the ground, where he and his friends had congregated, tracing the path of planes landing at Midway, across the street. The trademark plastic spit still turned in slow circles on the roof, a shapeless brown beacon open to wide interpretation—dinner, waste product, burnt tree trunk. Clearing was named for its lack of trees, and a century later, covered in asphalt, squat row-houses, and bungalows, the neighborhood still felt exposed, so barren and low, the spit was visible a mile away.

Out of the cold November breeze he stepped into a comforting blast of heat and fried onions. He hadn't eaten, and the thick odor made him nauseated and hungry at the same time. Sully sat smoking in the last booth, his vacant eyes fixed over the rim of a paper cup. His cheeks were as ruddy as the face of a waking baby but hollow and hatched with veins.

"Yo, what's happening?" he said, suddenly alert, touching a small suitcase on the seat beside him.

Chuck slid into the booth and realized he was disappointed. He'd called the Comfort Zone yesterday only to give Sully phone numbers, but he'd begged for a ride to New Horizons, a halfway house near Chuck's condo. Chuck finally agreed only to get Sully off the phone, confident at least one of them wouldn't show.

"You don't look so good. Rough ride? Traffic aw-ight?" Sully punctuated each sentence with a gulp of water.

"When's the last time you had a drink?"

"I haven't drank nothing in five days."

"Bullshit." Telling the truth wasn't as tough as the guy at United Way thought. Seeing Sully was harder. He'd been the good-looking one, blue eyes and crow-black hair—an unlikely, compelling combination. Endless women thought so. Now, at thirty-nine, he was mostly gray. He looked like he'd gone back to the haircut, or lack of one, in style when they were kids, but his face had aged prematurely, making him seem at once boyish and too old.

"Let me see…Wednesday. Tuesday. Monday. Sunday. Today. Yep. Five in a row." Sully stared at the ceiling as if Chuck wasn't there, ticking off days on his fingers. "I been drinking ice water. Non-stop. And coffee. Ugh, a ton of it." He straightened and took a sip, as if to demonstrate.

"What are you using for cream, grain alcohol?"

"I'm fine." Sully lit a cigarette. "I got a little heavy with that vodka—her drink. Should of stuck to Guinness. We usually never drank hard stuff in the neighborhood, did we?"

Chuck ordered coffee and a gyros. He ate little when he wasn't sleeping but found himself craving the greasy staple of his teens. He chewed in silence while Sully rambled about his girlfriend, Consuelo, and her asshole son, who wouldn't put him up even for one night. He explained how his last boss had cheated him while pretending to give him a break. The landlord was out to get him, too, had been from day one. Sully claimed to have run his own painting business for a while (probably a few side jobs, Chuck thought), until Jim O'Rourke, his friend and partner, screwed him over. He puffed furiously as he complained, smoke blooming like gray foliage. From details Sully let slip, Chuck guessed that these people actually had tried to help, but of course, he would never see it that way. He wanted to blame everyone and everything—except drinking—for his problems. If Chuck couldn't see that ragged face across the booth, Sully might have convinced him his life was perfectly normal apart from some puzzling betrayals and a run of bad luck.

As soon as he finished it, Chuck regretted the sandwich, which lurched in his gut like a living thing. He would sleep better if he didn't eat out so much, but he rarely felt like cooking. When he did, he ate leftovers for a week.

As he led Sully to the car, a growling northbound jet seemed to hover over Midway, frozen in its ascent. The noise, no more noticeable than his pulse when Chuck lived here, now sounded like the roar of some beast freed from a fairytale. Watching the plane's labored arc, he realized how the restaurant had changed. The old place had been torn down and rebuilt to the exact same proportions fifty yards east, probably for plane clearance when the airport expanded. How had he not noticed that right away?

Chuck bounced the car out of the parking lot. He didn't have real plans for tonight but always felt vaguely late for something. The later he felt, the tighter the bubble in his gut. It had expanded steadily as he drove south, past the rusted semi-trailers, empty rail yards, and weed-filled lots that lined the Stevenson. The trip had the opposite effect of his dull conversations with Tony, he supposed, because on the phone he could imagine his friend's existence on the South Side from a safe distance. Visiting the old neighborhood left no buffer, nothing between him and the grim sights of a life barely averted.

"They have all kinds of people," Chuck said of New Horizons, "tradesmen, lawyers, bums off the street. They all have a problem. That's why they're together."

Sully grunted, shifting in his seat, unable to get comfortable. "Fucking Sammy. Four years I worked for him, then I sit home while kids who can't hold a paintbrush get calls."

"A lot of these guys, their lives are fucked up because they can't see they have a problem." Chuck surprised himself by repeating the clichés he'd mocked yesterday, but he had to make Sully see his situation, to cut through the thicket of excuses that obscured it.

Sully pulled out cigarettes, squinting into the pack as if he had no idea what it contained. His hands shook trying to light a match. Had he controlled this shaking earlier or was there something about heading north, away from the security of the South Side, that made him nervous? He inhaled deeply twice then stubbed out the butt on his palm. Carefully, he returned the unsmoked half to the pack.

Pretending not to notice, Chuck sipped his coffee, which was both bitter and too sweet. He knew he shouldn't drink it. Caffeine at any hour aggravated his insomnia.

They passed the terminal for the new el line that connected Midway to the Loop, a futuristic building of glass and steel. Cicero Avenue was widened as part of the airport expansion. Landscaping and shops replaced seedy motels. Only the Comfort Zone remained. Chuck was almost relieved to see the familiar building, a metallic seventies structure perched over its parking lot on brown pillars whose paint flaked off like diseased bark—the last of the hourly-rate motels. He wondered if the prostitutes were gone too. In high school, they made a game of approaching working girls, then peeling out, reluctant to admit that an experience appealing in theory was, up close, squalid and frightening. One time, a girl jumped in the back seat and refused to budge. They sped away blindly to shake her, but the farther they drove, the more she seemed in control, refusing to get out until someone paid. Chuck finally took up a collection. She left then, but her perfume lingered, so powerful that for years, when the windows were closed, he thought he could smell it on his upholstery.

"She said she'd call me at your place tonight," Sully said casually.

"My place? You're not going to be at my place."

"Just for tonight."

There was a hint of the old confidence, Chuck thought. Amazing. This was Sully's plan all along. He never intended to check into New Horizons, just wanted a fresh nest to shelter old habits. What made him think that Chuck, Chuck of all people, would agree to that? Sully begged and wheedled, but he held firm. If Sully wasn't going to New Horizons, Chuck said, he'd drop him off now, wherever he wanted.

"Fine. Consuelo. Take me to Connie's." He pouted like a petulant five-year-old, but panic flashed across his face when

Chuck turned the car around. He didn't feel guilty. He was doing exactly what the experts at the hotlines encouraged.

"I hope she's there." Sully's resentment was gone, their argument already forgotten. A few raindrops pelted the car. "I always find her. We joke about how good I am at finding her."

Chuck imagined Sully's panicked searches for his lush of a girlfriend, the desperation that conjured her face on distant bar stools and anonymous corners, the places, unlikely and familiar, where he discovered his love. *Consuelo* sounded Hispanic, but he couldn't imagine Mexicans hanging out in the neighborhood, or Sully dating one. He'd grown up in the Village, the most insular, narrow-minded part of Clearing. Maybe she wasn't Mexican—someone just liked the sound, and the name didn't mean a thing.

No one was home at Consuelo's son's house or at the house she cleaned twice a month. As the rain grew heavier, Sully's shakes went from noticeable to uncontrollable. He slapped his hands onto his thighs, but after a few seconds, they flitted around like birds without a branch to land on. He's starting to feel it, Chuck thought, withdrawal.

"Where could she be?" Sully said, frantic and soaked from dashing through rain to knock on doors.

His pathetic quest for her, which angered Chuck at first, now softened him in a way that the shaking and the eviction story and the sad pretense of being okay hadn't.

"Tommy, look at me," Chuck said. "You need help, man. You need a doctor."

All he needed, he insisted, was Connie. They sat in the stuffy car, windows fogging while they argued. Twice Sully scrambled out the door, and Chuck coaxed him back like a parent bribing a moody child. He felt as if the rain was falling inside his groggy head. He hadn't slept in three days and wanted nothing more than to go home. If they'd reached this point when Sully seemed all right, Chuck would have left him on a corner, but he'd heard of guys slipping into comas, hurting themselves, even dying from withdrawal. He had to get Sully to a hospital.

He made a deal. Sully could stay with him tonight if he saw a doctor first. He had no intention of bringing Sully to his place, but if he could get him to the emergency room at County, which was on the way home, no doctor would release him in this state. They would stick him in detox, and Chuck could leave cab fare to the halfway house.

As they reached the expressway, clogged with rain and rush-hour traffic, Sully rocked in the passenger seat, sweating and shaking all over.

"Ah. I can't do this," he moaned. "I need a can of beer. Something."

The bubble beneath Chuck's ribs contracted in painful spasms. He didn't know withdrawal could appear so suddenly or with such wrenching physical effect. It reduced Sully to a pathetic mess, willing to sacrifice all for the thing that landed him here in the first place.

"You'll be okay." Chuck's words sounded weak in his own ears. "They'll give you something to take the edge off. You need something."

"Yeah, a big creamy pint." A laugh gurgled in his throat but came out a whimper.

When they turned onto Wilson Avenue at 3 a.m., Sully roused himself and locked the car door. Another delusion, Chuck thought, but he supposed anyone from lily-White Clearing, especially the Village, would be paranoid in East Ravenswood. The men drinking in front of the Uptown Tap were Black and so was the woman in the yellow mini-skirt smoking on the corner. On the South Side, Whites left when Blacks moved in. Neighborhoods changed for the worse or not at all. Here, you could see subtle improvements every week. Second-hand stores were becoming hip instead of seedy, attracting a younger crowd each year. Once-threatening dive bars grew comfortable, and streets that Chuck wouldn't have driven in daylight, he now walked alone at night. The value of his place could double, the realtor said, if he stayed put while the neighborhood changed around him.

"He's going to be okay," the emergency room doctor had said, releasing Sully over Chuck's protests. "He's lucky to have family."

"I'm not family," Chuck said, but the doctor was gone, already on to the next patient.

By then Chuck was almost delirious himself, eyes swollen, legs trembling from lack of sleep. In the waiting room, a nurse starting her shift asked if anyone had checked his vitals and didn't seem to believe him when he said he wasn't a patient. The air of desperation typical in emergency rooms was worse at County not because of poverty, Chuck thought, but because the sick were so inured to their suffering. No one complained about his ailment or the wait, not even a man with a grizzled beard who sat holding a bloody cloth to his head until he gently slumped onto the floor and was whisked away on a gurney.

They waited five hours for a doctor, five hours while Sully saw double, shaking like a cartoon character beaned by a falling branch. He returned from smoking out front to report a conversation with Pete "the Greek" Panayiotis, who'd died in high school. He talked to Jon Glab and Mikey Boylan, jailed for manslaughter at twenty, and Conn Keehan, the owner of Chief O'Neill's pub, came by to apologize.

At his condo, Chuck guided Sully down the steps. He sat him on the couch while he put everything risky or valuable out of reach, quietly disposing of mouthwash, isopropyl, beers, cash, and credit cards. He and Lennie had child-proofed the condo in a frenzy when her sister showed up unexpectedly with the kids, but this was the first time he had to drunk-proof it.

He caught the scent of Lennie's apple shampoo as he covered the couch with a thick down comforter, her only forgotten possession. He sometimes thought of her showing up to claim it. They'd be nervous at first, but he would make a joke and disarmed, she would sit, noting that the apartment hadn't changed, other than the gaps left by her furniture and prints. They would talk while he looked for the comforter, catching up on family and mutual friends, warming to conversation.

"What'd you say?" Sully asked, and Chuck realized he'd mouthed his interior dialogue.

"I said, I'll fix that pill for you." He gave Sully water and sawed a Valium in half as the doctor instructed. Half because they'd already pumped 1,200 milligrams through his I.V., enough to knock Chuck out for a week, the doctor promised, though it only eased Sully's anxiety slightly.

"What are you waiting for?" Chuck asked.

Sully's shaky hand scattered water like a sprinkler when he tried to drink. Exhausted, Chuck grabbed the glass, tilting it against his lips until he'd swallowed.

The next morning Chuck woke in a sunlit room. He lay still, his eyes adjusting to beams that slanted through the blinds like a ladder, motes of dust briefly illuminated by its rungs before drifting into hidden corners. The sight was strange both because the weather had been gray for days and because he rarely slept past the morning's first light, filtered weak and drab through the garden apartment's high windows. Stretching, he savored the smell of sleep, the pleasant ache of unused muscles, the weight of partial consciousness. He might have stayed in bed longer, even dozed off again, if not for Sully's smoke. The cigarette in the next room sharpened his senses, and he realized he was starving.

He called in sick to work and brought Sully with him to the Mexican grocery on the corner. They made a wide arc around two kids drinking in front of the boarded door of Uptown Liquors, but Sully didn't seem to notice. In the small store, Chuck bought bacon, potatoes, eggs, and tortillas. At the last minute, a pack of Kools and a bottle of water with a no-spill top.

Chuck ate more for breakfast than he had in days. Sully ate well, too, once Chuck rolled his eggs and potatoes into manageable burritos. He couldn't keep food on a fork.

"Where are we?" Sully said.

The question took Chuck by surprise. Sully seemed fine while they were eating, no conversations with phantoms or descriptions of things Chuck couldn't see.

"My condo."

He knew that, Sully said, irritated. How far north? Chuck explained that they were just off Lawrence, in East Ravenswood.

"I think it's Uptown."

Chuck smiled. "You're close. They call this section East Ravenswood. It's a little nicer than Uptown."

"It's dangerous." Wild-eyed, Sully watched the kitchen window, just above sidewalk-level, as if someone was attempting to break in—ridiculous, since it was protected by a steel grate. He was alert but couldn't seem to connect the details around him or see himself in a context rooted in reality.

Chuck postponed talk of New Horizons. He knew the argument about taking Sully to the halfway house would go better after a Valium, but despite the shakes and paranoia, he wouldn't take one. He obsessed over the pills—*How many'd they give me? How many'd I take? How many left?*—but refused them precisely because they gave relief, the idea of the drug more important than actual comfort. As the last dose wore off, he grew fuzzy, anxious, forgetful.

"I don't have a TV because I don't want one," Chuck said for the third time, Sully pointing out yet again that the price of TVs had dropped.

"Yeah, you should probably save up for furniture first," he conceded, "or see what old stuff your mom has. The apartment'll be aw-ight when you move in all the way. You should drywall over that rock, though, keep the damp out. Always drywall for a basement. I could do it, you want."

Chuck started to explain that his mom was dead, that he'd lived in the condo twelve years, that exposed stone was in, but stopped himself. Even if Sully weren't in a stupor, he might not know how condos worked or believe that Chuck's garden "apartment" was worth more than most houses in Clearing. Apparently, Sully thought a place had to be sloppy to look lived-in, which meant only the living room qualified, thanks to him. His rumpled blankets and pillow covered the couch, and the contents of his filthy bag overflowed onto the floor. Cigarette stumps formed a tiny clear-cut forest in the bowl he'd converted to an ashtray. That kind of mess normally would have set Chuck on edge, but fortified by a full night's sleep and a big breakfast, he hardly saw it. He needed to take more days off. How could he expect to sleep when he obsessed endlessly over work?

"No one's sticking me in a box," Sully said, convinced he would be locked in a cell at the halfway house when Chuck finally brought it up.

The more Chuck insisted that the people at New Horizons only wanted to help, the more Sully was convinced they were out to get him. He said he would leave rather than go there. He shuffled to the door to exercise that option, hugging his bag, disoriented and weaving, pulling on his only jacket, a windbreaker.

Irene called from the office during their argument, looking for a spreadsheet.

"So how are you doing?" she asked.

"Fine," Chuck said, thinking of how well he'd slept, then realized she meant Sully. "But I don't recommend Cook County Hospital, if you can avoid it," he added.

"My God, that bad? You poor thing. Is he there now? I knew you'd take him in."

"Well, a night or two," Chuck muttered.

"What have you been doing?"

"Talking. Maybe too much. I think he misses TV more than booze."

She was as shocked as Sully to hear that he didn't own a television. She had a small set, an extra, she said, and would bring it over. Chuck told her not to trouble. She insisted.

When he hung up, he told Sully he could stay through the weekend. Chuck would feel like a fool if Irene showed up with a TV for someone who wasn't there, and abandoning Sully in this state would look worse to Tony and the guys than if Chuck had done nothing at all. The doctor said that in three or four days he should be out of the woods, meaning through detox and the worst physical symptoms of withdrawal. After that, Sully could go to the halfway house, back to the South Side, or wherever he wanted.

"There's one rule," Chuck said. "No booze. One drop and I'll throw your ass out. I mean it. And if you're staying here, you go to AA meetings. Every day."

That evening Chuck met Irene outside his building. She wore a short black skirt and a blue silk blouse untucked beneath her jacket. She had changed out of her work clothes before coming to see him. He left her on the sidewalk while he brought Sully the TV and then took her to the Uptown Diner, across the street. The restaurant wasn't his first choice (homeless men sometimes wandered in looking for change), but from a window booth, he could watch the entrance to his building. He felt liberated when he walked outside, breathing deep, as if free of Sully, his babble, and his smoke for the first time in years.

"You actually eat here?" Irene asked, smoothing a tear in the vinyl seat patched with curling duct tape. She leaned across the booth, her face close to his.

"Usually just coffee. It's better than it used to be, if you can imagine."

She arched her eyebrows and laughed. He wanted to return her interest but found himself looking over her shoulder at his building. He'd saved the leftovers from lunch and pictured Sully trying to heat them on the stove with those shaky hands.

"You like Uptown?" she asked.

"Hmm? Well, I like East Ravenswood," he said. "This part of the neighborhood has big potential. It's more gentrified. Gentrifying, I guess."

"*East Ravenswood*. Fancy. No ravens and no woods, I bet, but sounds nice."

He'd scoured every inch of his place—no more money or booze, nothing containing alcohol—but felt as if he'd missed something important. He could see both exits, so there was no way for Sully to leave without his knowing. He fingered the bottle of Valium in his pocket. The doctor had warned him of desperate addicts self-medicating in ways that stopped their hearts as well as distress.

"You poor thing. You seem sleepy." She laid her hand on his.

"No, I slept well," he said, and then remembered: Halcion. Half a bottle on his nightstand, more in the drawer. The sleeping pills were such a part of his routine he didn't even see them when cleaning out his condo. "Sorry, I've got to go. I forgot something."

Irene insisted on going with him. Chuck waited at the door, antsy while she collected her things and paid the bill he'd forgotten.

Back at the condo, Sully sat on his usual perch, watching the news, less than frantic for the first time since he arrived. The sleeping pills were untouched.

Sully thanked Irene for the TV.

"Know who she looks like?" Sully said. "You remember Maeve, from O'Neill's?"

"Hotty?" Irene asked.

"Dreamy but not in your league," Sully said, a trace of the ladies' man showing through the wreckage.

Chuck promised to call Irene later, leaning in for a hug when she left. His arms curled inside an open coat whose soft lining enclosed them so comfortably, he lingered.

"Hey, get a room!" Sully laughed, and they parted.

Each night, Chuck stayed up watching reruns with Sully—*Happy Days, Gilligan's Island, Lost in Space*—shows he loved as a kid but twenty years later found painful. When he finally crept to bed, Sully woke him every few hours—smoking, mumbling, crying. Chuck would pretend to get up for water or the bathroom and then sit in the living room. He told every old story he could think of and when he ran out, invented new ones. He delivered pep talks so confidently, even he felt better. One night, he woke at 3 a.m. to the sound of Sully's tearful singing:

> Last night as I lay dreaming of pleasant days gone by,
> My mind being bent on rambling, to Ireland I did fly.
> I stepped on board a vision, and followed with a will…

Chuck scrambled to interrupt before the neighbors pounded.

"You ever see Tony Almos?" he asked, water in hand. He sat on the arm of the couch, pretending interest in an infomercial for a garden tool called the Weed Waster.

"No." Sully's voice cracked. Neither of them acknowledged that he'd been crying. "Sounds like a bong, man, don't it?

Tired of being half stoned? Get higher than you been in years with The Weed Waster." Sully sat up. "Hey, you don't have any—"

"I haven't smoked in forever."

In silence, they watched a bearded man with a trimmer clear a border in seconds, smiling as if mowing down the barriers to a better life.

"Tony don't ever want to go out," Sully said. "When he does, he won't shut up about kids. Had so many, thinks he's everyone's daddy now. If I wanted to get shit about drinking at the Crow's Nest I'd talk to my old man."

Chuck laughed. "The Crow's Nest? Not Chief O'Neill's?"

Sully waved a hand in disgust, signaling that he'd moved on from his old haunt for good. "What about Al?"

"Al don't stop working long enough for a beer." Sully paused after the word, which hovered in the room, ghost-like. "You remember his cousin Beaver, from Blue Island? They opened a business. Landscaping and tree removal, out of the space back of Dmitri's. Quit their jobs and everything—same time I did. Hey, you think Al knows about the Weed Waster?"

Chuck laughed. He could imagine what sort of business that would be, grown men mowing lawns for a living. He wondered about Sully's "business," too, whether he really started one or put a brave face on the work he scrounged after getting fired for drinking on the job.

Sully banged his heel on the old cedar chest where his feet rested. A cracked leather strap circled the stuffed box like a belt restraining a gut. The beat-up antique looked like it belonged to some unlucky marauder, stuck with the treasure other pirates let go.

"I can't believe you carried this up here. You still keep the old records in there?"

"Haven't dusted one off in years, but yeah, they're in there," Chuck said.

They talked about music, arguing about *The Grateful Dead* (both fans but for different reasons) and comparing notes on the concert that changed their lives, *The Rolling Stones* in '89 for both, though they went separately.

"Why didn't you call me?" Chuck asked after a moment. The Weed Waster flashed again on the TV, along with a bonus attachment, available for a limited time only.

"You had your own ticket," Sully said.

"I mean when you were stuck at the Comfort Zone. You called everyone else."

"Yeah, Tony said I should call you."

"He did?"

"Yeah. He said, 'The one you should call is Chuck. It'd be good for him.'"

He could see Tony planting the idea in Sully's cloudy head and having a laugh, then coaxing Chuck to call Sully, too, for good measure. No wonder Sully had been confident Chuck would let him stay. As a joke on Chuck, Tony's setup was warped, but screwing with Sully that way was cruel.

"So why didn't you call me?" Chuck asked.

"I didn't know we kept the same hours." Sully smiled, waving a shaky hand. "Or that you'd want the company."

Chuck couldn't decide if he was more angry or amused. Did Sully think 4 a.m. was his regular bedtime? Did he think Chuck always lingered over big dinners and bad TV, leaving his condo only for groceries? He had no idea how he upended Chuck's life.

By Saturday, Sully's foggy perception began to clear. His body still buzzed like a chainsaw, but the anxiety eased. With each meal, color seeped from the ruddy circles on his cheeks into the rest of his cadaverous face, and Chuck began to take pride in his cooking: steaks, fajitas, linguine with clam sauce, each meal more elaborate than the last. He had less success with the idea of AA. Sully had a way of refusing to attend a meeting and then, as Chuck got angry, promising that he would go the next day, when he felt better.

On Sunday, he made yet another round of calls trying to locate Consuelo. He propped the pathetic suitcase to which his life had been reduced onto his lap, spreading scraps of paper with names and numbers across the makeshift desk, muttering to himself as he decided which ones to dial. When he'd finished, the arm of the couch where he'd sat smelled like a diaper. Chuck realized Sully hadn't taken a shower since he'd arrived and talked him into one. The clothes in his suitcase were dirty, so Chuck loaned him some. He added Sully's things to his own and together they hauled a massive load to the laundry room.

Shampoo bottles, towels and a bar of soap littered the floor after Sully's hour-long shower. Water covered every surface. The curtain was torn where he'd clutched it. After washing up, he sat wrapped in a towel on the toilet seat for a shave. Chuck pulled up a chair, their knees brushing in the cramped space. His hand trembled as he held the razor.

"I didn't know the shakes were contagious," Sully said.

"Laugh away, wise guy, I'm holding the blade." It was easy once Chuck plunged in, finding the right angle and pressure for someone else's face, as long as he didn't think too much about what he was doing.

"You ever consider going back to Karen?"

Sully shrugged. Only his hands appeared to shake, but through the razor, Chuck could feel his whole being tremble.

"They used flat in here." Sully rolled his eyes upward while trying to maintain a steady face. "Should have gone semi-gloss—ain't no exhaust. Sloppy, too. Look at that trim."

"What happened, Sully?"

"You know hardly anyone calls me that anymore. Everyone gets half a name with you. Woodchuck." Chuck held the razor away as Sully laughed. "No one's pulled that out in a while, I bet." He ran a hand across the clean left side of his face before offering the lathered right. "She turned into a bitch is what happened." He said this after a preoccupied minute, as if replaying old arguments in his head. "*Where you been? Where you going? You know how late it is?* Try living with that broken record. I never liked orders."

Chuck wanted to hoist him in front of the mirror. Did he think he was better off now, homeless and alone, dependent on another man in this embarrassing way?

"Not just with Karen, though, I mean everything," Chuck said. "How'd you get here?"

He nicked Sully's chin, wincing as if he'd cut himself, but Sully didn't notice. He launched into the same speech he gave at Mythos Gyros the day Chuck picked him up. He blamed his boss, his landlord, his wife. Consuelo's son and their old friends from the neighborhood. *He* was fine. He would get some work, a decent apartment, and he'd be fine. *Fine.* But he couldn't muster his earlier conviction. Listening, it became clear to Chuck why Sully kept drinking. Drunk, he no longer had a failed marriage, he had freedom. He wasn't homeless, he just had less to take care of. He was never lonely either. There were always people in a bar and after a few drinks, he was one of them, part of the friendly, anonymous crowd.

Chuck cleaned the razor and left Sully to dress. He started fifteen minutes later when Sully emerged from the bathroom, Chuck's khakis and wool sweater floating around his gaunt frame. He looked like a boy lost in the men's department, trying on things that would be out of style by the time he grew into them.

Chuck set Monday as the deadline for getting Sully into a halfway house. He'd missed two full days of work and had a meeting on Tuesday that he couldn't skip, but when he got out of the shower that morning, Sully was gone, the backdoor open. He pulled on his clothes. At the corner, Chuck spotted him crossing Lawrence Avenue. Sully walked straight toward him, then continued, as if blind.

"I talked to those guys," Sully said after Chuck guided him back to the condo. He had trouble focusing his eyes as well as his thoughts.

"What guys?"

Two men from AA had stopped by while Chuck was in the shower. They tried to talk Sully into rehab, but he wouldn't go. Chuck had given the man at the United Way hotline his name but no address. Did they look him up just to check on Sully?

"They said, *Come with us, Tommy. Give New Horizons a chance. Please?*"

"Did you buzz them in?" Chuck asked.

"They met me up on the street when I went to get Lifesavers. They walked me back here. I needed something sweet."

"Sully, that was me. I met you on the street. We walked back together just now."

He looked as if he couldn't decide whether his version of things or Chuck's made more sense. "Pete 'the Greek' warned me about them," he said, as if this was a key point, evidence in his favor. "He told me not to go."

Chuck pictured Pete halfway to manhood, the point when a car accident froze his memory forever: arrogant and insecure, childish and muscle-bound, a heap of adolescent incongruities. Sully's wandering eyes rested over Chuck's shoulder and he felt a chill, afraid for a moment that if he turned around, he, too, would see Pete "the Greek's" shade. Sully was as disoriented as the last time he'd conjured Pete, on the steps of Cook County Hospital. His pupils wandered, black specks lost in a blue fog. Once again, he needed Chuck's help every time he sipped water. They were supposed to go back to the hospital if his condition worsened, but Sully refused. Chuck tried to bribe him with the prospect of Valium—he'd taken his last pill the night before—but not even that promise could lure him back to County.

Chuck went to bed that evening dreading insomnia, which returned as if by appointment. Sully whimpered in the next room, but Chuck knew that if he got up tonight, he would lose his temper. The harder he tried to relax, the faster his heart pounded.

The rasp of a lighter flicked in his ears four times, five, seven, until Sully finally lit his cigarette. Chuck counted the seconds until he smelled smoke—six exactly. A few more, and it began to smother him. Eyes closed, he imagined the room filling with smoke. He turned onto his back, his stomach, his side again, his mind racing to the rhythm of Sully's babble. Toward dawn, he dozed for an hour. He dreamed that he was trapped in a forest fire, branches snapping, smoke stinging his eyes, a painful heat fanned by wind and his own flight. He ran as fast as he could, but the fire engulfed everything at his heels and eventually, his clothes. Choking on smoke, he collapsed in an open field burned to stubble.

That morning, Sully's usual calls to find Consuelo took on a new urgency.

"You gave her my number, right?" Chuck asked. "And she hasn't called you once. She can't pick up the phone to see if you're breathing, and she's all you think about."

"I care about her. I don't like being this far from Connie."

"*Connie, Connie, Connie.* You think she's worrying about you right now?" The question burst from Chuck like a sob. "Shouldn't you worry about yourself?"

"I'm fine."

"Fine? You're living on my couch, and you look like death. You spend your nights talking to people who aren't there. You've lost your wife and your home and your friends and everything else that won't fit in that bag. And you think you're fine? You need help."

"I don't need help."

The old Sully would have swung at him, and the weak response worried Chuck as much as anything. Consuelo, who possessed him as powerfully as alcohol, was a major obstacle. As long as Sully had her, or imagined he might, things could always be worse—something, however insubstantial, stood between him and complete despair. He needed to see rock bottom. It was close enough to touch, but he would never recognize it with Connie there to keep him company.

"You should be out of this phase by now." Chuck spoke more softly, to himself as much as Sully. "I have to go back to work. I can't watch you twenty-four hours. This wasn't the plan. The doctor said you should see him if things got worse, but you won't go. You said you'd go to the halfway house, but you won't. You said you'd go to meetings—"

"I'll go to a meeting."

He reached for this option like a stumbling child who grabs a branch covered in bird shit to stop a fall, but Chuck couldn't help feeling a flash of hope.

"Today? There's one at New Horizons in an hour."

Chuck could taste cigarettes as he entered his condo. The walls were cured in smoke. Smoke had fouled his furniture, his clothes, the bedroom carpet—more present somehow than when Sully was there, camped out on the couch with a lit cigarette. He'd left a window open, a risk even with the steel grate, but it only turned the place frigid. Methodically, he mopped the hardwood floors in a fog, steam billowing in the cold air. There wasn't much furniture to move, and he worked quickly. When he finished, the place still felt somehow shabby. He continued cleaning until there was nothing left—every book shelved, corner swept, appliance scrubbed. Smoke lingered under the piney scent of mopped floors, but the condo was almost back to normal.

The bubble in Chuck's gut swelled, his discomfort all the worse after a pause. He hadn't noticed its disappearance, distracted by Sully's antics, only its return. He drew a hot bath, thinking that might help. He was chin-deep when the phone rang. He hoisted himself and ran to the living room naked, water cascading over freshly mopped floors.

"Chuck, what's wrong?" Irene asked as soon as he said hello.

"Nothing. Everything's fine. How have you been?"

"Is it your friend?"

He told her that Sully left that afternoon. "He fell off the wagon. No surprise there."

"Oh, Chuck, I'm sorry. Do you want to talk?"

"No, thanks. I'm fine. Really."

She offered to come over, to buy him dinner, to go for coffee. He practically had to hang up on her to get her off the phone. She sounded so determined, he wouldn't be surprised if she showed up anyway. He'd thought of her calls and the loan of a TV as simple kindness. Now they seemed pushy. He unplugged her television and placed it near the door, so he would remember to return it tomorrow.

Sully had gotten ready that afternoon and gone to the meeting as agreed. "I hate shit like this," he said on the way. "I hope they don't think I'm talking or nothing." Chuck had to steer him into the hall, where he sat behind a pillar— the one obscured spot in the open room—like a kid hiding behind a tree to avoid chores. He worked to ignore everyone around him.

Chuck waited at home for the meeting to end. He felt trapped. His boss wouldn't give him any more time off work. He couldn't leave Sully alone in the condo and couldn't kick him out—he had nowhere to go. Sully's suitcase overflowed onto the floor. Chuck searched the filthy bag as if it contained answers. He rummaged through the clothes he'd washed and folded, Sully's tattered phone book and papers. His shaving kit. A framed photo of Consuelo. At least, Chuck assumed it was her—thinning hair and swollen eyes, fat a man could get lost in rounding her middle. As he shoved the clothes back, Chuck noticed something red peeking from his cedar chest. He opened it. A shirt was caught in the hinge. He unhooked it and poked through more outdated clothes, old photos, worn yearbooks. Records by bands long defunct.

He didn't know what he was looking for until he found it, actually not even then. He pulled the empty fifth of Southern Comfort from the bottom of the chest and stared, unable at first to connect it to Sully. How had the bottle gotten here? Sully had left the apartment during the night a couple times—for air, he said later when Chuck found the deadbolt undone—but how had he found the means? The one place Chuck didn't search that first night was Sully's own bag. Maybe he brought the whiskey with him. Maybe he had money hidden away. Whatever its source, his relapse was no longer a mystery. He had gone through withdrawal, briefly satisfied a need, and then started withdrawal all over, a deadly cycle.

Chuck was waiting outside New Horizons when the AA meeting ended. He handed Sully his suitcase and the empty bottle.

"That's from before," Sully said. "I haven't drank nothing."

"You want, I'll take you to rehab right now."

"I didn't drink nothing."

They argued, Sully protesting, Chuck turning the conversation back to rehab but getting nowhere.

"If you decide you want to change your life and go to rehab, call me." Chuck walked away, Sully still pleading and wheedling, following him to his car like an aggressive beggar.

At the corner, he glanced back. In Chuck's oversized clothes, Tommy O'Sullivan clutched his suitcase in the street, a solitary figure, frozen and rattled, blindsided by yet another person who'd actually tried to help. Chuck had done his best to strip away Sully's excuses and illusions. He gave him an opening to see what he'd become and the space in which to change. Sully had his moment of clarity and denied it. Chuck slowed for a moment, transfixed by the man framed in his rearview mirror, then forced himself to drive on.

Lost and Found

"Please, don't get off at North Avenue. It looks like a bomb hit it," she said. "Construction. Take Division instead."

Dakhil Ben-Ali had seen only a flash of pink as the bony figure in the bright suit alighted in his cab like a flamingo. Now he noted her tense eyes and brow, the portion of the earnest face that fit in his rearview mirror. She was late seventies trying to look forty, makeup so thick it resembled a mask. He'd noticed this drawn look on the faces of wealthy old women in this country. Plastic surgery, someone explained, flesh gathered and stretched taut over bones, then tucked in to tighten the skin. They always looked severe, such women, as if they lost natural feeling along with their wrinkles.

Thinking that the flash of curious eyes in the mirror meant that he did not understand her, Candace Pound repeated herself in the slow, strident tone often substituted for a common language. "Do you know Division Street?"

"Of course," he said. "I will take it if you like."

She could not see his expression—just a coal-black cheek in need of a shave, half a curving walrus moustache—but his tone was haughty. There is no need to get excited, he seemed to say, or to talk to me as if I were your child. Well, why didn't he acknowledge her then instead of looking vacantly in the mirror? She had uttered some pleasantry when climbing into his cab at the jewelry shop (a handsome tip paid in advance, like the fare, because they gouged you on long trips unless you got a flat rate). He'd offered only a tight-lipped smile in response. How was she to know his English was good?

The Division Street exit was backed up, cars almost touching as drivers worked to close the gaps others might squeeze through

"Oh no. It's a beautiful day at least, isn't it?" Candace said, to show she hadn't meant any harm. She was not the type to talk down to cabbies and clerks. She was closer to Sergio, her doorman, than to any of her neighbors.

The driver gave a curt nod, and she realized how dull her observation must sound.

"My son is arriving Thursday from California, and he hates the humidity. He refuses to come back to the city in summer. Or winter—too cold. We have the worst of all worlds, he says. There's only a brief window when seeing each other in Chicago is even a possibility."

She spoke, a little breathlessly, through a square opening in the bulletproof wall of cloudy plastic that separated the front and back seats—the confessional, some drivers called it, and had to explain that odd rite of redemption to Dakhil. The slot was just big enough for financial transactions and could be sealed by sliding closed a small panel, also bulletproof. The biggest risk in keeping it open was not theft, but customers like this, people who went on as if they'd purchased a lover, not a lift.

"San Diego has a nice even temperature," she was saying, "but California feels so fake, everyone concerned with meeting the right people, being seen, making connections…"

Sixteen hours, he thought. Anything less today and he would not make rent. The old Jew had put him on notice: one more late payment and he would find himself homeless.

"Michael hates to leave the sun and beach even for a weekend. It's been three years since he was home, nearly a year since I saw him."

One year. Dakhil maintained a blank expression—even a flicker of annoyance could be taken as invitation. He had not seen his family in nine years and wondered if he ever would again. He woke sometimes and, lost at the feverish intersection of dawning consciousness and lingering dream, could hear his father snore, taste Nimo's sambusa, smell salt waves battering the strand. For an instant, he truly felt the place he was—only he wasn't there at all. When fighting cut Marka into hostile little zones and he crossed into Ethiopia, UNHCR labeled him a "displaced person." At first, he thought they said "misplaced," which felt more accurate than "refugee," a word he later learned came from "refuge" but meant something like its opposite.

"A year…" She shook her head, sad, amazed, excited.

The taxi jerked to a stop at Halsted. In a trash-strewn lot on the corner, a man sold giant rugs from a van. Gaudy squares emblazoned with animal designs surrounded him like woven cages. Gorillas, peacocks, and tigers stared blankly ahead as if pretending indifference while plotting escape, each unaware of his neighbors' parallel plans. The CHA highrise behind the van had suffered a fire. Soot was smeared like eyeshadow above rows of boarded windows.

The car's locks snapped shut. She started. He sensed her reaction and smiled in the mirror, a sincere smile, but apologetic or amused? She felt a flash of panic, as if he'd locked her in to drive down an alley where he might rob her or force some unwanted intimacy without obstacle. Instinctively, she reached for her purse and realized she'd been clutching it to her chest with one hand, keys gripped like a gun in the other as they drove through Cabrini-Green, past shabby towers and aimless young men, drinking and smoking on the street, walking blindly into traffic, ignoring the possibility of collisions against the blare of horns.

He'd noticed her unease, of course. He'd locked the doors for her.

Candace felt relief but also embarrassment. She did not want to be seen that way. She couldn't imagine what it was like, being part of the fractured families that populated the projects' grim, identical blocks. She looked for potential in every face she passed. Forcing herself to lean back in the cab, she uncoiled the strap from her hand and set her bag casually on the seat.

"My son's fiancé couldn't make it," she said. Her nerves, already taut, strained in the silence of the stuffy cab. She wanted to open a window but was reluctant to do so. "I met her last year, in San Diego—barely. She's very busy. It's too bad she couldn't come on this trip, but it will be nice in a way, just the two of us."

There was no one Dakhil knew well enough to ask for a loan or, if it came to that, a place to sleep. He'd spent his first nights in Chicago at The Babylon Arms, a flophouse on the West Side where chicken wire separated your ten-by-ten square and the wooden palette at its center from the next man's. Nothing separated you from the rants of the drunk and insane, though, the odors of sweat and piss and alcohol pressing on every side. He would sleep in a park before he returned to a place like that. Idly, he wondered if his father saved anything from the small amounts he sent home. Of course, Dakhil could never ask him for money.

"I've planned other trips to San Diego, but Michael's work always gets in the way. Once I booked without checking.

I was going to surprise him. I'll never do that again." She rolled her eyes and smiled.

Another tight-lipped nod. Was he this cold to everyone or only those who tipped in advance? She knew she was running on, but the cabby's silence and the feeling that she'd offended him created a space that some part of her needed to fill. And then there was Michael's visit. Her emotions rose closer to the surface with each day it approached. She found herself going on about it to hairdressers, waiters, bank tellers. It was only four days, a long weekend, but after that last fiasco in San Diego, she was determined to do everything right. She took care of the most important detail today at the jewelry store. The surprise had struck her in an instant, one of those revelations that transcends life's tidy compartments to make a connection so basic you wonder you didn't see it all along. She only hoped she could hold out until Sunday. No matter what else happened, that final gesture, recognizing old bonds and marking a new one, would guarantee a goodbye that felt like its opposite, like the start of something.

In heavy traffic, they inched across the narrow no-man's land along the el tracks, the weedy strip between Cabrini-Green and the Gold Coast. A truck double-parked, blocking the street. Dakhil honked. Lazily, the truck's shirtless Mexican driver raised his middle finger. Dakhil found himself stuck in the intersection, harassed by cross-traffic. He laid on the horn a full minute, until a break in the oncoming cars allowed him to pass.

"Where are you from, Dak-ill?" she asked nervously, mispronouncing his name from the city license posted on the dashboard.

"Marka. Somalia—I did not want to come here," he blurted as if she accused him of something. "My father made me come here." In his mind, he faced the truck driver, yelling the things he hadn't said when he had the chance.

"Why?"

He glanced in the mirror to see if she was serious. "You heard of Somalia? Mogadishu? The city is at war." It was best to pretend poor English, but he'd slipped. It was too late.

"Yes. Yes, of course." She thought of the way she'd described the construction on North Avenue, *like a bomb hit it*. Had that offended him? Finding your way as a foreigner in Chicago could not be easy, but they seemed so defensive and short-sighted these days, ignoring the opportunities in front of them until it was too late.

"Your poor mother."

"I don't have a mother." Dakhil imagined clamping one hand around the Mexican truck driver's throat and hitting him square in the face with the other.

"I'm sorry," she said.

"Why, did you know her?"

Her skin went cold, the hairs on her arms bristling against her blouse. "I didn't mean—forgive me. It's just something one says."

For the first time since she'd entered the cab, the old woman was silent, but she shifted anxiously, and he feared she would start again.

"We lost her in childbirth. She died giving birth to me." In the rearview mirror, he saw her mouth open to speak, and he cut her off. He described the blood that stained his mother's bed, the screams that filled the night, the blame his father attached to him, though he was only halfway in this world, stuck in its doorway when accused of the crime.

"Oh, they're doing more construction on LaSalle too." She clucked her tongue.

"My father was happy when the fighting got worse. An excuse to kick me out."

Her face twitched. Should she ignore him, smile in empathy, express the horror his story inspired? How had this happened? She'd managed to offend him by trying to avoid just that, talking about the weather, directions, his home, nothing really. He offered hardly a grunt in response but now felt compelled to relate dark family history.

"As a boy, I used to imagine my mother was alive." His eyes returned to the street. His voice grew quiet as he forgot himself and his passenger. "One day, I thought, she will find me. We will talk, and she will take me away. I waited for her at our door, searched the eyes of passing women through the openings in their hijabs for a sign that they knew me, but…"

He pulled into the horseshoe drive on Dearborn. A large man in a dark blue suit approached, favoring one leg.

"Hello, Mrs. P." He opened the car door and attached himself to her elbow.

"Thank you," Candace said to the driver, flustered as she bustled out of the cab. She hesitated, propping the door open with her hip, one foot on the pavement, the other in the taxi. She turned to say something else, but before she could find the words, Sergio led her away.

At her kitchen sink, Candace hummed as she turned the apples in her palm, paring awkwardly, red peels spreading like blood on white porcelain. As a girl, she'd removed the skin quickly, in one continuous ribbon, so fragile and fragrant it seemed a small miracle. She no longer had the patience or hands for that, but peeling a little at a time was satisfying, too, the naked fruit glistening and pure for a moment before exposure turned it.

She chopped the apples, sprinkled them with sugar and lemon juice, and set the bowl aside. Michael had loved her apple cake as a boy but would feel bad if he knew she'd baked it just for him. She would invent another reason. He was considerate, Michael, generous and sensitive, too sensitive for Chicago, which he found rough, provincial, even mean. He'd offered to take Candace West, but she'd lived in the Gold Coast nearly fifty years. He did not understand what it meant for a woman her age, having the whole world, the best of everything, in twenty square blocks—Oak Street boutiques, fine dining, familiar faces, the freedom to walk whenever you wanted, at least east of Wells.

She remained in the discarded part of Michael's life labeled *Chicago* as the barriers between it and his new home grew each year. He immersed himself in his work in San Diego, where he made partner before forty. She asked about his cases, genuinely interested, but he never said much, as if her questions were mere politeness. Unfortunately, his lawyerly reserve stirred the panic she felt at gaps, that nervous urge to fill them with chatter. She went on about having lunch with Mr. and Mrs. Ibis at the Standard Club—he'd been to school with their daughter Jael, did he remember?—the gold bracelets she'd bought at Barreaux d'Or, her revival of the family membership program at the Lincoln Park Zoo, where come January she would be number two on the auxiliary board, the interesting novel her book club had read, *Steppenwolf,* which apparently—did he know this?—was where the theater got its name...When she paused to catch her breath, she was met with silence, as if he lived in Mongolia, not California, and, rusty in her language, didn't understand a word.

Candace would ask about Susan then, as she always made a point to. He answered warily, expecting disapproval. That, Candace would never give, though the girl was cold, single-minded, the kind who put career above everything. She was all business whether ordering dinner, meeting Candace, or tending their pets—two African greys so territorial they were kept in separate rooms. The creepy parrots reminded Candace of Susan herself, solitary, intelligent things that puffed against their cages to stare, poised to bite any finger passed through the bars.

It seemed from the start as if Michael was trying to provoke his mother with Susan, to separate himself from home and family by pairing with the most exotic girl he could find. Not that Candace cared. Susan's family had come to the

U.S. from Vietnam with nothing and now owned a business and a nice home, all four of the kids college grads. They were obviously hardworking, the girl had come far. It was just the surprise of the thing, not realizing who this person was standing at the apartment door when Candace visited California last year.

Michael had been in the shower that first night in San Diego, when Susan startled her, arriving at the door just as Candace was stepping out for air. "Yes?" Candace said, staring blankly at the stranger, blocking the doorway, though she didn't mean to. She simply hadn't understood for a moment, even after the girl said, "I'm Sue" (*Susan*, Michael always called her). She might have been from the building or at the wrong door. Then Candace saw the leather briefcase and dress by Chanel, a tacky, ostrich-like affair. She recovered quickly, but her surprise must have been obvious. After that, the girl regarded her archly, with an icy grin.

Candace drew the blinds in the room she still thought of as Michael's and checked the bedding. She wanted him to feel at home. She had loved moving into the condominium on the twenty-third floor as much as she had circulating among Richard's set here, especially in those early years, when she realized she could hold her own with—even impress—the lawyers, bankers, and politicians who came to the parties she planned so meticulously. Her parents had been comfortable, fairly well-off actually, but not seating-charts and hired-chef well-off. Richard came from an established North Shore family, one with enough money that he didn't have to work—and yet he finished near the top of his class at U of C Law. She did not feel the sort of animal attraction for him that some men inspired but he was handsome and sweet, brilliant, a little shy. Her loquacious nature drew him out. His serenity calmed her. They seemed to complement each other so well, those first years felt like a dream.

And then one day—they slept in separate bedrooms by then—she realized she didn't love him. She hadn't noticed his carefully compartmentalized drinking until it was a serious problem. He developed a cruel streak. Their conversation faded into guarded pleasantries. The smallest misunderstandings turned ugly. They went days without seeing each other, but none of that explained why, in an instant—she remembered the Saturday evening it struck her—he seemed unrecognizable. One minute they were managing, and the next, she couldn't imagine continuing with him, any more than she could imagine serving a life term in a maximum-security prison.

Candace decided to move out. They would separate. She made detailed plans more than once, but inertia was her enemy. The more she considered it, the more insurmountable the situation became. So many things kept them tethered, none more complicated than Michael. In the end, she stayed for him. Richard literally had written the book on divorce, the one used in most Illinois law schools. He could make things ugly, apply financial pressure, maybe even gain custody, and Michael had such a nice life here—wonderful friends, the best schools. Where would they go if Richard declared war? She put on a brave face to keep Michael in the home he loved, but living there with a man who was suddenly a stranger, Candace felt more lost each day. The apartment seemed to shrink around her. Its roomy floor plan made her strangely self-conscious, aware at all times of where Richard was and of her own position in the condo, its place in the building, the building's location on the block, the block's within the city, and so on.

Michael went to California. Her friends retired, moved South, died. The group Candace called "the firm wives"—obsessed with complex workouts and simple cocktails—seemed to lose her number once Richard no longer worked with their husbands. Loneliness was bound to increase with age, but she kept busy—bridge on Tuesdays, a book club she loved, volunteer work for several charities and the Lincoln Park Zoo. She walked to wonderful restaurants each week—Spiaggia, NoMi, Les Contraires.

Candace's bohemian niece, Cynthia, visited regularly and moved in for a month after she left her live-in boyfriend, John. The unlikely pair went out for dinner and drinks, saw shows at the Art Institute, joked about attractive waiters and men generally. Candace felt like a girl again. If you looked past Cynthia's tattoos and outrageous clothes—and of course, Candace's skin—Cynthia almost seemed the older of the two. She liked to stay in, obsessed over black-and-white movies, loved elaborate home-cooked meals and old jazz.

"Was marriage the issue?" Candace asked on the couch over a bottle of merlot. *Side by Side*, a Duke Ellington album the girl loved, played low. She and John had stayed together, childless and unmarried, for a decade. "Did you want kids?"

"Only John—and I didn't know he was a kid until too late. When's the last time you saw someone? Any gentleman callers darkening your door?"

That was it. Next topic. Cynthia prided herself on openness but wouldn't discuss what had come between her and John. She said she didn't want children, but searching the girl's room for a lost book, Candace found pamphlets on artificial insemination. The term was as distasteful as the idea, fine for thoroughbreds but not her family. How could you trust a life to something so random? There would be information on the fathers, but could you be sure that the profile you planned so carefully matched what wound up inside you? Cynthia should have had a child naturally with John. The girl was determined to isolate herself, pretty but neglectful of her appearance, a romantic who mocked romance. She was desperate for warmth but, with an abrasiveness she labelled honesty, repelled anyone who came too close. Candace loved her because for a moment they'd been thrown together by circumstances, plans dashed, and through that unguarded crack, she glimpsed the real Cynthia. Most wouldn't.

Candace checked on the cake. She wanted it perfect for Michael, just like the ring. The jeweler had done a beautiful job, straightening the bent gold floret and resetting the loose side stones. Candace's great-grandmother had given it to her grandmother for an engagement ring. Candace's mom offered it for her wedding, too, but Candace wanted something new. In a rare moment of sharing—an auspicious sign, she thought—Michael had complained of his trouble finding a ring Susan liked, enough trouble that they stopped looking. Still, the idea did not strike Candace until she stumbled across it in a jewelry box that had been locked for years, opened by chance one day, nearly too late. As Michael started a new family, the ring would remind him of an older, bigger one, a link strained on the surface perhaps, but powerful, primal, still strong at its core.

The stink in Dakhil's studio was milder at mid-day but still powerful. The Indians were the worst, with their overpowering curries, but in long hallways, that odor combined with others, from Mexico, Turkey, Russia, who knew where. Aromas that were probably fine on their own clashed in tight quarters, and by dinnertime, the building smelled like a barn. His windows sat below the sidewalk, covered in steel mesh that blocked thieves but also sun and air. Odors did not escape his subterranean box easily. Breathing through his mouth, he took off his shoes and collapsed on the couch that was also his bed. He was desperate for a quick nap, but his mind bounced like a speedometer at rush hour, endlessly calculating what he had, how much he needed, the hours until rent was due. He thought of the prostitutes he occasionally brought back to this couch, the loneliness that caused him to buy them worse after the sad, brief pretense of love. He could feel their silent scorn when he grunted the fake names they gave, words he did not mean mumbled in their ears. He wanted to mean them, those words that came spilling out but worried that he never would, as if pretending had hurt his ability to speak the truth. He told himself that he rarely bought them and never spent much, but knew that the amount he lost this way would more than cover what he lacked now.

He was not attached to the apartment. He would be happy to leave it on his own terms, security deposit in hand, decent place waiting, but what job could he do that would pay for a better unit? He struggled his first year here, berated and cursed as he groped for addresses. In time, he absorbed Chicago's plan, the tidy grid with street numbers that fixed your location relative to State and Madison. He did not love this world but had grown comfortable in it, could now find blocks that even natives couldn't. He knew the official neighborhood boundaries, and the unofficial ones separating Black and White, Latin King and Vice Lord, posh and poor. He knew that women were bad tippers. He knew never to drive south of 18th Street or to stop for Black men under sixty. Some days, his cab felt like a cell on wheels. He longed for work that would let him move around, but knowledge of this city was his only American skill. He could not give up the money he made hacking to earn minimum wage on a loading dock or yard crew.

He had made good tips so far today, the best from that chatty old woman. Anger rose as he recalled her endless talk, but it was directed mostly at himself. She was harmless, boring but polite, better than most. Why had she bothered him so? Why did he make up that story about his family? When he was a child, Dakhil's mother had left his father for a Kenyan, a naturalized French citizen working at the Medecins Sans Frontieres clinic where she screened female patients. Somali mothers did not leave their families, not ever—only, his did. He often wanted to ask his father about her—their first meeting, what she liked, why she left—but couldn't without a beating. His father was cold, sometimes violent—understandable in a man whose only wife left him with three sons—but he never sent Dakhil away or treated him worse than the others. He'd said so only to shock the old woman, he supposed, to shut her up. He realized, though, as he said it, that the last part was true. He always imagined his mother searching for him, even as he hated her for leaving. After twenty-five years, would he even know her? She could be right here, he sometimes thought on crowded city streets, and we would pass each other by.

Unable to sleep, he shaved quickly. When he finished, he stood over a can of baked beans at the kitchen sink, swallowing cold mouthfuls like a cow at a trough. He wiped sauce from the can with a slice of bread, then grabbed the purse glaring at him from the end of the couch. He'd considered turning it in, but it might get picked over in the lost and found, and if she kicked up a row, suspicion could fall on him. He distrusted even the name, one of those English expressions he never fully understood. (Wasn't something lost only until it was found? How could it be both at once?) Of course, he'd known immediately whose purse it was. The old woman had grasped it like a shiny black shield, so anxious he imagined her collapsing if it was stolen from that cardboard box of missing phones, wallets, keys, and glasses, the things easiest to misplace and hardest to live without.

He dumped the contents of the purse onto his couch. An unlabeled bottle of thick white liquid. A roll of lozenges, a cell phone, a small box, makeup containers. A paperback called *Carnal Instinct* advertised a muscular, shirtless man and a woman in an old-fashioned dress on the verge of a kiss, seeming at once to embrace and pull away. A wallet contained thirty-eight dollars. He opened the box, saw the diamond ring, and snapped it closed as if he'd glimpsed something obscene. The ring looked valuable. He wanted to forget about the purse until Monday, but she was so nervous, the old woman, losing something this precious would put her in a panic. He would have to return her things today, when he could least afford the time.

He opened the box again and slid the ring onto his finger. He squeezed some lotion, more than he intended, into his hand. It smelled of ginger and something sweet but not overpowering like the perfumes that choked his cab. He held his hand to his face and breathed deep, rubbing the lotion into his dry palms, wiping the excess across his cheeks. It tingled after his shave, at once soothing and stinging. The scent was familiar, but he could not say what it was.

On her giant flip phone, he scrolled through a short list of contacts: Checker Taxi, a salon, a dry cleaner, a Dr. Latimore. Restaurants he knew from fares. Her own number and one for a "Michael" with no surname. The son. He was flipping across this entry while glancing at the ring and did not realize he'd connected until too late.

"This is Michael," the voice said, friendly but busy.

"Sorry, wrong number."

"Who is this?" Less friendly, less busy. "You're on my mother's phone."

Dakhil hung up. The phone rang a moment later. He didn't answer.

She did not describe him until Michael insisted. Very tall, very Black, she said, a nice young man, from Sudan or maybe Somalia. There was no trace of anger in Michael, who was impossible to rile. Candace wished he would get angry. She might have felt less like a client, her story dissected, words parsed, revelations coaxed, as if she were being deposed. Like a good lawyer, he wanted to protect her, to learn all the facts and most of all, avoid surprise. He didn't know how condescending he sounded.

"It's okay," she said. "He's bringing it tonight. I baked a cake, so I can give him some."

"A cake? Mom, you don't even know him. That's not a good idea."

"I know him well enough. We had a long chat. He came here to escape the wars."

"Which wars?"

"In Somalia. Or Sudan."

Michael pointed out that the normal thing would be for the driver to leave her purse at the cab company's lost and found. Why would he want to deliver it personally? He was in possession of her credit cards, phone, and ID, and now he was coming into her home. Why had he made calls on her cell, hanging up on Michael when he heard a man's voice, refusing to answer when he called back?

"Certain types prey on elderly women, Mom."

"Which *types* do you mean?" Candace bristled, though it was not his implication about Black men but the phrase *elderly women*—the box he put her in—that angered her.

Michael sighed. "Sorry. You know what I mean. I worry about you in that place on your own."

"The only thing of value is the ring, and he told me it's safe," she said, making her voice light. Michael would be here in two days, and she did not want awkwardness over this, or anything. "He could have kept it."

Even after Michael asked, it took Candace a moment to realize what she had done. The surprise was ruined, and before he'd even arrived. She wanted to sob.

"I'm sorry, but we found a ring," Michael said. "A couple weeks ago."

"You never mentioned. You said you stopped looking."

"We did, and once we stopped looking, we found something perfect. Did you tell this driver about the ring?"

I have made a mess of everything, she thought.

"Cancel your credit cards, just to be safe. He's been going through your stuff. How else would he know about the ring? He could be using it as a way in."

Michael's suspicion grated on Candace, but also made her think, unwillingly, of something the driver had said: *My time is money.* He'd said it politely on the phone but with emphasis, explaining that he could only estimate when he might arrive with her purse. He would have to come when a fare took him near the Gold Coast, he said, because today more than ever, his time was money. She frowned at her thoughts, Michael's thoughts really, invading her own. Losing the purse was her fault. The driver was simply being gracious.

"Call Sergio and let him handle this at the front desk. Do not let this man in. Okay?"

"When did you become such a worrier?" She forced a small laugh. "Everything will be fine. You'll see when you get here."

Candace's last sentence drifted in silence, and she felt the walls closing in, the air fleeing her chest, an invisible vice crushing her with slow insistence.

Dakhil did not bother to look on the street—nothing opened up in the Gold Coast at this hour—but left his cab in the high-rise drive, hazards flashing. He would only be a few minutes, and doormen gave cabbies a small window to get tenants. He sped past the empty front desk to catch a waiting elevator. He did not know if he would make rent—it might be the last hour that saved him—but if he was quick about it, returning her purse wouldn't change the math.

Across the lobby from the elevators, Sergio Paredo, the doorman, sat in the receiving room, trying to reach management after hours. Several boxes of building supplies were missing again, the Flip who delivered them late and stinking of booze again, and Sergio's impatience filled the small windowless room.

The delivery driver also sat, but he might as well have been kneeling as he cowered before Sergio, an enormous man with shoulders wide as the door. The driver feigned broken English, slipping into Tagalog and pretending not to know how items got lost. Sergio was on hold when he glimpsed a figure racing to the elevator—soon as he was occupied, of course.

His instructions were clear: don't let the cabdriver in, retrieve the purse and its contents. No one gets hurt, but rattle his cage, so he knows to leave her alone. This from the old lady's *pinche* son, who sent Sergio a hundo at Christmas, and on his birthday every year, a bottle of El Tesoro reposado, which Sergio gave away (he hated tequila). That was all it took to ease the son's guilt and, in his mind at least, keep Sergio on retainer, friendly with the old lady, available for whatever. Almost wasn't worth it, given the kid's cocky-ass attitude, but he liked the old lady and, for today's service, he would be paid extra. He'd worked twenty years as a cop, mostly in the jungle—Englewood, Garfield, Pullman. No one would believe the animals he locked up, losers who made you wonder what species, never mind families, they came from. He had so many scars—some from the job, some from growing up Mexican in Marquette Park—half his skin felt like leather, not to mention the limp that got worse each year.

Cops were the bearing walls that held this city up. They gave it everything, and what did they get in return? At the time of his injury, Sergio and half a dozen others were being investigated for their interrogations. "Torture" was the word used now, like conscientious cops were the Viet Cong or some shit. He never tortured anyone, bloodied up a suspect, or forced an innocent man to confess. Not once. He never leaned on someone who wasn't guilty, and he never leaned hard, even on the ones who were. In Chicago, the confession was as good as the crime: no one with clean hands volunteered for a cell at Stateville. You had to act tough sometimes, sure, that was the job, but it was an act. Did people really want to take their chances in a war zone without cops who got results? Would they rather have nothing between them and the animals out there? Go right ahead.

The department was happy to get rid of Sergio with disability and a three-quarters pension when he got stabbed on the job—a leg wound, nerves permanently damaged. He agreed to a quick settlement, OPS lost a file. A union connection found him this job, which paid just enough to keep him locked in another eight years, when he would hit sixty-three and could really retire. He cantered around a mahogany lobby all day—a high-dollar holding pen— pasting on a smile, pretending that he loved to open doors and kiss ass. No, he wouldn't mind taking care of this. He missed police work. He missed protecting citizens like that old lady from scammers and punks. He missed the way people used to look at him, and he hated the way they saw his gimpy ass now.

Still on hold, Sergio carried the phone into the lobby and saw the taxi's lights flashing in the drive. He finished with management and made another quick call before heading upstairs.

When she heard the knock, Candace thought for a moment that Michael was at the door. She'd broken down after his call that afternoon, unable to contain her feelings, which proved impossible to corral once they got loose. Only Michael let himself up and then knocked, and the rap on her door came at the exact time he was to arrive, though two days early. She was upset, but at the best of times, her mind played such tricks on her. The towel draped over a chair became his jacket, the noise that woke her his snoring, fresh flowers in the kitchen his cologne.

She opened the door a crack to see the cabdriver, who held her purse gingerly with two hands as if delivering a bomb.

"Oh, you." She did not mean to sound rude. "I'm sorry. I thought for a minute—my son was coming, and I've been…" She shook her head, collecting herself. "Won't you come in?"

"I cannot."

"Please, for a minute."

She backed up, opening the door wider, and he stepped hesitantly into the narrow entry. She wondered at his scent, difficult to identify mixed with the sweat of work and the odors of city streets, but it was one she knew.

From the dark box of the foyer, Dakhil looked into a massive room. An L-shaped couch long as a limo was parked at its far end. Three steps led to a raised area that looked like a stage—an armchair, end table, and television bounded by a low rail. The door closed, and he glanced back, as if locked in. The old woman sniffed. She had been crying.

"I left my—I am in a bad spot," he said.

"I can't thank you enough for finding my purse. Can I take your coat?"

He smiled weakly. It seemed like something his face had grown unused to, a pity since now that she saw more than a profile, he was handsome. He had shaved, but dark flesh bulged beneath his eyes. She had not noticed these bags earlier or the seam under his left arm where his shirt needed a stitch.

"Can I offer you some coffee? Beer? I don't drink beer, but I bought some in case Michael…A pity to waste it."

"I do not drink alcohol," he said. "I must get back to work." She was older than he'd guessed. The makeup was gone. Her face looked less taut, her eyes raw. Their purple-veined lids were thin and pink, delicate as a newborn's.

"A piece of cake then. Apple. I made it today."

He shook his head. Earlier, she'd imagined how awful Michael would feel if the cabbie forced his way in and murdered her, ransacking the place, stealing her valuables. The image was not only ridiculous, it would prove him right.

He would be annoyed, though, to learn that the cab driver returned her purse intact and that she served him cake.

"I don't know how I forgot it. Overexcited, I suppose, thinking my son was coming…"

Her voice caught, and he worried she might resume crying. "People lose things in cabs all the time," he said quickly. On the end table, two books, reading glasses, a cup, and several remote controls competed for space. The armchair next to it was the only piece of furniture that looked used, a depression marking the seat, fabric on its back worn thin.

"Your son is not coming," he said, as if drawing this conclusion from the apartment.

"No. Unexpected business." Still sniffling, she couldn't trust her nose, but she knew that scent. "You're sure you won't have some cake?"

"I'm sorry about your son."

"I should not have been surprised. I never loved his father." Candace's own words shocked her. They seemed to hover in the dim foyer, independent of her. She was glad to be rid of them. "I told myself that I fell out of love with Richard because he became a drunk, distant, cruel in small ways, but I never loved him. I wonder now if learning that was what made him drink, or made it worse. What I loved was this." She waved vaguely at the apartment and the skyline beyond its glass wall.

"Well, I am sure…"

"I told myself I stayed in the marriage for Michael, but the truth is, I stayed for an account at Saks and a new BMW every year. Extravagant parties, exotic vacations, a circle of people I never really knew." *Why am I telling him this?* she wondered. Upset from Michael's news, in the uncontrollable crying that followed it, she grew tired of pretense. It felt good to tell another person, and he was there. In her state, it seemed reason enough.

"Your son is lucky to have a mother who cares."

"My son grew up watching two people who couldn't stand to be in the same room pretend that they had a connection. He spent eighteen years trapped between an alcoholic, depressive father and a vain, venal mother. We made a sham of marriage."

Dakhil murmured an automatic protest, but as he looked away, his eyes stopped on the single worn chair, the cluttered table. He nodded.

"We turned him against the idea, but now, older and alone, he is about to make a bad marriage of his own. Of course, I can't tell him that, or anything of substance. I spent so long pretending, we can't have a real conversation."

"The ring is for him?"

"I had it repaired for his fiancée. It's a family heirloom, precious to me. When I told Michael about it, he said he'd already bought a ring. A lie."

"No. A misunderstanding…"

"The last thing he wants is a wedding ring from me. He's right. It would be a curse on the marriage. His fiancée hates me, but I'm not sure she knows the reason. It's because we aren't so different, she and I."

"Your son is lucky," Dakhil repeated. "Truly." That is her life, he thought. In this magnificent place, it is confined to thirty square meters around a worn chair. He imagined her world shrinking as she aged, from the city to her building to this apartment and finally, to that tiny square, as apparently, her family had shrunk to the bounds of her shriveled body.

"I'm sorry," she said. "Going on like this. I forget, you never knew your mother."

Abandoned by her son, she has no one to tell but a stranger, he thought, a stranger who lied to her. Photos of the son hung on the walls, with his mother, at the beach, one in a graduation gown. Dakhil thought of his own mother. Did she have a photo of him?

"My mother didn't die," he said. "At least, I don't think so. She left when I was small."

"I see."

"I do not know why I said that. I used to wish she was dead. I hated her for leaving."

Dakhil's father was too indifferent to be truly hostile—even his beatings felt distant. Real anger required something long gone from his makeup, if it was ever there. He became that way because a wife left him alone with three children. This was what Dakhil and his brothers said, blaming their mother, hating her, but what if this was always his way? What would have happened to his mother had she stayed?

"Do you remember her?"

"Some things. The smell of spices in her hair—cardamom, coriander. She sang sometimes, but the words are lost. I can't remember the songs or even her voice."

For years afterward, Candace would go over what happened next, trying to make sense of it, thinking of things she wished she'd said.

"Please, let me get you something. Come in."

"I do not want any money," he said, and she froze. She wondered why he was talking about money—she meant coffee, something to eat—and in the same instant, she recognized the scent he wore. It was her own. There was no mistaking her lotion, a mix of ginger and pomegranate custom made at Bolster's. She felt a jolt of fear.

Dakhil held the purse out to the woman, and her face turned pale as the wall. The bag dropped to his side. He touched her arm, afraid she might faint. She flinched.

In her mind, she heard Michael's warning: *Certain types prey on elderly women.* She was relieved when another knock came.

"Making yourself at home?" Sergio asked, propping the door open with his lame leg and squeezing the driver's shoulder. "Nice job, except I saw you sneaking through the lobby."

"Sergio, no," Candace said. "I left my purse in this man's cab and—"

"Don't worry, Mrs. P. I talked to your son. I know all about this guy."

"What is this?" Dakhil said. "You know what about me?"

"You've bothered this lady enough, chief. Let's have the purse."

Dakhil instinctively held her purse away as the doorman reached for it. Deftly he twisted an arm behind the cabbie's back, forcing him to drop the bag.

"Sergio, my God, no," Candace said.

"Let me go." Dakhil struggled in the entryway, but the man was much bigger and despite his limp, easily able to hold him.

"Check your purse, Mrs. P. Everything there? Check it again."

In her confusion, Candace did as he said. Nothing was taken.

"Now, we're going to go have a little talk, so you know exactly where you stand. And because I'm a nice guy, I'm going to tell you where they towed your cab."

"You're hurting me." The driver moaned.

"Sergio, please." Candace's mouth was dry. What was he doing to this man? What had Michael told him? They struggled at the open door, Sergio pulling the driver through it. The cabbie's eyes, so sympathetic a moment ago, darted like a cornered animal's. They locked onto Candace's as he bounced against the jamb, half in the hall, half in her apartment, and she wondered how she could have thought for an instant, that he might harm her. It was after nine, and he'd been working since this morning. His hair was tussled, the seam under his left arm torn wide. They jerked backward, the driver's feet lifted off the floor like a child's. His shirt flew up, ribs rippling through tight skin. When was the last time he'd eaten a good meal? She imagined herself cooking one for him while he rested on the couch or in Michael's room. She saw herself drawing a bath, mending his shirt while he soaked, perhaps even dozed in the tub. Over coffee, he told her about the mother he'd lost and the family he still had, about coming to the U.S. and his plans in Chicago. He could keep the ring. He might give it to his own fiancé one day or sell it. What good was it to her? He would meet Cynthia, her niece, and they would become friends or—why not?— perhaps more. Candace did not have to dispel doubts as she had before. She simply saw him as he was: a frightened man alone in a foreign world, exiled, in need of care.

She had to tell the driver that she was sorry, that this was not her idea, but she found herself stuttering, groping for his name. What was it? The words wouldn't come. First she must insist that Sergio ignore whatever Michael had said, explain that he'd got everything wrong, but she could not find the words for that either.

"My son…" was all that came out as the driver's face hovered in the narrow opening, and then the door closed.

Acknowledgments

"Chez Whatever" was published in *The Chicago Tribune* as grand prize winner of the 2019 Nelson Algren Award; "Out of Egypt" was published as "Accidents" in *Other Voices;* "Creatures of a Day" and "Clearing" were published in *The Colorado Review;* "Chief O'Neill's" was published in *The Cimarron Review.* "Dibs" was published as "Snow Chairs" in *Cagibi;* "Swing Night" was published in *Puerto del Sol.*

The fictional South Side bar in "Chief O'Neill's" bears no resemblance to the excellent establishment of the same name which opened on Chicago's North Side some years after that story was written.

* * *

Special thanks to Robert Boswell, Rus Bradburd, Antonya Nelson, and Connie Voisine, dear friends who gave me invaluable advice and shelter of all kinds while I wrote these stories.

Thank you to the great, ever patient Dr. Ross Tangedal and his talented staff at Cornerstone Press, especially Brett Hill, Sam Bjork, and Sophie McPherson, for making this book a reality.

Thanks to the Chicago Department of Cultural Affairs and Special Events (DCASE), whose Individual Artists Program provided a generous grant for this book.

Thanks to the Illinois Arts Council, Lee Abbott, Jennifer Acker, Ree M. Amezquita, Melissa Andres, Noel Archard, Michael "Duke" Austin, Allie Field Bell, Elizabeth Blackwell, Leslie Corbett Chenoweth, Will Clattenburg, John Conroy, Joeff Davis, Stuart Dybek, Andrea Mama Eff, Gautam Emani, Don Evans, Peter Gianopulos, Michelle Granger, Alex Hallwyler, Tripp Hartigan, Emily Haymans, Jon Jablonski, Ruth Kellar, Matt Lee, Marina Lewis, Kevin McIlvoy, Anne and Rob Merritt from The Perfect Cup (Chicago's best coffee shop), Achy Obejas, Bayo Ojikutu, Ray Quinn, Rick Radun, Alex Shakar, Deirdre Sugrue, Elizabeth Taylor, Jessica Terson, Jeff Jefe Vance, Rob Hog Wilder, and Joe Zekas.

BARRY PEARCE won the Nelson Algren Award for fiction in 2019. His fiction has been published in *Colorado Review, Cimarron Review, Cagibi,* the *Chicago Tribune,* and elsewhere. He grew up on the South Side of Chicago, the son of immigrant parents in a diverse working-class neighborhood. He still lives in Chicago, where he works as a ghostwriter of nonfiction books.

www.ingramcontent.com/pod-product-compliance
Lightning Source LLC
Chambersburg PA
CBHW031032310726
48969CB00007B/1949